Red-hot raves for the novels of Louisa Edwards

TOO HOT TO TOUCH

"*Too Hot to Touch* is a satisfying, emotional and touching read."
—*Read, React, Review*

"I can see that this series is going to be another keeper on my shelves. A great start to this new foodie series, it makes me want to learn to cook . . . almost."
—*Smitten with Reading*

"Edwards always amazes me with her descriptions in the kitchen and food. Be sure to read this book on a full stomach, or else the hunger pains might get ya!"
—*The Book Pushers*

"Jules and Max scorch the pages . . . very well-written characters with flaws, issues and depth."
—*Badass Book Reviews*

"I loved this book. It was funny, sexy, the love story was touching, and the characters were likeable. As a fan of contemporary romance, this is exactly what I'm looking for when I buy a book. I can't wait to read the next installment. This one is a keeper so don't waste more time and go get it!"
—*Romance Around the Corner*

"If you like food, televised food shows (especially the popular Bravo series *Top Chef*) and books with happy endings, you're in for a treat."
—*San Angelo Standard Times*

"Scorching romance and delicious passions ignite behind the scenes of a high-stakes culinary competition. Today's hottest chefs vie for fame, fortune . . . and each other's hearts." —*Fresh Fiction*

"Yowza! There's nothing like romance in the kitchen to get juices pumping and hearts pounding, especially when the writing sizzles like it does in Edwards' latest." —*All About Romance*

"Every woman who's made the painful discovery that great sex is not enough to make a man realize he's in love will sympathize. *Too Hot to Touch* flips the power balance." —*BN.com Romance Reviews*

"I enjoyed the banter between all the characters. We get a little hint as to whom Danny's heroine will be as his book will pick up where this one leads off. It's overall an enjoyable read, and I'll be picking up Danny's book when it comes out." —*Happily Ever After Reads*

JUST ONE TASTE

"The third addition to Edwards' contemporary, culinary-based love stories is a rare treat that is certain to satisfy readers with its delectable combination of lusciously sensuous romance and irresistibly clever writing." —*Booklist*

"Laugh-out-loud funny, *Just One Taste* [is] a surprisingly tasty story of two unlikely people meeting and falling in love . . . A fun, light read with plenty of humor and passion, *Just One Taste* makes it to my keeper shelf and has me searching for the book preceding [it]." —*Affaire de Coeur*

"Awesome characters, delicious food and even more fabulous sex makes for a super-sexy and fun read! Edwards does it again. Her stories are fun but so meaningful, and I will definitely be reading her next book!"

—*The Book Lush*

"This is a wonderfully tasty series. Once you take the first bite of this story you'll be hooked to the very last bite."

—*Once Upon A Romance* (5 Stars)

"There are a lot of elements in *Just One Taste*, and Edwards juggles them like a pro. The addition of mouthwatering recipes at the end of the book enhances the excellent reading experience, and draws you into the world of cooks and cooking. A very enjoyable contemporary romance with plenty of bite and heart."

—*Sacramento Book Review*

"I absolutely love *Top Chef* and *Iron Chef America*, but have never really picked up a food/chef-related novel before. I'm happy to report that *Just One Taste* was fun, sweet, and deliciously romantic."   —*PS I Love Books*

"This is my first 'taste' of a Louisa Edwards book, and I'll be going out for the others in this series. If you want a story with sweet romance, definite sensuality and enough laughs to make your day, then you need to read *Just One Taste*."   —*Long and Short Reviews*

"Rosemary is probably one of the most intricately sketched heroines I've ever seen in a book, and the romance is, in a word . . . intense, and the blending of the story was richly presented. Make it a point to read this Perfect 10 today!"

—*Romance Reviews Today*

Hot Under Pressure

LOUISA EDWARDS

St. Martin's Paperbacks

This is a work of fiction. All of the characters, organizations, and events portrayed in this novel are either products of the author's imagination or are used fictitiously.

HOT UNDER PRESSURE

Copyright © 2012 by Louisa Edwards.

All rights reserved.

For information address St. Martin's Press, 175 Fifth Avenue, New York, NY 10010.

EAN: 978-0-312-53440-0

Printed in the United States of America

St. Martin's Paperbacks edition / April 2012

St. Martin's Paperbacks are published by St. Martin's Press, 175 Fifth Avenue, New York, NY 10010.

10 9 8 7 6 5 4 3 2 1

This book is for every woman who said to me,
"It happened to me, too." We are not alone.

Acknowledgments

Thank you to Deidre Knight for giving me the support and encouragement I needed to tackle this story, and Rose Hilliard for giving me the space to write it—and for loving the result. I'd be a very different (much worse!) writer without the two of you in my corner.

My other big supporters were, as always, Kristen Painter and Roxanne St. Claire! Sisters of my heart and two of the best writers I've ever come across. It's a true joy to wake up every morning to an email inbox full of your wit and wisdom!

If you're not a big fan of epilogues, you can blame Kate Pearce and Bria Quinlan for the monster at the end of this book. My fearless beta readers felt the end needed a little something more . . . and I couldn't resist the chance to check back in with some of my favorite characters. Seriously, without Kate and Bria, my books would be much less shiny, so big thanks to both of them.

Recipe props go to my mother-in-law, for introducing my husband to grilled PB&J sandwiches, and especially to my dad. It's his masterpiece of a recipe for paella in the back of the book, so send your mental enjoyment and gratitude to George Edwards when you make it!

My mother is my first and last reader, sees every draft, and never fails to offer real commentary along with the unstinting praise. And requests for more of Kane and Claire, so if you're a fan of that couple, you have my mom to thank for getting to see so much of them in *HUP*.

And last but certainly not least, I need to thank my husband, Nick. You know it's true, everlasting love when you can spend an entire year both working from home, and not kill each other!

Chapter 1

"Ready. Get set. Go!"

Beck ripped off his blindfold and blinked furiously to accustom his eyes to the harsh fluorescent lights of the kitchen. His focus narrowed down, the exact same way it did in battle, the world around him going grainy and slow like an out-of-focus news broadcast.

Five minutes on the timer, counting down relentlessly as he spent precious seconds assessing the situation.

It was a relay challenge. Each member of the team had five minutes to make the raw ingredients into a polished, perfect dish—with the added bonus of not being able to communicate or watch each other as they took their turns at the stove.

The stakes? An unnamed but highly desirable advantage over the other two teams going into the final round of the Rising Star Chef competition.

As soon as the RSC coordinator, Eva Jansen, had explained the challenge, the rest of Beck's team had huddled into a circle to divvy up roles.

"Win, you've got the best knife skills, you start us on prep. You get us going. Max, Danny and I will muddle through the middle. You? You're the clincher," Jules Cavanaugh had pronounced, poking Beck in the chest. "We'll set you up with something great, you take it home."

Anticipation warred with Beck's hard-won composure, forcing him to ice everything down just to stay calm.

They trusted him. His team trusted him to close out the dish and take it up to the next level.

He wouldn't let them down.

Five chef contestants per team, each chef with five minutes to cook.

Twenty-five minutes total for the three teams to create something delicious enough to wow three world-famous food-snob judges.

Beck had spent the first twenty minutes of the challenge at parade rest, legs braced apart for balance, hands folded at the small of his back, every sense on high alert as he worked to filter the sounds and scents of the competition kitchen.

The other two teams were ranged around him, a constant low-level distraction of chatter, noise, tension, the whiff of an achingly familiar perfume . . .

Ignore her. Ignore all of them. Focus. You learned to tune out gunfire and explosions, you can learn to block her out, too.

All that matters is the food.

Beck caught the rhythmic, high-speed staccato of a chopping knife hitting a wooden block with the same rapid-fire precision as a burst of machine gun fire. That had to be Winslow Jones, the East Coast team's own prep chef. Beck would know that signature rat-a-tat-tat anywhere.

Something light and green on the air, woodsy and fresh, with a hint of black licorice. Herbs, Beck decided. Tarragon, most likely. His tactician's brain immediately began working through the proteins and sauces that paired best with tarragon, clicking over the possibilities, everything from chicken to lobster.

Could be chicken—Winslow could break down a bird into eight perfectly portioned pieces in less than sixty seconds flat. Time was a factor here, because the further each prepping chef took the dish, the more Beck would have to work with as he refined it and added flourishes at the end.

The scrape of a dull blade against a hard surface made Beck frown under his blindfold. Was Win shucking oysters?

"Switch!"

The first five minutes were gone.

A sauté pan clattered onto the stovetop on Beck's six. He tensed and tracked the movement behind him, but didn't turn around.

He hoped to God that Jules, who was next in the rotation for their team, wasn't getting the oysters sautéing now—they'd be ready to shoot from a rubber pellet gun before Beck got them up to the pass.

Nothing you can do about it. Wait for your chance. Be ready.

Forcing himself back into the moment, Beck kept his senses trained on the activity around him, the eddies and currents of bodies moving quickly through space, sometimes brushing against him, sometimes cursing, the air of tension and effort as palpable as if he were standing stock-still in the middle of a firefight.

Finally, it was Beck's turn.

He blinked away the dazzle of the lights and cast his gaze from side to side, sizing up the kitchen with a single glance.

A single glance that turned into a long, time-eating hesitation when the first thing Beck saw was a woman, her strawberry-blonde hair haloed around her sweet, heart-shaped face and an expression of excited determination firming her soft pink mouth.

Skye Gladwell.

In terms of strategy, if her team had set out to pit Beck against the chef most likely to make him choke, they couldn't have chosen better. Not only had Skye proven herself a formidable competitor in the last round of the competition . . . but Beck had proven he was nearly unable to focus when she was around.

An avalanche of emotion crashed over his head, obliterating his carefully constructed walls and gouging holes in his focus like a sucker punch straight to the heart.

Sorting out how he felt about Skye Gladwell was like trying to untangle a bowl of cooked spaghetti, but as the seconds ticked down and the pressure mounted, the red-hot coil of determination tightened his gut and overwhelmed everything else.

Skye had already raced over to the West Coast team's table and was busily taking over dicing whatever her teammate had left lying on the chopping block. As if feeling Beck's eyes on her, she glanced up.

Their eyes met across the kitchen, and Beck's vision tunneled down for a short, disorienting moment where all he could see was Skye.

The one person in the entire world who could destroy his composure without even trying.

His gut clenched, his heart rate doubled, and the hair on the back of his neck stood up. In that moment, Beck was a knife's edge away from snarling at her, at his teammates, at the unbelievable twist of fate that had brought him face to face with the one woman he'd give anything to forget.

A clatter of metal, the sound of a pot being dropped by the third competitor, jerked Beck back into the moment. He shook his head as if he'd just surfaced from a dive.

You can't do any of that right now, dickhead. So focus. Get your head out of your ass and move. Go. Go!

Jolted into high gear, Beck slammed the door shut on the part of his brain that couldn't help keeping tabs on every move Skye Gladwell made.

And why the hell did that internal voice have to sound so much like Lt. Martino, his drill instructor back at Navy Boot Camp? Shaking his head clear like a dog coming out of the water, Beck tuned out everything but the various elements of their dish in the final stages of cooking as Danny Lunden wiped his brow and jogged over to the other side of the kitchen where the rest of their team waited.

The other competitors were already running, scrambling, zooming back and forth between the pantry, the walk-in coolers, and the stoves, but Beck forced them away from his consciousness and took his time to taste everything.

He'd been wrong. That scraping he'd interpreted as Winslow shucking oysters had actually been the cracking of a mound of local Dungeness crabs.

Winslow Jones must be some kind of psychic genius to have chosen crab as the base of their team's dish. If there was any ingredient in the world that Beck knew better, he couldn't think of it.

He'd grown up eating Dungeness crab, setting his own traps and checking them, boiling water over an illegal open fire on the rocky beach and steaming the spiny brown crustaceans. He'd hacked them open with a pocket knife, cutting his fingers on the jagged edges of the shells, the only thought in his mind to get at the briny, shockingly juicy sweetness of the crab meat.

His team's crabs were all prepped and ready to go, white-tipped claws stripped of meat and piled in a small mountain to the side of the stainless steel work surface beside shallow prep bowls filled with garnishes.

Beck lifted the bowls in turn, inhaling deeply and identifying the contents by smell. Fresh tarragon; chopped ginger; thinly sliced shallots. Beside the bowls lay stacks of peeled, seeded cucumber in perfect two-inch batons, crisp and faintly green.

Spinning to check out the stove, he found a sauce reducing on the back burner of the stove, glossy and pale yellow. A quick dip of a clean spoon, and he tasted egg yolks and cream. It needed something more, another flavor element to bring the whole thing together . . . .

Plus, it was getting thick, it and it would need to be thinned out for the dish he already had in mind. He could use the cooking water from the crabs, he decided as he checked the enameled cast iron stockpot bubbling merrily beside the sauce.

The pot held plain boiling water, he ascertained from a sniff test, which was a good strategic move on someone's part. If Beck wanted to blanche a vegetable as a base for the crab, or make some very al dente pasta, he was all set up to do it.

An idea flickered to life, and without questioning his instincts, Beck snagged a bottle of champagne vinegar, a canister of sugar, and a clean, small saucepan. Carefully ladling out a cup of the boiling water into the new saucepan, he added an equal amount of vinegar and cranked the burner up to high so he could dissolve the sugar into the mixture as quickly as possible.

The already hot water came back up to the boil in seconds while Beck put the cucumber into a wide-bottomed bowl, hesitated a brief second, then added the ginger and sliced shallots to the mix, along with a few red pepper flakes for kick. Then he poured the hot brine over the vegetables and rushed the steaming bowl of quick pickles to the blast chiller to cool down.

On his way back to the stove, he snatched the tarragon

from the prep table. Adding it to the sauce, Beck tasted and corrected for flavor, thinning with the salty fish broth as he went, until he had a delicate, savory sauce, rich with fatty egg yolks and redolent of summery tarragon.

It was still missing something, though—and with the brine at the top of his brain, Beck got a flash of inspiration. Darting to the walk-in cooler, he searched the shelves for the bottle he was sure he'd seen earlier.

Ah ha! There it was, the green glass beaded with condensation. Beck grabbed it and hustled back to the stove where he popped the cork with a satisfying, festive burst of bubbles.

Champagne would add a light tang to the sauce, especially if he tamed the yeasty, acidic flavors by quickly reducing it to a thin syrup. Pouring a small amount of the sparkling wine into another saucepan, he cranked the dial and let it foam up and then back down again before stirring it into his sauce.

Another taste . . . Beck grabbed a clean spoon and dipped, then had to remind himself not to double dip.

Damn, that was tasty. Clean and bright, but with a creamy fattiness that would contrast beautifully with the simple crab.

Then it was quick, back to the blast chiller to rescue his pickles, which he drained on paper towels before portioning them out between three appetizer plates, carefully cross-hatching the cold, crispy cucumbers into squares dotted with the dusky purple-pink of the shallots, which hadn't spent enough time in the hot brine to lose their color, just the right amount of time to soak up enough sweet-sour flavor to offset their sharp, oniony tang.

He hoped.

Each plate got a mound of snowy white crab meat on top of the pickled cucumber and shallots, and Beck flicked his eyes up to check the wall clock.

Thirty seconds left. He became aware of the chef contestants who'd already had their turn cooking standing on
the kitchen sidelines, chanting along with the dwindling
numbers on the timer, counting down the seconds in a
frenzy of encouragement.

Adrenaline pumped into Beck's blood, and he felt the
same odd reaction he always got. His heart slowed, every
beat like the tick of the second hand in his ear. The hot air
of the kitchen felt cool against his temples as the sweat
there cooled.

When he lifted careful spoonfuls of his champagne sauce
and swirled it into artful semi-circles around the edges of
his plates, his hand was rock steady.

"Five . . . four . . . three . . . two . . . one!"

Beck dusted the chopped tarragon from his fingertips
onto the last of the judges' plates just as Eva Jansen said,
in her official announcer voice, "Time! Step away from
your plates."

The physical act of backing up a pace seemed to cut
the cord that had bound him to his work, and Beck felt
the rest of the world come back online, background noise
and awareness of the other two chefs who'd finished their
teams' dishes flooding his head in a rush.

Skye Gladwell was right next to him, her heady, earthy
scent of nutmeg and cream hitting him like an open-
handed slap to the face. Beck had to close his eyes for a
long moment to thank his combat training for giving him
single-minded focus and drive.

Because this particular challenge was perfectly cali-
brated to tap into Beck's primal fight-or-fuck instincts.

Skye? He'd had ten years to get over her, but apparently
that wasn't long enough to blunt the edges of his desire.

He didn't love her anymore, obviously, but damned if
he didn't still want her as badly as he had at the age of
twenty. It had been a surprise to him in Chicago, that un-

expected surge of physical need, but he was over the shock of it now, and working to kill the desire as dead as his softer feelings.

Until he managed it, though, he had to acknowledge he was pretty messed up in the head when it came to Skye Gladwell.

The third contestant in this final challenge, however . . . Beck's feelings on that guy were a whole lot less complicated.

On Beck's left stood Ryan Larousse, the cocky, smarmy head of the Midwest team. They'd already gotten into it once or twice during the competition, to the point where Beck had humiliatingly and completely lost his cool and actually knocked the skinny little weasel on his ass.

Drawing serene blankness around himself was like strapping on body armor, and it helped as Beck worked to slow his breathing and return his heart rate to normal. Eyes straight ahead, waiting for the judges to come over and pronounce a winner.

Feel nothing. Feelings are for people who have the luxury of acting on them. You do your best and accept the rest.

It was a decent mantra, as far as survival went, but Beck couldn't help but feel a mirroring tingle of the excitement in Skye's eyes as she shot him a sideways look.

"This is amazing. I can't believe we're both here," she breathed, her wide, cornflower eyes tracking the progress of the judges, who'd started with the Midwest team's plate.

All the work Beck had done to slow his pulse and regulate his body temperature went up in smoke. "I can't believe you still look at the world that way," he said.

"What's that supposed to mean?" The sudden ramrod tension of her body said more than her stiff words.

Beck shook his head. He'd always loved the innocent pleasure she took from life—but it drove him crazy, too, the way she refused to see the world as it really was, in all its harsh, ugly reality. Especially considering what she'd gone through while their relationship was imploding.

Let it go, he told himself, gritting his teeth. *You're over this, remember?*

"Nothing. Forget it. Congratulations on making it to the finals." Beck thought that was safe. Polite, distant.

"You too," Skye muttered as the judges exclaimed over Larousse's handmade gnocchi with pea shoots and shiitake foam. "And hey, congrats on finally finding your balls again."

Beck felt his head snap back on his neck as if he'd taken a clip to the chin.

"What?"

Skye turned to get a better look at his face, brushing the flyaway softness of her red-gold curls against his arm. Beck fought not to flinch, not to grab her and shake her, not to betray his agitation by moving a single muscle.

"Your balls," she said clearly, eyes flashing darker than he'd ever seen them, even that last, awful night. "You must've found them, if you finally got up the guts to show your face in this city again."

The bitterness in her voice stung like lemon juice in an open cut, and Beck had to fight with everything in him not to react.

"Nice talk," he said, unable to help the hoarse thickness of his voice. "You kiss your mother with that mouth?"

She looked away, back to the judges, who were finishing up with Larousse. "I'm not the sweet kid you left ten years ago, Henry. Don't think for even a second that I'm going to go down easy. I'm here to win, not to make new friends or relive ancient history."

"Don't worry," Beck snarled under his breath. "Once this is all over and my team has won, I'll be ditching San Francisco and heading back to the East Coast."

"Perfect," she said. "Except my team's going to be taking home the prize money and the Rising Star Chef title. And before you run back to New York, there is one little thing I'm going to want from you."

The judges were thanking Larousse and sauntering down the table toward Skye as Beck said, "What's that?"

He didn't know what he expected—money, maybe, or a demand that he go to hell. In the farthest, undisciplined depths of his mind, there might've even been a hint of a thought that maybe she'd ask him for one last night together, for old time's sake.

Instead, what she whispered out of the corner of her mouth just before smiling brilliantly and greeting the judges knocked Beck off balance and stopped his heart.

"I want a divorce."

Chapter 2

How in the hell did we get here?

Skye closed her eyes; but that just made it worse—the heat of Beck beside her, the wild, masculine scent of his skin, like pine needles and the wind off the water—and suddenly, without warning, vivid memories rose up and enveloped her.

The sign said DAY USE ONLY. *Skye squinted up at the amber-orange clouds over Kirby Cove.*

It was sort of daytime. Okay, maybe the sun wasn't technically still up, but the moon and stars weren't really out yet, either.

Staring at the metal gate blocking the steep trail down to the cove, Skye tried to imagine what Annika Valanova would say if a Golden Gate National Park ranger called her to come bail her daughter out of park prison.

She could practically hear her mother's throaty, dramatic voice pronouncing all rules petty and unimportant in the face of Art.

Annika always said the word Art *like that, with the kind*

*of emphasis that let you know she meant it with a capital A,
as serious as breathing.*

*For sure, more serious than a piddling little park reg-
ulation or two.*

*And then there was her father. Peter Gladwell had
made a career out of breaking the rules and defying ex-
pectations. If he could see Skye now, waffling around and
wringing her hands over going against posted signage,
he'd probably disown her.*

*Promising herself she'd get the images she needed and
get out of the park before dark, Skye ducked under the
metal bar and hurried down the path.*

*When it came right down to it, she'd rather get a slap
on the wrist from a park ranger than face her parents'
disappointment when she proved, for the zillionth time,
that she hadn't inherited their dedication to Art and civil
disobedience.*

*An hour later, she was still perched on the flat rock
she'd found near the edge of the water, sketchpad abandoned beside her as she gazed out over the bay. The
lights blazed up along the Golden Gate Bridge, a bright,
straight line leading to the city of Skye's dreams.*

San Francisco.

*She sighed, curling tighter over her knees as a crisp
breeze swept the rocky beach. The skyline beckoned her,
so close and yet so far, promising freedom. Anonymity.*

*Man, what she wouldn't give to walk down the street
and be just one of the crowd, instead of the love child of
a scandalous artist and a famous playwright.*

*A sharp, shocking rustle in the bushes behind her
startled Skye out of her daydreams. The city might be
nearly close enough to touch, but the park was still home
to a surprising array of wildlife. On walks with her mom,
Skye had seen raccoons and skunks, and she'd heard of*

campers running into bigger stuff like bobcats, coyotes, mountain lions . . .

Heart drumming in her chest, Skye scrambled to her feet, eyes on the dark tangle of tall grass and thick brush up the side of the hill. Why hadn't she stayed on the trail?

The bushes shook again, the crackle of twigs snapping and leaves crushed underfoot reminding Skye of the hiker who'd told everyone in town she'd seen a bear last summer.

As Skye skipped backward, the heel of one of her flat sandals slipped against the rock and she toppled off, arms pinwheeling in a desperate bid for balance. She hit the ground below the rock, air rushing out of her with a woof as her back slammed into the gravelly sand.

"Hey! Are you okay?"

Skye blinked up at the moon and wondered if she was having an auditory hallucination. Bears didn't talk, right?

"God damn," the voice swore. "Hello?"

Although if they did, they'd probably sound a lot like that voice, *Skye thought, lifting a heavy hand to probe at the spot of warm pain radiating out from the back of her skull. The voice was deep and a little rough, with a velvety earthiness that made Skye think of thick, luxuriant fur rubbing against her skin.*

Enough with the bear stuff, already.

"I'm okay," she called, sitting up and putting a tentative hand to her throbbing head. "Ouch."

She squeezed her dazzled eyes shut and wished she dared shake her head to scatter the strange cobwebs from her brain, but she had a feeling that would hurt.

"Ouch doesn't sound good. Here, give me your hand."

Skye tipped her head back and opened her eyes as the world swirled around her in a dizzy rush of stars and clouds and moon, all blocked by the tall, broad-shouldered silhouette looming over her on the rock.

She blinked, dazzled again, but this time in a much less cerebral, more low-down-in-the-body kind of way. Skye sucked in a breath, feeling everything inside her tighten up and throb a heated pulse of excitement through her jarred system.

The man, because he was certainly a man and not a bear, leaned over one knee and held out a long-fingered hand. Everything about him was in shadow, with the moonlight behind him, outlining him in black, but Skye could see that he was big. And dark. Not all of the darkness came from the gathering night, either—his hair made wild, black waves around his face. Even his clothes were black.

He was like something out of a novel, Heathcliff on the moors, and that thought had Skye scrambling to her feet without taking his hand, because she'd never really understood the attraction of a surly, bad-tempered, violently aggressive thug—even if he was smokin' hot.

And what kind of guy wandered around off-limits parks after hours, dressed all in black?

Conveniently ignoring the fact that she, herself, was wandering around the park after hours, Skye dusted off her jeans-clad rump, unusually grateful for her extra padding back there. Packing a lot of junk in the trunk meant she'd have nothing worse than a bruised behind. That skinny bitch from school, Laura Hayden, would probably have broken her tailbone taking a tumble like that.

Not that anyone other than Skye would ever be such a gigantic klutz as to fall off a perfectly flat rock.

"I guess you're okay, then," the guy said, straightening up. Skye narrowed her eyes, trying to make out some *details of his face. She was supposed to be an artist. She was supposed to be good at this kind of thing.*

Too bad she'd never been very good at "supposed to."

"I told you I was." That sounded kind of ungrateful. She didn't really want to antagonize the guy, did she? "Thank you for stopping by, though. It was nice of you to make sure I wasn't dead or concussed or something."

There. Polite, even in the face of potential mugging.

"Oh, I don't know." The earthy voice sounded a breath away from laughing at her, and Skye wondered if she'd been right about him being a man.

Well, he was definitely male, but maybe not as old as she'd originally thought. Crossing her arms the way that squashed her too-big boobs down a little, Skye lifted her chin. "What don't you know?"

The guy lowered himself to the rock and kicked his legs out in front of him, leaning back on his hands. "You might still be concussed. I'd better sit here with you a while, just to make sure."

Skye did some more waffling. He sounded reasonable, nice even, but he was wearing black jeans and clompy leather boots, and every time he moved moonlight glinted silver off the zippers and safety pins holding his leather jacket together over a black T-shirt. He looked tough, in a way that no one Skye went to school with in tiny, artsy-fartsy Sausalito, ever looked. But as her eyes adjusted to the dim light and she began to make out his features, she saw that he was young, too. Probably not any older than she was. Maybe a year older. He could be eighteen.

Feeling jittery and weird, Skye glanced back in the direction of the path. He wasn't blocking her escape in any way. And with him sitting like that, she could make a break for it, no problem. Skye was shorter and rounder than cheerleaders like Laura, but she was fast.

"I'm not going to hurt you, if that's what you think."

Skye whipped around at the guy's quiet voice. He sounded . . . sad. Or something. Disappointed, maybe, and guilty shame flooded Skye's chest. He'd been nothing but nice to her, and here she was, judging him by how he dressed and looked, just like those dumb girls at school always judged Skye, with her peasant blouses and paint-stained corduroys.

"I don't think that," Skye denied stoutly. "I'm sure you're a very nice person. It's just that it's getting late, and I should probably head home."

"Whatever." The guy shrugged and leaned back on his hands again, looking off to the side, away from Skye, exposing his sharp, chiseled profile.

Skye felt a little like she'd fallen off the rock again, the world tumbling around her for a brief, disorienting moment before she caught her breath.

He was gorgeous. And all big and dark and scary. And gorgeous.

The moon was higher in the sky now, casting a blue-ish light over everything. Skye could finally make out his expression, the way resignation had twisted his hard, sensual mouth into a flat line. He tipped his head down, just a little, and the shadows lengthened over his strong, uncompromising face.

It was the face of a man Skye would've said she'd never want to meet in an alley, or alone on the moors, or in a deserted public park—but as she stood there and watched him realize that she hadn't run off yet, watched the softening of his lips and the widening of his dark eyes as he turned back to find her still there, Skye knew this guy was telling the truth.

He'd never hurt her.

A surge of confidence had her rounding the rock and scrambling up the loose dirt and gravel of the hill to get *to the top again. She plunked herself down right next to him, pulling her knees in to her chest and giving him a sidelong look.*

"Decided I'd better not risk it."

Confusion narrowed his eyes and made her notice his short, masculine eyelashes, black as soot when he blinked. "Risk what?"

"Concussion." *She shrugged.* "Not to mention how dangerous it is to run in the dark over bad terrain. Knowing me, I'd find the one rain gulley and sprain my ankle, or fall off a cliff into the bay."

"A little accident prone, are we?" *The smooth amusement was back in his voice, and a warm glow filled Skye with fluttering wings of pleasure.*

The hottest guy she'd ever seen in real life was sitting in a secluded, romantic cranny of nature with her, talking to her. Maybe even flirting with her!

"More than a little," *she said, aware of how breathless she sounded, but utterly unable to get a good, deep gasp of air into her giddy lungs.* "My mom won't even let me in the studio with her anymore, I've knocked over her easels so many times."

"Your mother's an artist? That's cool." *He said it so simply, like he was interested, but didn't really care all that much.*

Skye strove to match his detached tone. "Yeah, she paints. Sculpts a little, works with metal. Whatever she feels like when the muse takes her."

His mouth twitched again, quirking one cheek into winking a dimple at her, so fast she almost missed it. "The muse. Is that what you were looking for out here?"

"Who, me? What makes you say . . . hey, give that back!"

Skye snatched at her composition book, but the guy

held it up, his long arms easily keeping it out of her reach.

"Are you an artist, too?" he teased, waving the notebook.

Jumping to her feet, Skye lunged for the book, her only thought to get it in her hands before he opened it and saw her embarrassingly horrible chicken scratch drawings.

The guy gave it up easily with a "Hey, okay! Sorry. Shit, I ought to know better—" but having braced for a struggle, Skye overcompensated and lost her balance.

She clutched the notebook to her chest and squeezed her eyes shut, the words "Not again!" flashing through her brain as her entire body braced for impact—before she realized she hadn't slammed into the hard, cold ground.

In fact, she was sprawled on something hard, but warm. A firm surface that gave when she pressed her hand to the cool leather of the guy's jacket . . .

Oh my God.

"I'm so sorry," she squeaked, mortified, as she tried to heave herself up off the poor guy she'd just flattened. "I must be crushing you."

"Don't apologize. You're not crushing me at all." His voice sounded strained, though, and Skye's cheeks went scorching hot with a mixture of arousal and humiliation. She felt enormous and ungainly, wallowing in his lap like a walrus, unable to get her balance back and get off of him—but part of her wanted to stay right where she was, for the rest of her life.

"Besides," he continued in that same, tense voice, "it was my fault. I was being a dick."

Annoyance rushed back in, overwhelming her embarrassment momentarily. "Yeah, you were. An artist's *notebook is sacred, okay? You never, ever mess with that. Ever."*

Never mind that Skye wasn't an artist and never would be, no matter what her parents wanted.

"I'm sorry," he said again. "You're right. Hey, I've got shit I wouldn't want some stranger poking through, either."

"Please." She couldn't help but scoff. This boy radiated 'cool' like it was seeping from his pores. *"What could you have to be embarrassed about?"*

"Right." He looked away, out over the water. *"Because a guy like me couldn't possibly have depths."*

Now Skye felt bad again. The yo-yoing of her emotions was wearing her out. *"No, I didn't mean—"*

"Well, I have depths," he declared, swiveling his head suddenly to give her a narrow stare. *"You're not the only one with a secret notebook, all right?"*

Skye felt a quickening of excitement. Something in common! *"You're an artist, too?"*

Fake it till you make it, baby. And if it would give her more to talk about with Tall, Dark, and Deep, here . . .

But he shook his head. *"Nah, can't even draw a good Spider-Man. But I . . . write stuff. Sometimes."*

Skye couldn't believe how nervous he seemed all of a sudden. But kind of defiant, too, like he expected her to laugh. Deliberately keeping her voice very serious, she asked, *"What, like stories?"*

He shrugged, staring down at his fingers picking at the frayed hole in the denim over his left knee. *"Not really. More like . . . poetry, I guess. It's lame, I know."*

"It's not lame!" Skye clambered up to her knees beside him. *"It's amazing."* Bracing herself to take a flying leap, she said, *"Would you maybe read me one of your poems sometime?"*

There was a swooping feeling in her belly, as if she'd

tumbled off the rock again, but it stilled when he glanced up at her from under his dark lashes. His hair fell over his forehead, almost hiding his eyes, but she could still see the way they crinkled when he smiled.

"Yeah? Maybe. Sometime. Anyway, sorry again about trying to steal your notebook. But you look really freaking cute when you're mad. Like a kitten with its fur rubbed the wrong way."

Skye huffed. Great. She was a kitten. Kittens were, roly-poly little balls of fluff—definitely not sexy at all.

Crap.

Skye gave him a disgruntled frown. "Yeah, thanks. And thanks for keeping me from falling to my death again, but I've got to go."

"Wait, don't leave. I promise I'll be good. What's your name?"

Skye paused, torn. She didn't really want to leave— and it wasn't like she had a curfew or a set of parents waiting at home for a family dinner or something. "I'm Skye," she said, bracing for recognition. "Skye Gladwell."

"Cool," the boy said, sitting up. He was watching her with interest, but nothing flared in his gaze at the mention of her famous father's last name.

Skye got a little tingle of excitement down her spine. The anonymity she'd always wanted, that she stared out across the San Francisco skyline and dreamed about, was sitting right in front of her. Embodied in the broad-shouldered, muscled form of a truly, knee-shakingly hot guy.

Skye thought maybe she'd found her muse.

"You live near here?" he asked.

Settling back down beside him, Skye felt the heat of his tall, young body all along her right side. "Pretty close. Sausalito."

He leaned in, his face right next to hers, close enough that she felt the delicate scratch of his unshaven cheek against her temple. Pointing out over the water with his long arm, he said, "I live way over there. A place so different from this, you can hardly imagine."

"Where?" She could barely breathe, shiveringly, achingly aware of every inch of him.

"Oakland."

"I've never been there," Skye confessed, a little ashamed. It seemed stupid—it wasn't like Oakland was some faraway country or something.

"You're not missing anything," he told her. "Don't bother. No, seriously, don't—sweet little thing like you'd get eaten alive in my neighborhood."

Skye stiffened, knocking him back a bit. "I can handle myself. I'm tougher than I look."

You had to be, when every kid in school wanted to make fun of you for your parents being crazy, and not married, and sewing you weird hippie clothes to wear.

"You're a cream puff," he said, and she felt his fingers stroking through her hair. "What's a nice girl like you doing out here? Looking for trouble?"

The tender, careful caress distracted Skye from the extremely unflattering comparison to fat, round pastries, and a delicious shiver skimmed over her skin, raising the fine, pale hairs on her arms and tightening her nipples into tiny pinpoints of sensation.

If she turned her face just the eensiest bit to the right, she'd be looking right into his deep, dark eyes. Their mouths would be close enough to brush together. His hand was in her hair.

The moment hung suspended and brilliant, like one of the stars overhead, while Skye's heart pounded out a new, terrifying rhythm. She wanted to kiss him. Did he want to kiss her?

Gathering all her courage, she closed her eyes and turned her face, lifting her mouth to his . . . and he handed her a twig with a bright green leaf attached to it.

"This was tangled up in your hair," he said.

Skye died, right then and there, of humiliation.

Or at least, she wished she could. But no, stubborn life had to keep marching on, trampling all over her hopes and dreams and dragging Skye with it.

"Thanks," she managed to get out, even though her voice sounded like someone had a choking grip on her vocal cords.

"No problem."

His face was still really close to hers. She could feel the warmth of his breath against the tip of her nose; he smelled like the salt breeze and smoke, like from a bonfire.

From this close, now that her vision had adjusted, Skye thought his eyes were deep brown, the rich, pure color of the paint her mother mixed in with gold to make the perfect shade to capture the cedars she loved to paint.

"You've got pretty eyes."

For a moment, it was as if he'd read her mind. But it only took Skye a second to catch up and realize he was talking about her own boring blue eyes. Disappointed, she lowered her gaze and fought to keep the tremble out of her lips.

"Thanks," she said again, more subdued this time.

Everyone complimented her eyes. Or her strawberry-blonde hair, or her creamy skin, or her great personality. Those were the things people talked about when you were heavier than the other girls in your class. She could just hear her mother's bewildered voice as her sharp gaze sketched over Skye's lackluster appearance: "You could be so pretty, if . . ."

"No, I mean it," the guy insisted, scooting closer until

Skye's hopeful heart picked up its pace again. "I've never seen eyes that change colors. And your mouth . . ."

His stare dropped to her lips, which parted on a startled gasp. This was new! No one ever talked about her mouth. Or looked at it like that.

Was she about to get her very first kiss?

Chapter 3

A stack of dirty pans toppled to the counter with a crash, jarring Skye out of that moment of infinite possibility and back into the present.

The shitty, depressing present that tasted of nothing so much as bitter failure.

She'd finally confronted Henry Beck.

This was supposed to be an empowering moment. Skye had always imagined it that way. She'd expected to feel strong, independent, even righteous. Instead, all she felt was a clutch of nausea and the burn of bitter tears behind her eyes.

Beck's face, of course, showed nothing. No reaction, other than a slight widening of his unreadable dark eyes. She could hate him for that alone, if it weren't against Skye's life philosophy to hate anyone, ever.

Even the husband who'd abandoned her when she needed him most.

The hardest part is over, she told herself, slipping a hand into the pocket of her chef's coat. *And there's plenty of time.*

Paper crinkled between her fingers, the printed-out

email already creased and worn from her nervous fidgeting and rereading. At this point, Skye had it memorized.

Keeping it short because internet is spotty out here, but I miss you so much, Sunshine. I think about you all the time. I'm going to try to make it back stateside to watch you compete, and when I get home, there's a question I want to ask you . . .

All my love,

Jeremiah

Mustering up a smile for the judges was easier when she thought about Jeremiah's email. He always made her feel good—and this particular email, with him dropping that hint about a question, made her heart thump hard against her ribcage.

Was he going to ask her to marry him?

The question rolled around her brain like a ball of bread dough in a mixing bowl, sticky and thick with potential. Potential joy, sure—but also potential problems.

Since Skye was already married. And had never quite gotten around to telling Jeremiah about her not-quite-ex.

That sucked the smile right off her face, so Skye had to work extra hard to get it back and make it convincing; somehow, the sight of Beck's sternly impassive features reminded her that she'd never really learned to fake . . . well, anything. But especially emotion.

Feeling uncomfortably like a liar, Skye plastered on a bright grin and hoped her overheated cheeks would be attributed to the warmth of the kitchen and the excitement of the timed challenge.

"Hello, Chef Gladwell," Claire Durand said, in her cultured French way. "It's lovely to see you again. What do you have for us today?"

Skye swallowed down the messy wad of adrenaline, bitterness, and grief clogging her throat. It took her a moment to even remember what they'd just cooked, but finally she managed. "My team and I did pan-roasted quail with a carpaccio of baby zucchini, strawberries, and avocado."

"Very pretty," observed the distinguished older gentleman who'd temporarily joined the judging team just before the finals, when celebrity chef Devon Sparks had to leave. Theo Jansen was a legend in culinary circles, although more so in New York than on the West Coast, since that's where his restaurant empire was based.

But every chef in the nation recognized him as the founder of the Rising Star Chef competition. The fact that he'd complimented anything about her food gave Skye a thrill that chased some of the gut-wrenching negativity out of her system—even if he might not be a judge for much longer. There was a rumor floating around that Eva Jansen was looking for someone to replace her father on the judging panel.

Until then? Skye was going to take the compliment and enjoy it. "Thank you," she said. "I hope you enjoy the flavors."

The third judge, Kane Slater, had been silent until now, but he was the first to grab a fork and dig in.

"Nice color on the bird," he said as he cut through the crispy, brown skin of the quail with a satisfying crackle. "Wow. The strawberry! I wasn't expecting that."

A trickle of sweat tickled its way down Skye's spine. She cast a nervous glance at the rest of her teammates. The strawberry had been her addition.

"I thought the dish needed a little more color and juice," she offered, twisting her fingers into a knot behind her back. "And fruit is traditional with game birds."

"Yes. Usually the fruit is cooked, however." Claire leaned over to cut a small bite. Skye noticed how meticulous she was about getting a tiny sliver of every single element of the dish onto her fork. "Hmmm."

Theo Jansen tried it, too, and gave Skye a smile before thanking her and moving down the table toward Beck.

Before she could freak out too much that she couldn't tell what Ms. Durand and Mr. Jansen thought of her dish, Kane Slater gave her a quick wink and a surreptitious thumbs up. It wasn't enough to totally melt the tension in her shoulders, but it helped. Skye smiled at him gratefully, mentally promising to go out and buy every single one of his albums, even though she was more of a jazz girl herself.

Now that the judges had moved on, Skye's teammates crowded closer, reaching for spoons to snatch bites of the dish they'd collectively created.

Skye's best friend, Fiona Whealey, licked the bowl of her spoon and scowled. "It's good. No thanks to me. Damn it, what am I doing here?"

Fiona was the resident baker at the Queenie Pie Café. Baker, not pastry chef, and God help you if you called her by the wrong job title. Fiona was proudly self-taught, and no one made bread like Fee's, but her talents were wasted on these short, timed challenges.

Before Skye could move in for a comforting pep talk, her grill man stepped up. Hugging Fiona close with an arm around her narrow shoulders, Rex Roswell said, "Shut it, Fee-wee, you know we couldn't get anywhere without our flour-puff girl."

It was an old joke, but a reliable one. Fiona laughed and ducked away from Rex to smooth down her perfectly straight, extremely non-puffy hair. The platinum-blonde locks were as baby fine and soft as ever, Skye observed, glad of the long years of practice at denying her own envy.

She didn't even want to think about what her crazy red hair had been doing while she talked to Beck.

"I still think we woulda won if we'd gone vegan." Their resident hippie health nut poked morosely at the perfectly crisped skin stretched golden and tantalizing across the quail's breast. Nathan Yamaoka, the only Asian Rastafarian Skye had ever seen, was on a perpetual, if lackadaisical, campaign to turn the Queenie Pie Café into a vegetarian restaurant.

"I had you all set up for a nice little veggie dish," he went on.

"Who added the quail?" Skye interrupted, looking around at her team.

Oscar Puentes raised his hand, totally unconcerned by the scowling of his shorter, much skinnier, dreadlocked teammate. "That would be me."

Skye waited until Nathan had turned away, muttering something about dead baby birds, before she gave Oscar a discreet thumbs up and a grin.

Nathan was a genius with vegetables, and they had a huge number of vegetarian customers who were kept extremely satisfied and enthralled by his many innovative uses for kale, but her team was in the RSC to win it.

And glancing around at her competitors' dishes, Skye knew a salad wasn't going to cut it.

The judges walked back to the front of the kitchen, snapping Skye out of her unhappy thoughts and prompting her to make a grab for Rex, who was deeply involved in the second half of the flour-puff girl routine, which consisted of him trying to get his hands into Fiona's hair and rub her head until he'd generated enough static electricity to power a small city while she squawked a protest but secretly loved it.

"Guys! Quit it! The judges are about to announce the winner."

Get a room was what she wanted to say, but Skye restrained herself.

Eva Jansen swiveled her slinky hips to the front of the judges' group, her shiny brunette bob swinging smoothly against her chin. Why was it Skye's fate to be surrounded by gorgeous size-two women with perfect, glossy straight hair? This wasn't exactly how she'd pictured the restaurant business.

"Thank you, chefs, for some lovely small plates. Midwest team, the judges loved your gnocchi—I actually heard the phrase 'light as a feather,' which is not something I often associate with tiny balls of potato dough. But they're getting a little tired of the foam, and felt it should've had more shiitake flavor to really add something to the dish."

"Oooh, somebody's mad," Fiona muttered out of the side of her mouth, her pale blue eyes avid as she watched Ryan Larousse's reaction to the critique.

Skye bit the inside of her lip. Yeah, the Midwest team had made some mistakes, but it was down to the final three now. The small stuff was where it would all play out, and perfect dishes were rare.

"Chef Beck," Eva Jansen said, moving on. "Your local crab with tarragon champagne sauce seems to have been a favorite with the judges. According to my notes, it was the quick pickled cucumbers and shallots that tipped it over the edge from a nice, if uninspired, French-inflected dish to something new and uniquely yours. Good job."

Sneaking a glance at Beck, Skye wasn't surprised to find him looking entirely unmoved by the whole thing. Of freaking course. She wondered, as she had so often during their brief, tumultuous year of marriage, what it would take to truly move Henry Beck.

She'd certainly never cracked the code.

And if there was a part of her that thrilled with quiet pride for Beck at hearing such positive feedback from the judges, Skye squashed it just in time for Eva Jansen to turn to her with that feline smile curling up the corners of her too-red mouth.

Skye bit her lip again, never more aware of the fact that her all-natural tinted lip balm, while cruelty free and completely organic, didn't have as much staying power as whatever industrial-strength lipstick slicked Eva's scarlet mouth.

"And last but not least, we have the West Coast team. The team with home-field advantage here in San Francisco."

When Skye reflexively stretched her mouth into a smile, she had to hide a wince as the expression pulled against the sore worry spot inside her bottom lip. For the millionth time, she vowed to stop biting her lip at the first sign of stress.

Tension coiled through her ribs and slithered down into her stomach, making it hard to catch a breath.

"Want to know what the judges thought of your pan-roasted quail? They enjoyed it very much. But even more than that, they enjoyed the inventive use of fresh fruits and vegetables, and the way you helped those simple ingredients to sing through the dish."

Relief flooded Skye, even as the wildly triumphant look on Nathan's tan face made her want to groan. He was never going to let them hear the end of this.

The rest of her team was smiling and hugging, patting each other on the back, and Skye had to grind her molars together to keep from shaking them. *It's not over yet*, she wanted to scream. *They haven't announced the winner!*

Or the prize, come to think of it.

"You all put up wonderful dishes, but the dish all three judges agreed they'd go back to again and again—"

"I wanted to lick the plate," Kane Slater put in, with his usual infectious enthusiasm.

"Is that a euphemism?" Eva shot back, a mischievous twinkle in her eye. "Anyway, as I was saying, the judges ranked one team's dish the highest out of all three, and that team was . . ."

Skye had been holding her breath so long, her lungs burned.

"The East Coast team, from Lunden's Tavern!"

Beck's teammates whooped and shouted, all but tackling him to the ground, while Skye stood there feeling like a punctured helium balloon.

"Settle down, chefs. There's more. The last two teams—it was neck and neck, and we couldn't get a unanimous decision. But the majority vote went to the Midwest team for second place."

Now Skye was a helium balloon that had been punctured, deflated, and run over by a streetcar.

Last place. Her team was in last place.

Eva's pointy features softened a bit as she looked at the Queenie Pie gang. "You had strong support," she said. "But in the end, the judges felt that the Midwest team was more inventive, pushed a little harder, took more risks."

That's not true, Skye wanted to argue. *We took the risk of not actually cooking our accompaniment. We took the chance that you'd see that food doesn't have to be a science project to be delicious and exciting.*

What the hell was risky about doing a foam, when practically every chef in the nation was experimenting with liquid nitrogen and agar-agar?

But she clenched her jaw and smiled through the frustration. Arguing wouldn't solve anything, and would only serve to make her look like a sore loser.

Which, okay. Maybe she was, a little bit.

This day was so not turning out the way she'd hoped.

It had been a few years since basic training, but Beck still knew how to stand tall with a hundred-and-sixty-pound weight on his back.

And a good thing, too, since Winslow Jones was clinging to him piggy-back style and showed no signs of wanting to come down.

"You the man," he crowed directly into Beck's ear.

"All right, boys . . . and girl," Eva Jansen said with an amused glint in her eyes. "Settle down. Don't you want to find out what you've won?"

All of Beck's senses went on alert. A valuable advantage in the upcoming challenge, she'd said when first explaining the relay. With a roll of his shoulders and a quick torso twist Beck managed to dislodge Winslow and set the kid back on his sneakers on the solid ground. He needed to focus for this.

"Thank you." Eva was being as carefully bland and polite as Beck had ever seen her, obviously conscious of the fact that she was addressing a group of chefs who all knew she was dating one of the men in their ranks.

Beck shot his teammate Danny a quick, assessing glance. The guy was mirroring Eva's sleek, satisfied glow.

Things had gotten dicey back in Chicago when Eva had taken her quest to get the RSC televised too far. But now that she'd ditched the Cooking Channel and sent the cameras home, Beck thought everything should work out fine for her and Danny.

For a while, anyway.

Not that he thought Eva and Danny were mismatched—in fact, the millionaire playgirl and the family-oriented pastry chef were weirdly perfect for each other. But Beck didn't have a lot of faith in forever.

"As you all know," Eva began, "the next few days will be pivotal. The next challenge will decide which team goes home and which two will continue on to the final round, choosing two representatives to go head to head for the title of Rising Star Chef."

A rustle of nervous murmurs and shifting bodies blew

through the crowd of chefs like wind stirring up sand. Beck kept his eyes front and center, all his attention lasered on Eva.

"Up until now, the challenges have been very teamwork oriented. But for the finals, we'll be judging the work of individuals. So to prepare for that, in the next challenge we will be asking each team to essentially give us a bio. We want one signature dish from each chef on the team, one dish that sums up your cooking style and tells us who you are as a chef."

This time the murmurs through the crowd were excited, and Beck felt his own heart rate increase by a few BPMs. This was a good assignment, one that would allow each chef to really stretch and showcase his or her talents.

"You'll have tomorrow to shop and prep, and the morning of the following day to cook. We'll expect one small, amazing plate from each of you tomorrow afternoon. But there's a twist. East Coast team, are you listening? This is where your win comes in."

Beside Beck, Winslow nodded vigorously, bouncing up onto the toes of his white sneakers. Beck suppressed a grin.

Eva didn't bother, letting her lips stretch into a pleased, proud smile for just one moment before she went back to her professional face. "Each team will be doing their shopping in a different location around San Francisco. There are three choices, and the East Coast team gets to pick first. Then the Midwest team, then the West Coast team."

This was a big deal. A chef was only as good as his ingredients. Beck glanced over to where Skye Gladwell stood with her team.

Her face was frozen in a small, strained smile that didn't reach her blue eyes, and he had to turn away before the wave of sympathy swamped him. Yeah, it sucked that she got last dibs, and he'd much have seen that douche-truck Larousse ranked third, but there was nothing he could do about it now.

Eva paused dramatically, flipping her short brown hair off her face with an imperious head toss. "The shopping destinations are the Ferry Building Farmers' Market, the brand-new Fresh Foods store in the Mission, and China-town. You may discuss."

Beck turned to his group as they huddled up, but there was little or no discussion to be done. Basically, they all took one look at each other and said "Ferry Building."

Well, duh. A farmers' market, especially one as com-prehensive and amazingly stocked as the one at the San Francisco Ferry Building, was a no-brainer. The best, freshest produce, all of it local, seasonal, and perfect—it was hard to imagine choosing any of the other options. Grinning and relieved, they left the huddle and waited for the other teams to make their choices.

Eva Jansen wasn't kidding—this was a major advan-tage. Beck watched as Skye stood silently with her team, lips pressed into a thin line. There wasn't much point to them debating, was there? They were stuck with whatever the Midwest team didn't choose, by default. He wondered what she was hoping for as she squared her shoulders and reached up to corkscrew a few red-gold curls back into the knot on top of her head.

Ten years ago, Beck would've known the answer to that without even thinking.

Finally, Larousse and his team resurfaced, high-fiving each other and looking smug.

"Ready with your choices?" Eva asked.

When everyone nodded, she looked to Jules Cavanaugh, Beck's team leader. In a clear, firm voice, Jules said, "We'll take the Ferry Building Farmers' Market."

Beck, who was watching for it, saw the way Ryan

Larousse wrinkled his nose in annoyance, but apparently he'd been prepared for that answer, because when it came to his turn, he didn't even hesitate. "We'll go with the Fresh Foods in the Mission district."

Interesting. And not what Beck would've chosen if he'd had command of the Midwest team.

Cocking his head to catch Skye's reaction, Beck thought he was probably the only person in the kitchen who could read the tug of pleased surprise at the corner of her mouth.

"Guess that leaves us with Chinatown, then," she said, neutral as grapeseed oil, but Beck knew. She was happy.

There wasn't time after that to analyze just why he left the kitchen filled with a certain warmth.

He tried to convince himself that it was nothing but the job-well-done, mission-accomplished satisfaction of having won the day with his team. There was certainly plenty of backslapping and jubilating going on around him as they decamped for the hotel where the Jansen Hospitality Group had secured rooms for the competing chefs.

But deep down, part of him knew that at least an ounce of that warm, liquid pleasure sloshing in his belly was the knowledge that even after all these years, he could still read Skye Gladwell like a step-by-step recipe.

Now all he had to do was figure out how to use that knowledge to win the Rising Star Chef competition.

Chapter 4

Claire Durand definitely did not storm out of the competition kitchen—but it was a near thing.

She wasn't a woman given to fits of diva drama. As editor in chief of an internationally renowned food magazine, in charge of a revolving staff of temperamental, artistic, flighty journalists, photographers, test kitchen cooks, and columnists, Claire was known for keeping a level head.

When dealing with a photographer held hostage in a jungle by militants, Claire kept her sangfroid. In the face of crushing workloads during all major holidays, rigid deadlines, and plummeting budgets, Claire was a tower of calm, cool strength.

But even she had her limits.

Being forced to sit on a judging panel with two men who had entered into a humiliating, caveman-style battle for the right to claim her? Pushed her right up to the edge of those limits.

The glancing touch of long, blunt-tipped fingers on her shoulder tossed her off the edge and into free fall.

Throwing off the warm weight of the hand she'd recognize anywhere, Claire whirled to face Kane Slater.

Again, more dramatic than she preferred. She'd managed to keep it together for most of the challenge itself, but now that their audience of chef contestants had left the coordinator and judges alone in the kitchen, it was harder to keep a tight rein on her composure.

Kane backed up a step, hands held up as if she'd aimed a loaded gun at his chest. "Hey, now. Go easy, gorgeous, and tell me what's bugging you."

Kane Slater, with his shock of sun-kissed hair and deep blue eyes; his tightly muscled, compact form; the youthful, energetic vibrancy of his presence . . . just a glimpse of him caused every nerve in her body to throb out a quick, ecstatic burst of remembered pleasure.

What a pity Claire's body was not as sensible as the rest of her.

"There are no bugs," she snapped, losing her grasp on American idiom in a rush of embarrassed anger. "Which is to say, I'm fine."

"Yeah, you are." His gaze traveled over her from head to toe, warming her skin like a touch.

Shivering, Claire wished Kane's flirting didn't have the effect of making her insides turn to molten chocolate.

It should've been foolish, so over the top—but instead, his artless, honest appreciation for all things Claire made her want to throw herself into his arms like the naïve, lovelorn young girl she hadn't been for so many years.

But there was the danger he might interpret such an action to mean that she'd forgiven and forgotten . . . and she hadn't.

Besides, they weren't completely alone. Eva and her father were carrying on a low, serious conversation over by the door, and the mere sight of Theo Jansen was enough to make shame and betrayal rise up to swamp the swirling attraction that clouded the air.

"I thought I made my position very clear," she hissed,

rounding on Kane. "Rather than choose between you and Theo, I choose neither. I choose to be alone."

He shrugged. "That's your choice. Just like it's my choice not to give up on you."

This situation was untenable. But Claire didn't have time for the scream of frustration that was building in her chest, because at that moment, Eva and Theo concluded their discussion and came over to begin the judges' meeting they'd scheduled for after the preliminary challenge.

"It's official," Eva began, her eyes sparkling like smoky quartz. "Devon Sparks is coming back for the finals!"

Relief made Claire a little lightheaded. "That is wonderful news." She caught Theo Jansen's eye across the group. This meant he wouldn't have any reason to stay here, thereby cutting the level of tension on the judging panel in half.

"His wife is doing better, then?" Kane asked.

"It was his wife who called me," Eva said, laughing. "Apparently, Devon makes for a very exhausting, intense nursemaid. She's importing her aunt, Bertie or something, from Virginia and kicking her husband out of the penthouse and back over to us."

"I'm glad," Kane said, and Theo shot him a glare.

"Of course you are," he growled. "With me gone, you'll have no more competition for Claire's affections!"

"Whoa, Dad," Eva said, stepping between the two men just as Kane scowled and ground out, "I'm glad because Lilah Sparks is a nice lady, and it's good that she's feeling well enough to send her husband away in the middle of a difficult pregnancy. You total and complete ass."

Claire supposed there were women out there who would watch two alpha males snarling over them and, rather than feeling like pieces of meat about to be torn in two, would feel honored. Important. Powerful.

Claire was not one of them.

Kane shook his head in disgust and turned away, his broad shoulders tense under his thin cotton shirt. Claire watched him go, helpless to stop the unwanted curl of heat that melted through her lower body.

Stupid, stupid body.

"Enough." Eva raised her voice just enough to let them all know she meant business. Despite her inner turmoil, Claire felt a flash of pride in her young friend—since embracing her own faults and mistakes, and rising above them to reach for the love of the man she'd wronged, Eva had gained in both poise and confidence.

Which was slightly frightening, really, given how confident Eva had always seemed. But where the younger Eva's spiritedness had bordered on bravado at times, she now seemed more grounded—settled and sure of herself and her place in the world.

"Probably the best thing about Devon coming back is that we'll cut down on distractions like this," Eva bit out. "Dad, you know I love you, and I would never bar you from attending the competition you founded. But it's time for you to leave."

My, my. Claire regarded her friend with renewed interest. If Eva was throwing her father out of the judges' meeting, she certainly had gained confidence. The old Eva had been desperate for her father's love and respect, to the point of making choices that later came back to haunt her. But now . . .

Theo sputtered for a brief moment before recalling himself to gravitas. Lifting his leonine head, he studied his daughter as if searching her for a weakness.

Evidently finding none in Eva's calm, implacable expression, Theo turned to Claire, an appeal clear in his eyes.

But Claire had no sympathy left to spare for him. Not after he instigated the conversation that had led to her discovering that the young man she'd . . . come to care for could betray her confidence by dragging their affair out into a testosterone-measuring contest between chest-thumping men.

Oh yes, she was angry with Kane. But Theo was just as culpable, and she'd be pleased to see the back of him.

Raising her chin a notch to Ice Queen stature, she said, "I agree. With Devon returning, we have no more need of your help on the judges' panel. Go home, Theo."

Thwarted, Theo pressed his lips together so tightly, they disappeared into his impeccably trimmed salt-and-pepper beard. But he hadn't built America's largest restaurant empire by fighting losing battles.

Instead, he shrugged dignity over his shoulders like a perfectly tailored blazer and inclined his head. "Very well. Since everyone seems to be in agreement, I'll step down."

Out of the corner of her eye, Claire caught movement as Kane shifted his weight.

"I'll step down," Theo continued, voice hardening, "but I'm not leaving San Francisco. I'm staying for the finals."

"Of course you are," Kane said softly, with a bitter amusement that was wholly unlike him.

Theo tensed but didn't respond. When he kissed Eva on the cheek and stalked out of the kitchen, Claire felt a large chunk of the stress and emotional upset she'd been carrying for days go with him.

"Now," Eva said briskly, "let's get down to business. Here's what we're going to need to watch out for in the next challenge."

As she began outlining the specifics they'd be facing, Kane rejoined the conversation by walking back to stand at Claire's side.

He was close enough that she could feel the heat he gave off, the restless energy of his presence ruffling the air between them like a caress against her skin.

Theo might be gone, and with him, a portion of her tension. But the larger part—the part that had caused her the most intense emotional upheaval she'd experienced in the last twenty years—was still very much here.

And Kane was still very much intent on stirring Claire up, if she were to judge by the swift, wicked grin he slashed in her direction.

It was going to take everything she had, every trick she'd learned at the hands of callous, cruel men and faithless lovers, to hold strong against that smile and what it offered.

Claire could only hope she was strong enough.

Chapter 5

Twenty-four hours after escaping his second airplane in as many weeks, it was still all Beck could do not to fall to his knees and kiss the gritty San Francisco sidewalk every time he walked outside.

The mercifully solid, right-under-his-feet, surrounded-by-clear-open-space sidewalk.

That was a feeling he never thought he'd have about coming back home, but Beck had learned not to try to predict shit like that. People reacted all kinds of crazy ways when their adrenaline was up and their defenses were down.

Take him, for example.

Beck hated airplanes. Not as much as he hated submarines, but close. They both gave him that messed-up, suffocating feeling of being an anchovy packed into a thin metal canister, barely able to move or breathe or think through the rising panic.

"You doing okay?" Winslow Jones, line cook and mother hen extraordinaire, put a concerned hand on Beck's shoulder.

Caught between embarrassment that he'd freaked out

enough lately that people were starting to notice, and gratitude for his teammate's quiet worry, Beck blanked his tone with the ease of practice.

"Fine," he said shortly, hoping his expression communicated both *thank you* and *drop it*. He didn't shrug Win's hand off his shoulder, though.

Even if Winslow Jones, with his intense enthusiasms and hyperactive kitten-on-catnip behavior, sometimes drove Beck crazy, it was nice to have buddies again, to feel like part of a team. He'd missed that since he left the Navy.

Even though this team was all about culinary battles instead of real ones, that feeling of being in it together was the same. Through the ups and downs of the Rising Star Chef competition, they had each other's backs.

That had never been more clear than during the past week, ever since they lost the last round in a humiliating upset and only advanced to the next level of the contest by the skin of their nuts.

Beck really, really didn't want to think about the reasons behind that epic failure in Chicago. Not when he was finally catching his balance after the turbulent flight and the shock of Skye's demand for a divorce.

Okay, so his personal life was a train wreck. Fine. All he wanted to do was bask in his team's win on the relay challenge, breathe in the achingly familiar breeze off of San Francisco Bay, and figure out what the fuck he'd find here at the Ferry Building Farmers' Market to cook that would tell the judges who he was as a chef.

If he could maybe get Winslow to quit looking at him with so much freaking compassion and understanding, that would be a big bonus.

Win nodded and curled his hand into a fist, bumping Beck's shoulder companionably. The thin, chill light of the northern California sun cast dramatic shadows on his high, brown cheekbones. "Good. Because no way can I haul your gargantuan ass up off the pavement if you faint on me, son."

Beck grinned. He knew what to do with this. "Come on, Jones. I know you work out. How much do you bench, one-fifty? One-eighty?"

Win sniffed, tossing his close-cropped head as if to brush his nonexistent long hair out of his light green eyes. "Bitch, please. I work out to achieve the Unattainable Gay Ideal Body, not to be able to actually lift heavy shit. Although . . ." Pursing his lips, he made a big show of looking Beck up and down. "You're not so far off from attaining that ideal, Mr. Universe. Where'd you get all those muscles, anyway?"

"You're not going to tease me into squirming," Beck told his winking teammate. "So you can quit licking your chops."

Pretending to pout, Win's eyes nevertheless held that sharp glint of intelligence so many people missed when they looked at the energetic, enthusiastic young chef. "You are a mystery, Henry Beck."

Beck frowned. He wasn't trying to be mysterious. He just didn't like to talk about himself. Or anything, really.

He liked to cook. That was it.

"Don't call me Henry," Beck said, a hint of growl in his tone. He didn't mean to be so gruff, but it was out there already, making Win's eyes widen with surprise.

See? This was why Beck didn't do talking. Words messed everything up.

"Sorry," he said, before Win could make everything worse by stuttering out the apology that was already clear in his eyes. "I just . . . I haven't been called that in a long time. It's not really who I am anymore."

Win got that all-seeing, all-knowing expression on his face again. Beck looked away, focusing on the crowds milling through the stalls piled with fresh fruits and vegetables. His mind catalogued their surroundings automatically, everything from the fanny pack–wearing tourist exclaiming over the free samples of late summer raspberries to the young woman in workout gear buying a pound of cedar-smoked salmon from the vendor on the corner.

November was always gorgeous in San Francisco, the last gasp of warmth before winter rolled over the city. Despite everything, Beck was glad the producers of the Rising Star Chef competition had set the final round of the contest here.

Like a sucker, Beck let his gaze expand across the Bay, sharpening on the dingy gray outline of office towers and apartment buildings that formed the Oakland skyline. It looked better, cleaner, from this distance, with the fog over the water softening its hard edges.

"What's over there?" Win asked, hooking one sneaker-clad foot on the lowest rung of the railing running around the Ferry Plaza. Unable to keep still, as usual, he proceeded to climb the guard fence as if it were a set of monkey bars, completely heedless of the drop into the choppy, dirty waters below him.

"Oakland." Beck kept a surreptitious hand out to spot Win, ready to grab him by the seat of his pants if it looked like he was about to go tumbling into the drink. "If you fall in, I'm not diving in after you."

"Pssh. I won't fall. I have the balance of a jungle cat. Rowr."

Hovering behind Winslow—*Who's the mother hen now?* Beck asked himself with a twist of the mouth—he wondered where the hell the rest of the team was.

This was why single-minded focus won the day. Because once you started letting other things—sex, relationships, love—into your head, it messed you up until you couldn't even remember a simple meeting time.

Case in point: Danny Lunden, their team's pastry chef, was probably off with the woman who ran the RSC, Eva Jansen. Their combustible relationship had definitely contributed to the failure of the Chicago round, but sadly Beck couldn't lay the whole entire fiasco at their feet.

Danny wasn't the only one who'd been off his game.

Danny's brother, Max Lunden, and childhood best friend, Jules Cavanaugh—who were, incidentally, all over each other and upping the soap opera quotient of the team by about a thousand—were another spanking new couple.

Add to that the fact that Max and Danny's father, Gus, was recovering from heart problems bad enough to land him in the hospital, and you had a team with more than a few distractions pulling their attention off the ultimate prize.

They were supposed to be meeting up first thing this morning to get their shopping done fast and head back to the competition kitchen for prep. But here it was, edging on toward nine o'clock, and no lovebirds.

Beck tightened his jaw and controlled his impatience. There was nothing to do but wait. And be glad he'd kept himself free of emotional entanglements and the mushy brain function they caused.

"So are you worried about competing against your estranged wife?"

Beck shot Winslow a quick look, but Win's head was ducked against his chest as he maneuvered his skinny, wiry body up to sit on the top railing.

"No. It'll be fine." *Please God, keep Winslow from apologizing again for that clusterfuck last week.*

There was a pause while Win wiggled his way upright and twined his feet under the bottom railing for balance. His light brown skin didn't really show a blush, but Beck was willing to bet the kid's cheeks were flaming hot under that sprinkling of dark freckles. "Okay, good."

Silence stretched between them for a long moment, broken only by the hoarse squawk of foraging seagulls and the cheerful clatter of produce vendors and shoppers behind them.

Win clearly still felt bad about the part he'd played in the whole world finding out about Beck's past. But Beck didn't hold a grudge. It wasn't Win's fault, and Beck recognized the signs of an impending shame spiral. He needed a distraction before Winslow had them both rehashing past events that couldn't be changed.

Nodding at the hazy Oakland skyline across the water, Beck said, "That's where I grew up."

Giving a start of shock, Winslow nearly toppled off the railing. Eyes wide, arms pinwheeling, he grabbed for Beck's arm.

"You what? You're from here? I can't believe you didn't say anything."

"I'm saying something now."

Win's eyes went from round as dinner plates to cat-eye slits. "Yeah, you are. Offering up tidbits about your childhood to try and stop me from gossiping about you and digging into your mysterious past?"

This time, Beck did shrug free of Winslow's hand. "Fuck off, kid. There's nothing mysterious about me. Nothing interesting, either. That's what I'm trying to tell you."

Winslow threw up his hands in exasperation and nearly fell off the railing again. "Nothing mysterious? You're nothing *but* mystery. You got hired on at Lunden's Tavern, what, six months ago? And shit, *Henry*, I only found out your first name, like, last week! You don't talk. No one knows shit about you. You're all tall, dark, and mean looking, but you're not mean, so what the hell? And you cook fish like you grew up . . . living on the ocean." Win twisted his torso to get a better look at the strip of Oakland shore that jutted out into the bay. "Huh."

"You're determined to turn my life into an episode of *Law & Order*. I hate to break it to you, Detective, but I didn't learn to cook growing up in Oakland."

Beck could only imagine the crap he would've taken if he'd shown any interest in something like that, back then.

Interest flared in Win's eyes as he swiveled back around. "No? Then where—?" But he closed his eyes, squeezed them tightly shut, and stopped himself. "Okay. Forget I even started this convo. I promised myself after everything that went down in Chicago, I'd quit snooping. Curiosity isn't going to get the best of this cat again, no sir. You got secrets? Keep 'em."

Beck let an arched brow speak for him.

"No, I mean it, man," Winslow said, hopping down from the railing, finally, and giving Beck an earnest look. "I should've been cool and just let you tell us your story in your own time."

The kid was trying so hard. Beck wanted to meet him halfway. Struggling for a moment, he came up with, "Thanks. That would be nice." And watched the light die out of Win's eyes as he deflated a little and turned away, like a puppy who'd been smacked on the nose with a rolled-up newspaper.

Damn it.

"It never bothered me that you wanted to know more about my past," Beck offered. "Because I knew, even if I didn't tell you, it wouldn't make any real difference."

Win frowned as he started back toward the cluster of food stalls. "What do you mean?"

What the hell? Might as well go all the way. "It didn't matter to you, not for real. You were curious, you made up stories about me—yeah, I knew about that. And for the record, I was never in prison, I'm not in the Witness Protection Program, and I'm not the missing son of some Balkan royal family."

"Oh man," Win whimpered, covering his face with one dramatic hand. "I need some coffee." Splaying his fingers, he peered at Beck. "That didn't bug the crap out of you?"

Beck shrugged. "You treated me the same, no matter what crazy story you believed that week. All of you, Gus and Nina, Danny and Jules, even Max when he came home—you accepted me for who I am now. The past is over and gone; it's done. That's why I don't talk about it. And in spite of the stories, I know you don't really care one way or the other. I'm just Beck, fish cook, to you. And I like that. Before Lunden's Tavern, I never really had that."

He flashed on an image of the restaurant that first day, when he came in to interview with Nina Lunden. Max and Danny's smiling, sharp-eyed mom was the first person Beck ever met who made him feel at ease from the get-go. He imagined that was how most people felt about coming home.

Dropping his hand, Winslow blinked up at him. "Wow. I think that's the most I ever heard you say at one time."

"Yeah, well, don't get used to it. I'm not going to start wanting to have regular gab fests or anything."

"Aw. And here I was hoping we could have a sleepover and braid each other's hair." Win bounced up on his heels, hooking his hands in the front pockets of his low-hanging jeans. "No, man. You go on and work that strong, silent shit. Somebody on this team has to be better at listening than talking."

Beck smiled, because there it was again, that casual, complete acceptance the Lunden's Tavern team tossed around like it was nothing.

But to him, it was everything, and he'd do whatever he could to repay them for it.

Winslow smiled back and offered his fist for a bump. "We're cool, man. And I was serious about that coffee. You want? There's a place inside the terminal that's supposed to be killer."

"No, thanks," Beck said. "But you go ahead. I'll stay out here and wait for everyone else. If we get too spread out, we'll never find each other again, and I think we should do a quick tactical before we start shopping."

With a wave and a head bop, Winslow melted into the crowd, and Beck turned his attention back to surveying the market itself, scanning for a glimpse of his other team-mates.

Standing head and shoulders above most of the sea of people milling around him, Beck crossed his arms and tried not to notice the wide berth the other shoppers gave him. When he caught himself scowling and ducking his head to let his chin-length hair swing across and hide his face, he jammed his hands into his pockets and moved out of the flow of foot traffic.

The market was a riot of color and life, scraggly-bearded organic farmer hippies in ripped tank tops rubbing shoulders with young mothers in yoga pants pushing strollers. An arriving ferry pulled in to the dock around the back corner of the building, disgorging a group of up-and-coming urban professionals in slim-cut suits, on their way from their homes in the 'burbs to jobs in the city.

Northern California's growing season extended well into November, and the vendors' tables were piled high with tail-end-of-summer goodies, mounds of sun-warmed nectarines and opulent globes of Italian eggplant glowing deeply purple in their baskets. The air smelled exciting, full of the ripe scent of fresh fruits and vegetables, the rich soil still clinging to them.

Beck's mind was conditioned now to see the potential

in ingredients like this. He wandered closer to a forager's stall, where a blackboard easel sported amazingly detailed chalk drawings of chanterelles and maitakes.

Mentally calculating the meatiness of a sautéed mushroom against the delicate brine of a seared diver scallop, Beck scrolled through possible accompaniments. A ginger butter sauce? Or maybe something with more acid, like a brown butter and lemon vinaigrette. He put out a thoughtful finger to the overflowing basket of grayish brown fungus, relishing the grit of the dirt under his fingertips.

"When did you start liking mushrooms?"

Chapter 6

Beck froze with one hand outstretched, his broad, blunt fingertip pressed to the smoothly rounded silken head of a dark portobello.

The chill brilliance of afternoon sunlight reflecting off of San Francisco Bay whited out his vision for a long moment—or maybe that was the swift blow to the head of hearing Skye Gladwell's sweet, bright voice directly behind him.

Turning to face her, Beck steeled himself for the sight he was pretty sure he'd never get used to: Skye as a woman, not a girl. Her hair was a cloud of strawberry-blonde curls around her pretty, heart-shaped face—so familiar and at the same time, so changed.

The face he'd once known better than his own was the face of a stranger now.

Still, it didn't take the familiarity of years to read the mocking note in her casual tone.

"I learned to like a lot of things, the last ten years," Beck replied. "Learned to hate a lot of things, too."

It wasn't hard to keep his voice even and calm. He'd had lots of practice, in way worse circumstances than standing in front of a vegetable vendor's tent, staring down the first person he'd ever loved.

His wife. Who wanted a divorce.

Good thing he didn't love her anymore, or that would probably hurt.

Curiosity sparked in Skye's changeable blue-green eyes, colors shifting like waves out at sea, but she didn't ask what else he'd learned.

She'd changed, too.

One swift glance was enough to take her in from head to toe. Clearly, Skye still favored comfort over style. Her ankle-length, gypsyish skirt was the color of denim but made of something much softer. She had a sweatshirt tied haphazardly around her curvy waist, rucking up the hem of her loose, flowing top and exposing a tantalizing sliver of tanned, smooth belly. She shifted and silver flashed in the sun, catching his eye.

Belly-button ring, his stunned mind processed, even as his mouth dried out and his heart rate increased to battle-station conditions.

A little mental discipline, please.

Forcing his mind away from the image of himself dropping to his knees and tonguing that new, taunting bit of jewelry and the warm, salt-sweet body beneath it, Beck studied the rest of her, taking in the details he hadn't had time to assess at the relay challenge the day before.

Her cheeks were pink with more than whatever emotion swamped her at the sight of the husband she no longer wanted, and her red-gold curls were escaping from the knot on top of her head in wild corkscrews. The fact that she had the sweatshirt at all when it was easily seventy-five degrees in the sun . . .

"Just come off the ferry?" he asked casually, and didn't even try to keep himself from enjoying the surprised dilation of her pupils.

"How did you—?" She faltered, glancing over her shoulder to the large transport craft still bobbing gently on the water. Swaying to her left made the bangle bracelets around her wrists jingle like bells. "Yeah, I'm meeting my team in Chinatown."

Wait a minute. "Your restaurant is in Berkeley."

She lifted her chin, "Queenie Pie Café," she said. "Corner of Shattuck and Bancroft."

Beck took a deliberate step to his right, more for show than because she actually impeded his view. Yep, he'd been right.

The orange lettering on the side of the boat spelled out "Golden Gate Ferry."

"That ferry didn't come from Berkeley," he said. "The Golden Gate line makes runs from . . ."

If her little chin got any higher, she'd be staring straight up at the clouds. "From Sausalito," she confirmed. "That's right. I'm living there now."

In spite of Beck's personal vow not to try to predict emotional reactions, he was still surprised by the sudden wash of disappointment that soaked through him.

Sausalito. The quaint, picturesque artist colony where Skye's free-spirited, radical parents lived, painted, wrote political rants disguised as plays, and kept their daughter gently but firmly ground under their vegan shoes.

Skye had hated Sausalito, had danced a wild, spinning circle around their first, tiny, crappy apartment over a grocery store in Chinatown, swearing she'd never go back. And now, here she was, a Sausalito resident—even though it meant an hour and a half commute every morning and night.

Maybe Skye hadn't changed as much as he thought, if she was still living her life to please her parents.

Goddess of the stars, could this get any worse?

Feeling the tickle of her stupid red hair frizzing around

her face, Skye impatiently yanked her hands over her head and tucked what she could back into the rubber band securing her bun.

She was windblown, exhausted from the trip home from Chicago, pissed about the loss yesterday, stressed after dealing with her parents on about three hours of sleep, and now this.

Henry Beck, standing here before her, in the huge, handsome, judgmental flesh.

He looked . . . big. Had he always been so tall? So broad through the shoulders? The heather gray of his cotton T-shirt stretched taut across his chest, his biceps straining the sleeves. The baggy fit of his jeans did nothing to hide the leanness of his hips or the strength of thighs.

And she might not have a good view of it at the moment, but Skye could draw up a mental image of his deliciously tight, muscular backside just by closing her eyes.

He was harder than her memories, though, in a lot of ways. There were creases in his angular face, lines beside his dark eyes that hadn't been there ten years ago. Probably from squinting into the blazing sun reflecting off an ocean on the other side of the world.

Henry's eyes, so dark brown they were almost black, had always been impenetrable. Impossible to read, unless he wanted to let you in on what he was thinking. Which was almost never, with most people, but Skye used to have an all-access pass to the inner workings of Henry Beck's brain.

Not anymore. She had to remember he wasn't her Henry any longer—he was Beck.

When she'd first seen him again, in that competition kitchen in Chicago's Gold Coast Arms Hotel, she'd nearly been sucked right into the black hole of those deep, shadowy eyes.

She'd stuttered and stammered, stumbled all over herself and acted like a complete fool. As per usual. While Henry—no, Beck—had stood and watched, as calm and impassive as if they'd never met.

Never laughed together. Never kissed. Never promised to be there for each other, no matter what.

As if he'd never abandoned her, left her alone in their studio apartment with nothing but a check that covered the next month's rent, a shiny new insurance card, and a baby on the way.

Swallowing down the familiar, careworn surge of grief, Skye reminded herself she didn't need Henry Beck and his Navy salary and benefits to get by anymore.

And she had living, breathing proof that he wasn't the only man in the world who could ever bring himself to care about her.

Bringing an image of Jeremiah, with his dark blond hair and twinkling green eyes, to the forefront of her mind calmed her down considerably.

Holding her head high enough to put a crick in her neck, Skye told herself she didn't give a damn what Beck thought about her living situation. He'd given up the right to comment on it a decade ago.

"So how are your parents, anyway?"

It was amazing how quickly it came back to her, that old sense of caution whenever the subject of her family came up with Beck. "They're fine," she told him. "Peter's got a new play up at the Royal, and Annika's experimenting with plastics. You know, business as usual."

He nodded and that was it. Awkward silence dropped over them like a blanket, muffling the sounds of the market. For pretty much the first time ever, Skye wished she wore a watch, so she could check it and have an excuse to get out of this awful conversation.

If she stayed here much longer, and she'd be in serious

danger of letting Beck see everything she hoped to keep hidden—namely, that he'd ripped her heart out when he left, and she'd never quite managed to get it back.

"Sounds like nothing has changed."

His voice was flat, heavy with the weight of a hundred arguments, but even through the blankness, Skye could hear his contempt.

"Not true," she countered, tossing her head in another attempt to get the wind-whipped hair out of her mouth. "I'm ten years older, ten years wiser, with ten years of restaurant experience under my belt. And no matter what our history is, I am going to wipe the floor with you in this competition."

The black arches of his brows shot up toward his hairline. "You *have* changed. You didn't used to be so direct. Or so competitive."

Yeah, well, I didn't used to be responsible for the livelihoods of an entire staff, not to mention my parents. And I didn't used to know that there was any way to be happy without you.

But all she said was, "Get used to it. We're almost to the finals, Beck." Unable to help the wave of excitement that crashed over her head when she thought about it, Skye grinned. "I mean, can you believe it? We started out competing against four other teams, and now it's just your team, my team . . ."

"And that asshole, Ryan Larousse," Beck growled.

Skye's thrill evaporated like fog over the bay. "Can't you let that go?"

Shock erased the blank expression from Beck's face. "He tried to trip you when you were carrying a pot full of scalding hot liquid."

Wincing, Skye pointed out, "But he apologized! I'm sure he just didn't think his actions through. He didn't really mean to hurt me—he was trying to get a rise out of you. And he succeeded!"

Beck's mouth firmed into a hard, straight line. It was the look that told Skye, without words, that nothing she said was going to change his mind. "I won't apologize for protecting you."

And Skye felt it again, that strange, conflicting welter of emotions she'd thought long behind her—the softening of tenderness spiced with gratitude bumping up against the tense, coiled unhappiness at being the cause of violence in the world.

Not only generalized, capital-V Violence, either, but violence done and risked by this familiar stranger standing in front of her.

Well, no more. "I'm not asking you to apologize," she said, dragging calm into her chest along with a cleansing breath. "Because I know that would be a waste of time. But I am asking you to respect my wishes. Once the final round of the Rising Star Chef competition starts, I don't care what Ryan Larousse pulls, you stay out of it. I'm a big girl, Beck. We might technically be married, but that's just paperwork. You're not my husband in any way that matters. And it's been a long time since I needed a street-tough kid in my corner to fight my battles for me. I meant what I said yesterday. I want that divorce, Beck."

His expression of cool detachment never faltered. "No argument from me," he said, without any inflection at all, and suddenly the tiny, faltering, brainless spark of hope Skye had harbored collided with a rage she thought she'd long ago come to terms with, igniting a stinging, burning fire in her chest.

"No, no arguments," she agreed viciously. "God forbid you should show enough emotion to fight for what you want."

"I thought you hated fighting." Beck arched one brow. "At least, that's what you said when I enlisted."

"What I hated was being alone in every fight. What I hated was never knowing how you felt—about anything! I hated . . ." *That you were leaving me.* Skye stopped herself before she could say it, breathing harshly.

There it was again. Hate. She didn't want to be someone who threw that word around lightly.

Trying for calm, she said, "This is pointless. You never understood, never even tried—you're not going to start getting it now, after ten years apart."

"Why do you want this divorce? I mean, why now?" he asked suddenly. "You could've brought this up back in Chicago."

Because last week in Chicago, she hadn't gotten that cryptic email from Jeremiah, promising her a brand-new future.

Panic buzzed through her. Should she tell Beck the truth? Would that make him more likely to give her what she wanted?

No way. Beck didn't get any more of her than he'd already had.

"I don't understand why we're even having this discussion," she hedged. "I'm trying to make it easier for you to do what you do best. Walk away."

Her words dropped into the pause between them like ice into a glass of water. When Beck spoke again, his voice was dangerously soft, and Skye tensed all over before she'd even registered what he was saying.

"You know what? No."

Her jaw dropped. "No? No, what? No divorce? You don't get to say no!"

"And yet, here I am, my mouth shaping the word and . . . huh, yeah, seems like my vocal cords are working okay, because no. Uh uh. Forget it."

Shock tightened her throat until she was the one struggling for words. "But you . . . you left me! A decade ago." A thought occurred to her, and she poked a triumphant finger into his wide, solid chest. "I don't need your consent! I'll claim abandonment."

Looking down at her from his great height, Beck seemed to loom until he blocked out the sun, and the sky, and the crowds around them, until it was almost like they were alone, the only two people on the planet. "A no-contest divorce would be so much faster, so much simpler."

Gritting her teeth until her jaw throbbed, she said, "But if you won't give me one . . ."

"I tell you what," Beck said, his dark eyes unreadable. "I'll play you for it."

Skye gaped again. "Excuse me?"

"I'm assuming our teams both get through to the final round—that dickhead Larousse is a one-trick pony who's already played out his entire act. So it'll be down to an East meets West matchup, in the end." Beck crossed his arms over his massive chest. "If your team wins, I'll give you your no-fault, no-strings, no-fuss divorce."

Skye's thoughts scattered like a bucket of chopsticks dumped on the floor. Groping for a rational response, she managed, "And what do you get if you win?"

He shrugged. "I'll still give you the divorce, but I'll want something in return."

Narrowing her gaze on his impassive face, she said, "Like what?"

A spark ignited deep in his dark brown eyes, sending a too-familiar shiver straight down Skye's spine. Beck leaned forward until his forehead almost rested against hers, his presence warm and overwhelming.

"One last night with you."

Chapter 7

Skye goggled at him. He couldn't be serious.

"You can't be serious!"

Beck straightened to his full, more than impressive height. "Why not? If I remember correctly, sex was never one of our problems. Why shouldn't we enjoy one last night, for old times' sake, before we vacate each other's lives for good?"

Because I've got a boyfriend, Skye though frantically. But now, more than ever, she couldn't say that.

She knew Beck. In this mood, he'd stubbornly do the opposite of whatever Skye wanted, just to prove he could. She understood where that impulse came from, but it didn't make him any easier to deal with now.

"Because we're getting a divorce," she tried, instead of the truth. "And I'd rather have a clean break."

"Guess you'd better plan to win the RSC, then."

"I haven't agreed to this stupid bet yet," Skye reminded him.

"You will," he said, in that simple, egoless way that always drove her bananas. He really wasn't being arrogant or commanding. He was just telling it like he saw it.

And the worst part was, he was almost always right.

"You'll agree," he continued, "because either way, you get what you want. It's a good deal, and you're too smart not to take it . . . unless you don't think your team can beat us."

"God, you're infuriating," Skye said, shaking her head. It wasn't like she couldn't see what he was doing by challenging her, rousing her competitive instincts and bringing them into the negotiations, but still. It was working.

She took one last stab at talking them both out of it. "Are you really gonna make a bet that relies on someone else's skill?"

He frowned. "I don't follow."

"From what I've seen, if the East Coast team makes it all the way to the finals, it's most likely to be Max or Jules who goes into that final cook-off. Not you."

A glimmer of hope shone through. She definitely had him there—Jules Cavanaugh was the East Coast team leader, and out of everyone on the team, Max had the most competition experience. Either of them was a more probable choice than Beck.

"Of course it won't be me." Beck's impassive dismissal killed Skye's last hope like a hand flipping a light switch. "I was hired on at Lunden's Tavern less than a year ago. I'm not the guy. Doesn't matter, we're a team. Their win is my win."

"So . . ." Skye floundered a little, having a hard time reconciling this team player in front of her with the fiercely independent loner she'd married. "You'd trust the outcome of our bet to someone else's cooking?"

His eyes shifted away from her, fixing on something in the distance out over the bay—or maybe on something deep inside, that only Beck could see. "I learned how to function as part of a group a long time ago. It comes down to trust. My team knows I've got their backs. And I know they've got mine. We're going to win."

He zeroed in on her face again, this time with an intensity that singed Skye's nerves like a jolt from a live wire. "And when we do, you'll be mine again for one final night before I let you go."

Skye's throat closed down tighter than a fist as everything low down in her body went taut and liquid with a sudden rush of unwelcome desire. Could she really risk this?

Her self-preservation instincts were screaming at her to turn him down—but it was so terrifyingly easy to rationalize accepting. After all, as he'd said, either way it went, she'd get her divorce. And she really believed her team could beat any other group of chefs out there.

Plus, whispered a tiny voice inside, *don't you want to find out if the reality of being touched by Beck lives up to your memories?*

Chances were, the memories were wildly exaggerated. Who knew? If she lost, she could find out that she didn't respond to Henry Beck any more than she did to Jeremiah. Talk about a win/win situation.

"Okay, fine. I accept the bet. With one condition."

He arched a brow as if he wasn't convinced she was in any position to make demands, but said, "Go on."

"This stays between us. No locker-room talk with the rest of your team, no gossip."

The last thing Skye needed was to finally secure her quiet, quickie divorce, only to have Jeremiah hear all about it if he managed to show up to watch the finals as he'd promised. It was bad enough that everyone in the competition knew she and Beck were still married, after that humiliating public spectacle in Chicago.

She could only thank her lucky stars that Eva Jansen had kicked the camera crews back to L.A. The last thing

Skye needed was to have the details of her marital status broadcast across the airwaves.

"Agreed," Beck said, satisfaction smoothing his voice to a low growl. He gave her one of his rare smiles, and Skye was dismayed by how much it still lit her up inside to see that stern, grim face crease into an expression of happiness.

Although this time, his happiness sent a bolt of fear straight through her chest.

What had she gotten herself into?

Beck trusted his instincts. He'd had to start relying on them when he was just a kid, and they'd kept him alive and whole this long.

He didn't think those instincts had ever prompted him to do something this crazy before—but as he stared down at Skye Gladwell's soft, flushed cheeks, her determined little chin and bright blue eyes, he couldn't regret it.

He could, however, ignore the voice inside that suggested he might've arranged this bet because there was more than a culinary competition and a backlog of sexual chemistry between Beck and his estranged wife.

Luckily, he didn't have much time to think about what other reasons he might have for not wanting to just give Skye her divorce, because he heard a voice shouting his name over the din of the farmers' market crowd.

Beck turned and threw up a hand in greeting, searching the sea of moving bodies for the familiar heads of his teammates. Spotting them over by the entrance to the indoor Ferry Building concourse, Beck glanced back to say goodbye to Skye, only to find she'd already gone.

He couldn't stop himself from scanning the crowd once more, this time for a small, strawberry-blonde woman, but she'd melted into the eddying current of foot traffic as seamlessly as if she'd had stealth training.

Beck made his way over to his teammates, frowning at the way people scurried to get out of his way like they thought he might go on a rampage and start cracking skulls if they didn't make space for him.

There was a weird, empty feeling in his chest. He didn't like it.

Rubbing at his sternum, Beck caught up to Jules, Max, and Danny just as Jules held up her phone and said, "Oh, a text from Win came through while I was on the phone. He's at the Blue Bottle Coffee stand inside. Let's go grab him and then have a conference about what we're each planning to cook for the challenge."

As Beck followed everyone else into the cool interior of the Ferry Building, he only vaguely registered Max's worried tone as he questioned Jules about the phone call from back home in New York.

Most of Beck's attention was on his surroundings. The Ferry Building sure hadn't looked like this when Beck lived in Oakland.

Even with its high domed ceiling and skylights, it felt dim after the glare off the water outside. Automatically adjusting for the decreased visibility, Beck barely listened as the rest of his team chatted excitedly about the produce they'd seen and what dishes they wanted to make.

The words of the challenge itself kept playing themselves out over and over in Beck's head.

One dish that sums up your cooking style, who you are as a chef . . .

So who are you, Henry Beck?

That was a question he'd avoided answering for a long time.

He knew what he could accomplish. He had absolute confidence in his own ability to survive, to overcome, to succeed. The Navy had given him that, and for a long time, it had been enough.

"I'm going to make ramen," Max announced. "With a sous-vide duck egg and barbecued pork belly. It's the perfect blend of ancient traditions and cutting-edge techniques and ingredients."

"So it's perfectly you," Jules said, squeezing his arm with an intimate smile. "I'm thinking about a play on steak frites, making my own skinny fries, some kind of horseradish crème fraiche. Maybe doing the beef raw, like a tartar or a carpaccio. Haven't decided."

"Talk about perfectly you." Her best friend, Danny, laughed. "Dad would bust his whites open, he'd be so proud."

Danny and Max were brothers, and their father, Gus, owned Lunden's Tavern, where the entire East Coast team worked. Jules was the executive chef at Lunden's, and she'd been working there since her teens. She liked to say the Lunden family taught her everything she knew about life, love, family, and red meat.

Beck wondered what that would be like, to be so accepted into someone else's family that they honestly thought of you as theirs.

Coming up through the foster care system, Beck had seen a lot of families interact with kids who didn't truly belong to them, and until he'd met Jules and the Lunden clan, he would've sworn that kind of unconditional acceptance wasn't possible.

It definitely hadn't been for him.

Danny, the team's pastry chef, was going on about some fruity creation he wanted to try, using some of the farm-fresh produce the vendors were selling outside, and Beck forced himself to tune back into the strategy session just as Winslow appeared at his side, holding two white paper cups billowing fragrant steam.

"Here, man," Winslow said, offering one of the coffees. "Got you some."

"Thanks." Beck was surprised, and covered it by reaching into his back pocket for his wallet. "What do I owe you?"

"Nothing, nothing, it's on me." Winslow grinned that bright, hundred-and-fifty-watt grin, but it didn't really reach his light green eyes.

Beck suppressed a sigh, knowing Winslow still blamed himself for the part he'd played in instigating the big confrontation with Skye back in Chicago.

Beck would have to find a way to let the kid know it wasn't a big deal, but now wasn't the time. They all needed to be focused on the upcoming challenge.

"So what are you thinking of making?" Jules asked Winslow, curiosity brightening her brown eyes to amber.

"Oh, you know," Win said vaguely. "A salad, maybe. To round out the meal. I'm cool with filling in, whatever the menu needs."

A slight frown creased Jules's forehead. "I'm not sure that's the point of the challenge," she reminded him gently. "They want us to come up with a signature dish. Basically, you on a plate."

"So I'm a salad." Winslow shrugged, avoiding everyone's gaze as he took a sip of his coffee. "Or a nice veggie soup, something light and bright and full of flavor. Like me."

He grinned again, and this time it lit up his whole face. "Ok, I guess I'm doing a soup. What's the Beckster got planned?"

All eyes turned to Beck, who froze for a bare instant before unlocking his muscles and lifting his coffee to his mouth, buying time.

"I'm doing fish," he said when he'd swallowed the hot, incredibly deep and intense coffee. Tipping the cup at Win, he silently acknowledged the greatness of the brew.

God, he'd missed West Coast coffee.

"Well, we know that," Jules said with a grin. Beck could practically hear the eye roll in her voice. "But 'fish' covers a lot of territory."

"What's your signature dish?" Max asked helpfully. "The one you've cooked for the most people or gotten the most requests for."

Beck's most requested dish? That had to be the linguini with clam sauce he'd whipped up after scamming a case of canned clams off the quartermaster of another boat when the submarine had surfaced near Greece.

The boys had gorged themselves on the pasta, slippery with salty, lemony sauce and the satisfyingly chewy clams, until they'd devoured every single can. For at least a year after, whenever Beck took requests before heading out on libo to forage for contraband and extra rations, he'd get at least a couple of seamen who remembered that clam sauce and asked for it again.

But this was the Rising Star Chef competition, he reminded himself, shaking the past away. He wasn't going to pop a tin of pilfered clams open and dump it over some noodles.

The judges weren't going to be as easy to please as a bunch of sailors who'd been cooped up on an underway sub for five months without a break.

"I haven't decided yet," Beck said calmly, aware that he was projecting enough fuck-off vibes to propel everyone around him back a step.

His teammates, though, God love 'em, weren't easily intimidated.

"Sounds good," Danny said, slapping him on the shoulder. "Walk around a bit, see what looks nice and fresh. That's my plan, too."

Everyone nodded, apparently used to Beck not talking or contributing much. Setting his jaw, Beck tried not to hate himself.

He'd come up with something to cook, and everything would be fine.

But as the rest of his team walked away, pairing off naturally as they went in search of their ingredients, he couldn't help but feel alone. Which was stupid, right? Because alone was exactly how he liked it.

Right?

As he wandered to the rear of what looked like a high-end grocery store, he found Ferry Plaza Seafood tucked away in the back. It looked like a casual restaurant, but up by the counter was a glass display case full of gorgeous seafood, and Beck found his gaze lingering on the pile of fresh, unopened clams mounded over the crushed ice.

Next to the gleaming fillets of deeply orange, wild-caught Alaskan salmon, the clams looked small and dirty, dull and unassuming and in no way impressive.

But when the young girl with the septum piercing and hot pink hair came over to take his order, Beck couldn't keep himself from adding a few pounds of clams to the side of salmon.

Opening the floodgates to the past wasn't as simple as it seemed, he realized, as he tried to stem the tide of memories.

Well, fine. Maybe the memories would be inspiring. He sure hoped so, because as of right now, he had no clue what he was going to prepare for the judges tomorrow.

Chapter 8

The thin light of early dawn filtered into the competition kitchen from a set of narrow windows set high in the white tiled wall.

Claire gripped her clipboard and wished fervently that she'd brought along an underling to send out for coffee.

But no. The magazine ran close to the bone on deadlines and staffers, the way all print media seemed to these days, and there was no one to spare for a frivolous job like following the editor in chief around and making sure she didn't work herself into a nervous breakdown.

Not that Claire was close to that. All she had to do before the chef contestants arrived at nine o'clock was to survey the kitchen, double-check the checklist of produce, proteins, and other product, and ensure that each team's station was fully stocked with all the tools necessary for the challenge.

None of that was difficult in any way, but somehow, *sans* coffee, it felt like a daunting task.

Perhaps because she'd barely slept the night before.

Taking in a fortifying breath of still and quiet—the

calm before the chaos of cooking that would erupt in this room in a few short hours—Claire mentally hiked up her slim, fitted heather gray trousers and wished the matching jacket had sleeves all the way down to the wrist. The bracelet sleeves might be stylish and becoming, but in the hyper-air-conditioned chill of the pre-competition kitchen, she could feel her teeth about to start chattering.

The bang of the door opening reverberated through her caffeine-deprived head for one flinching instant before she registered who stood in the entryway, blinking dazedly.

Kane Slater.

Immediately, Claire felt a flush of heat warm her entire body. Whether it was sexual awareness (likely) or frustrated anger (even more likely), she couldn't say. All she knew was that she was no longer shivering with cold.

"I didn't know anyone would be down here," he said, shoving awkward hands into the front pockets of his tight, dark blue jeans.

"I didn't know you ever rose from your bed before the crack of noon," Claire retorted without thinking. And then, of course, all she could think of was the vision of him in his bed, the gorgeous, lanky, somehow elegant sprawl of him as he took up every available inch of mattress real estate and tangled the sheets around his strong young limbs.

"Yeah, well. Believe me, I wish I were still in bed."

Snapping herself back into the moment, Claire pursed her lips and turned away from the all-too-tempting vision of him as he stood before her, rumpled and sleepy eyed. He looked, as usual, as if he'd rolled from his bed and yanked whatever clothes were nearest onto his body— this morning, scuffed jeans and a white V-neck undershirt so soft and thin from washing as to be indecent—and yet, he made the ensemble appear timeless. Classic. Sexy, in the most unstudied, natural way possible.

But the part of her that had held this man in her arms and soothed a tender hand down his trembling back after an explosive hour of lovemaking couldn't help but notice that he did appear to be exhausted. Even the thick rims of his fashionably chunky black glasses, which he only wore when he was hungover or trying to go incognito, couldn't hide the deep purple shadows like bruises under his blue eyes.

The largest part of Claire felt a vicious sort of satisfaction about this. If she couldn't sleep, why should he be able to?

But the small, tender part—the part that didn't care that Kane had betrayed her trust and reduced her to an outward expression of his male ego—somehow had control of her tongue.

"What is the matter? Can you not sleep?"

His wiry shoulders, always a little slouchy in that casual American way, straightened as if someone had pulled a string attached to the top of his scruffy, dark blond head.

"No, no. I'm fine. Just . . . working on a new album concept. When inspiration strikes, I have to go with it. You know how it is."

Claire did know. More than once, she'd woken up to the soft scratch of pencil and the flutter of discarded pages of composition paper layering the bed.

Steeling herself against the memory, she said, "Tell inspiration to wait until the RSC is over. For the next few weeks, you will need your rest, and I—we, I mean, will need your full attention."

Cheeks burning at her slip of the tongue, Claire walked briskly away from him, aiming blindly for the walk-in cooler. "So you may as well go back to your room," she said over her shoulder.

"Noted. But there's no way I can get back to sleep now. And since I'm up and everything, I'd like to help with whatever it is you're doing."

Merde.

Kane kept pace with her, his casual, ambling walk somehow eating up as much ground as Claire's staccato march. Damn her vanity for demanding she wear these ridiculously high Yves Saint Laurent pumps.

"I'm taking stock of the provisions for the challenge," she told him, but before she could explain that it was really a one-person job and she didn't need any help, *merci beaucoup*, Kane frowned and said, "Isn't that Eva's job?"

Derailed, Claire paused with her hand on the commercial refrigerator door handle and glanced back at him. "Yes, technically. Eva or one of her minions usually handles this. But with all the extra work of settling Devon Sparks back into his role and dealing with the fallout of canceling the television contract, I said I'd help."

The softness in his eyes was echoed in his voice. "You're a good friend to her, Claire."

Uncomfortable with the sentiment, Claire frowned and went back to trying to open the cooler. What in the name of heaven was wrong with this door? "That has nothing to do with anything. I am a professional—my publication's name is on this competition, so there you go. It's my job to make sure it runs smoothly."

"Don't give me that crap. Your job means a lot to you, I know—but it doesn't mean everything." He sounded unaccountably fierce, but there was a note of uncertainty, a need for confirmation, that had her ready to turn and face him when Kane's warm, nimble-fingered hand covered hers on the door handle, holding her in place.

I'd know this hand anywhere, Claire found herself thinking nonsensically, *in the dark, in my sleep. Anywhere.*

Kane's fingers were long and tapered, interestingly

callused from hours of plucking guitar strings, tapping at piano keys, and handling drumsticks. The way they'd felt running up the backs of her thighs, pressing gently at the insides of her knees, tickling down the slope of her neck . . .

Claire shuddered, heat soaking through her.

The action somehow managed to jiggle the walk-in cooler's handle exactly right, and with a pop of unsealing rubber lining, the door swung open, forcing her back a step.

Directly into the circle of Kane's tanned, muscular arms.

"Oops," he said, dropping his hands from their immediate, steadying grip on her shoulders.

"What?" Claire shook her head and scrabbled for her composure, which was somewhere on the floor with her balance and her ability to string words together.

"Nothing. I didn't mean to startle you." He stepped around her to inspect the door, which was smooth on the inside, an older model with no emergency-release mechanism. "Wow, guess we'd better make a note to keep this door propped during the challenge, or we'll end up with someone getting stuck in there."

For once in her life, Claire didn't want to talk about business. Dropping her clipboard to the floor with a clatter, she put her hands on her hips and faced down the most confusing man she'd ever slept with.

"We need to clear the air."

"Oh? I thought you felt you'd been perfectly clear." Those sleek golden brows winged up in what appeared to be genuine surprise.

It had been one week since she'd walked up to the competition kitchen in the basement of a Chicago hotel to hear her current lover and her ex-lover fighting over her like two junkyard dogs snarling over a bone, and in that time, she'd barely slept more than four hours at a stretch.

One week ago, she'd decided that if Kane and Theo were going to treat her like a commodity to be traded, then she wouldn't be with either man, and she'd made her position perfectly clear.

One week ago, she'd shut the door on her relationship with Kane Slater . . . but he'd stuck his foot in the opening and stubbornly refused to let it close completely.

And for seven long days, and longer nights, Claire had been left to pretend that no part of her was furtively, intensely glad of his persistence.

Not that any part of his persistence had included an apology.

She threw her hands up in the air, vaguely aware that she was behaving like a Marseillaise fishwife, but unable to stop herself. "Fine. You're right. There is nothing more to say."

"Wait. I do have something to say to you." Determination throbbed through Kane's rich, musical voice, adding a rough gravel that rubbed down Claire's spine like a touch.

Kane cocked his head to one side as he regarded her with the intense interest that always made Claire want to squirm away from him and check her hair for new threads of gray.

Letting the cooler door swing shut—they obviously weren't going to be getting to the inventory any time soon—Kane leaned his narrow hips against the stainless steel and tucked his hands back into his front pockets. He looked like some pop artist's depiction of young masculine Americana, the immortal cool of a James Dean or a Bruce Springsteen.

And yet, he was so emphatically himself; no comparison could really do him justice.

God, how she wanted him.

"I know you want me to say I'm sorry, Claire. But I'm not."

She stiffened, every muscle going rigid. "No. I inferred that you regretted nothing from the way you continue to bait Theo, engaged in some ludicrous battle of machismo and ego that has, at this point, nothing to do with me."

He laughed softly, but there was no mirth in it. "Don't kid yourself, Claire. It has everything to do with you."

Once, many years ago, Claire had allowed teenage Eva Jansen to tease her into accompanying the young girl to Coney Island Amusement Park in New York. It wasn't as vile as Claire had anticipated—in fact, the memory of her first Coney Island hot dog had inspired an award-winning *Délicieux* feature on frankfurters—but the entire experience had been marred by one ride.

The Tilt-a-Whirl.

As the name suggested, it had consisted of otherwise sane, rational people strapping themselves into a creaky metal contraption that then tilted at an alarming angle and whirled them through the air. The world had become a blur of nausea, vertigo, and anger at the entire universe for inventing such a ridiculous pastime.

Claire could close her eyes right now and imagine she felt the hard iron bar of the ride's restraint cutting into her midsection. The emotions she was currently flooded with were identical.

"You're wrong about something else, too."

The challenging tilt of Kane's chin jolted her out of her musings. "What?"

"There is something I regret."

Claire snorted, brought back to the point of this conversation with an unpleasant lurch. "Of course. The fact that I overheard your conversation at all."

"Nope. I regret that you only heard half of it."

"I heard enough," Claire told him, but even she could hear the confusion in her voice. Firming her tone, she said, "It was enough the moment I heard you and Theo discussing my affection, my self, as if I were a prize to be won."

But Kane shook his head. "Yeah, but you missed all the buildup. I promise, I didn't go from zero to macho-mode in seconds. You want to know what I said when Theo first brought it up, when he first told me I should give you up, for your own sake?"

"Wait, that's how the conversation began?"

"Yep. And I told him to go take a flying leap, because neither one of us could make a better choice for you than you could make for yourself."

Claire felt her knees wobble precariously. As if reading the shock on her face, Kane spread his hands and shrugged in a self-deprecating gesture.

"Hey," Kane said, smiling a little. "It's no accident I've got more female fans than male. And it's not just 'cause I'm so stinking cute. I've got sisters at home; I know how women think, and I know what's going to piss y'all off beyond belief."

Claire shook her head to try to clear it. "Wait. So you knew it was wrong and disrespectful . . . yet you allowed Theo to bait you, anyway? Because the way I remember the end of that conversation, you did not sound quite so enlightened."

"I've asked myself that same question over the last few days."

She swallowed hard. "And how have you answered yourself?"

Kane blew out a frustrated breath. "When Theo challenged me for you, when he tried to convince me that you'd be better off without me, and if I cared about you, I'd step aside . . . it made me so mad, Claire. Not because he was saying anything new—God knows, I've had those same thoughts, wondered if it was fair to ask someone like you, with your professional reputation, to step into the crazy, glaring fishbowl that is my life."

He paused, a far-off look in his eyes, and Claire had to close her fingers into a tight fist to keep from reaching for him.

She needed, with every fiber of her being, to hear what he would say next.

"No." Kane huffed out another, unamused laugh. "I resented the implication that I didn't care about you, but I don't think Theo had it all wrong—didn't, even then. And I probably wouldn't have let him goad me into a fight, except that all of a sudden, there was someone in front of me I *could* fight. And it felt good."

Claire was completely lost. This conversation wasn't going at all the way she'd anticipated. "What do you mean?"

He looked her right in the eye. "I mean, when I told Theo I'd fight to keep you, I was really talking to you."

She'd never seen him so intent, his steely determination naked and exposed, with all his usual mask of lazy amusement and carefree joie de vivre ripped away. Claire wanted to retreat from the sense of purpose in his direct gaze, but there was nowhere to go.

"You didn't know I was there," she sputtered.

"But you were there in my head." Nailing her with a glance, he said, "You'd been pushing me away for days . . . hell, for weeks, since before we even got together. You let me have your body, but you never let me get closer than skin deep, and for a long time I let you get away with it. I played it your way, even though it sucked and it didn't make either one of us happy, but it didn't help. You still kept me at arm's length."

Claire wanted to protest, to deny it, but that would

mean admitting that he'd gotten under her skin from the very start. Raw fear stopped up her throat like a cork in a bottle, and all she could do was stare at him.

Clearly taking her silence for agreement, Kane smiled grimly and went on. "So when Theo pushed me, I snapped. I said to him what I should've said to you—that I'm ready to fight to keep you."

Heart battering at her ribs, Claire could scarcely hear over the rush of her blood in her ears.

Kane fell quiet, gaze locked with hers. Everything Claire wanted to say collided in her throat, clogging her vocal cords with emotion. Silence stretched between them, thick with expectation and unspoken promises.

There was so much she wanted to tell him, but the very idea of exposing herself that way made her soul shrivel like a grape left out in the sun. She stared at him, mute with misery, wishing there were a way to communicate her feelings telepathically, straight into his brain, so she wouldn't have to lay herself open.

And as she stood there, struggling to overcome decades of clean, simple, balanced, emotionless living, the light died out of Kane's eyes, and he turned away.

"But it's no good if you won't fight for us, too," he said quietly, jamming his hands into the front pockets of his tight jeans. The muscles in his wiry, tanned forearms stood out, stark and tense. "So I guess that's it. Theo's leaving, I'm backing off . . . you're safe now."

With that, he turned and walked out.

And Claire let him go.

Her heart turned to lead, weighty and solid in her chest. She had to work to breathe around it, almost as hard as she was working to convince herself that this was the way it had to be. That it was better to make a clean break now than to invest more time and emotion in a relationship that couldn't—just *couldn't*—last.

She stood alone in the empty kitchen and stared down at her clipboard on the floor, every beat of her heavy heart whispering that she'd lived up to one of her countrymen's ugly stereotypes.

Instead of standing her ground and fighting for what she wanted . . . she'd surrendered to her own fear.

Chapter 9

"What do you mean, he wants to play you for it?"

Skye did a quick over-the-shoulder to make sure no one was close enough to overhear before elbowing Fiona and hissing, "Shh! Would you keep it down? I'd rather the rest of the contestants weren't privy to any more details of my private life, thanks very much."

Fiona waved one slim, pale hand in an airy circle before going back to shelling fava beans into a stainless steel bowl. "Paranoid much? Everyone's too busy prepping to pay any attention to us. So chill, babe, and spill the details on hubba hubba hubby!"

"Don't call him that." Skye pointed her whisk at her best friend with a narrow-eyed glare. "He's not my husband. At least, not in the way you're suggesting."

Fiona gave a neutral *hmm* that buzzed across Skye's skin like a pesky mosquito.

"I mean it," she insisted, frustration driving her right arm to beat the egg whites in her ceramic bowl so vigorously she'd have meringue in half the usual time. "Beck is the past. Jeremiah is my future."

Perfect Jeremiah, with his perfect dark blond hair and perfect cheekbones, perfectly tanned from all the time he spent outdoors, working to build schoolhouses and clinics in developing countries.

Ignoring the twinge of inadequacy was easy; Skye had been shoving that feeling down since she was a little kid. It felt familiar. Safe.

"Wait, don't tell me—Hunky Hubby doesn't know about Mr. Perfect." Fiona ripped open the green pod in her hands so violently the uncooked beans exploded against the side of bowl with a clatter.

Resisting the urge to call more attention to this conversation by shushing Fiona again, Skye cut her eyes left, to where Beck and his team were set up.

No matter what kind of chaos was going on in the competition kitchen—and with only a few hours to cook today, the chaos factor was huge—Skye seemed to always know, instinctively, where Beck was. It was like she had some kind of internal radar set for Tall, Taciturn, Crazy-making Ex.

Better than thinking of it as the response of furry, helpless prey in the presence of a scary, toothy predator.

"There's no reason to tell Beck about Jeremiah," she said, aware of how prim she sounded, but unable to do anything about it. "It's not any of his business."

"Not his business!" Fiona widened her pale blue eyes comically. With her ultra-fair skin and wispy platinum hair, she didn't look like she'd seen a ghost—she looked like she *was* the ghost. "Well, I declare. He is your lawfully wedded husband."

"Whatever relationship existed between Beck and me ended years ago. All that's left is a stupid piece of paper—and pretty soon, even that will be history." Skye peered into her friend's bowl, her own meringue forgotten for the moment. "Here, don't shell those—they're small and tender enough to roast and eat whole. That'll be a nice contrast to the blanched favas in the salad."

"Ah, yes. And now we come to it." Fiona grinned, a crafty look coming over her elfin face. "Handsome Hubby agreed to the quiet quickie divorce in exchange for . . . what?"

"It's more like a bet than a straight transaction." Skye went for lofty and unconcerned, and she almost pulled it off. "But it's a win-win for me, because I get the divorce either way."

"Yeah," Fiona drawled. "And you've also now got built-in motivation to lose the RSC competition—because if you lose, you've got an awesome excuse for one last whirl with your ex before you move on to Mr. Perfect. Who probably only knows the missionary position."

"Stop it." Skye couldn't help it, though. She had to laugh. "Don't worry, I'm not going to try to fail, just to get to experience Beck one last time. That's not even an issue."

"Oh, come on! You're going to give up that—" They both turned and glanced at Beck, standing over his station with a dark, forbidding look on his hard-edged face. Skye had to work to contain the shiver that tightened her chest. *Prey response*, she told herself. *That's all.*

"Damn," Fiona breathed before skewering Skye with a skeptical glare. "Seriously. You're giving up Mr. Sex on a Stick for a guy who doesn't believe in staying exclusive when he's out of the country?"

"Jeremiah doesn't think it's practical to expect fidelity of each other when we're apart so much," Skye said, the primness returning to her voice. "And I agree with him."

"Practical. Jesus, be still my heart. Did he at least throw you a little slap and tickle before taking off for Malaysia, or wherever the Peace Corps sent him this time?"

The barb sank home, but Skye covered her wince with

an exaggerated scowl. "He's in Burkina Faso. And I am never drinking with you again. You know too much—I'm afraid I'm going to have to kill you."

"Okay, fine. But if I get one final deathbed request, it's that you tell me the truth—while Jeremiah's off doing who knows what with every pretty do-gooder he can find, have you ever once availed yourself of his 'What Happens When We're On Separate Continents Stays on Separate Continents' clause?"

No. Of course not. Because, as Jeremiah said fondly, she had the lowest sex drive on the planet.

"Look, sex just isn't that important to me," she tried to explain, but of course Fiona wasn't having any of that.

Giving her a raised brow sharp enough to leave a scar, Fiona said, "Sugar. Sex is important to everyone. It just doesn't mean the same thing to all of us."

This was starting to sound like one of the discussions at Skye's parents' parties—the kind of conversational dilemma that could only be solved through the discreet application of mind-altering substances.

"All right, enough," she said firmly. "We need to concentrate on our menu, not my sex life."

"Or lack thereof."

"Or lack thereof," Skye agreed through gritted teeth. "Get back to work!"

Fiona saluted smartly and clicked her heels together, her wooden chef's clogs making a loud clacking sound. "*Oui*, Chef!"

Skye caught her friend's elbow as Fiona headed over to claim an oven to roast the smallest of the whole fava bean pods.

"Seriously, Fee. Keep this bet thing with Beck just between us, okay? I don't want the rest of the team worrying about it."

The perpetual twinkle in Fiona's eyes softened for a

moment. "You know it, babe. Your secrets are always safe with me."

"I do know that." Skye gave her a grateful smile and went back to her egg whites. Fiona was the only one who knew the whole story—everything that had gone down with Beck. And she'd had a front row seat for the years of dating limbo, when Skye felt torn between anger at and loyalty to her absent husband, and allowed the patently ridiculous hope that he might come back one day to keep her at home every Friday night.

Or, as Fiona had put it when she staged her mini-intervention, the years when Skye had hidden behind the specter of Henry Beck to keep from having to put herself out there again.

Faced with Fiona's indomitable will and her own mounting loneliness, Skye had tentatively started dating. And then, after several blind dates so awful she still had nightmares about them, she'd met Jeremiah Raleigh at one of her parents' deadly dull parties full of intellectuals smoking pot and talking about the situation in Africa.

Jeremiah had been invited as someone who'd actually been to Africa, and his genuine passion as he spoke about what he'd seen there captivated Skye.

So different from Beck, she'd thought, helpless against the comparison, and when Jeremiah turned his radiant smile on her, the warmth of knowing exactly how interested he was fed something inside her that had gone hungry for years.

Realizing she had a soft, goopy smile on her face, Skye pressed her lips together and went back to beating her egg whites. She could've used a mixer, sure, but an electric mixer meant she lost the connection between the force of her arm and the pressure of her hand around the whisk—it was too easy to overdo things when modern technology made them so simple and effortless.

She remembered the first time she'd cooked for Jeremiah; she'd said something like that to explain why she didn't own a microwave, and he'd given her that look. That shining, expectant look, the one that lit him up from inside.

That was the first time he'd invited her to come along with him on one of his overseas trips.

But it wasn't the last.

Shaking her head to rid herself of any thoughts that weren't kitchen related, Skye set her ceramic bowl down on the cutting board at her station and gently dipped her whisk into the egg whites to check them.

Holding her breath and praying she hadn't overworked the egg whites while her mind was flying off on the Jeremiah tangent, she lifted the whisk. The stuff clung to the end of it, drooping off the tip of the wire balloon like a glossy, white parrot's beak.

Perfect medium stiff peaks.

She'd already blended in the cream of tartar and the tiny amount of sugar she needed in order to hold out any hope of the meringues keeping their shape in the oven.

Normally with meringues, the sugar in the mix would do all the work of helping to keep the sweet little cookies puffed and crispy on the outside before they crumbled and melted in the mouth.

But Skye had taken the judges' comments about innovation at the relay challenge to heart, and she was attempting something a little crazy—a savory meringue.

Which meant less sugar, less structural integrity, less of an idea of how the heck this was going to turn out . . . and approximately six thousand times the amount of stress.

How's this for taking a risk, she mused as she set her jaw and reached for the knobbly chunk of parmagiano reggiano cheese.

Her hand closed on empty air, and she frowned down

at her *mise en place* in confusion. The rest of her *mise* was perfect, all her ingredients set out close to hand and easily accessible: fresh green chives, cayenne pepper, salt. But no cheese.

Oh come on. Had she really been so wacked out and worried about flying by the seat of her pants on this recipe that she'd forgotten to grab the main flavoring ingredient from the walk-in cooler?

Flicking a quick glance at the wall clock counting down the minutes to the end of their prep time today, Skye bit back a curse. She'd wasted an entire hour of prep time on that conversation with Fiona and the mushy-headed daydreaming afterward. There were only three hours left on the clock, and she still had to grate the cheese, finish mixing up the meringues, pipe them out on baking sheets, and dry them in the oven for at least two hours.

Maybe more.

Feeling each tick of the second hand like a gong ringing in her ears, Skye hustled across the kitchen to the corner with the walk-in and the dry goods pantry, dodging chefs with hot pans spitting bacon grease and sharp knives flashing as they diced and chopped for all they were worth.

Mind finally full of nothing but the next task, the next ingredient, the next step on her mental checklist for this parmesan chive meringue recipe, Skye planted both palms flat on the cold metal door to the walk-in cooler and shoved it open. Immediately scanning the shelves in the dim lighting of the overhead fluorescent bulb, she heard a quiet *snick* from behind her.

There was a strange rush; the noise from the busy kitchen cut out abruptly, and the air in the cooler went still as even the lone light bulb went black.

Chapter 10

Oh no. I let the door close.

Claire Durand's words of caution came back to Skye in a blazing instant of pure self-derision—how could she have been so careless? So stupid? So forgetful?—while she groped for the door, her fingers finding the smooth seam and scrabbling frantically, pointlessly, for a handle that didn't exist.

"This isn't happening."

The disembodied growl came from the back corner of the cooler, and Skye whirled to face the voice, heart slamming hard enough to jar her body against the door.

Not hard enough to budge the door open, though.

"I'm sorry," Skye blurted. "I feel like an idiot, after Claire warned us and everything, but I just wasn't thinking."

There was a huff, almost a snort, and Skye narrowed her eyes as if squinting would somehow give her night vision. "Who's there?"

"You don't recognize my voice. I think I'm hurt."

The deadpan delivery combined with the shock of awareness that skittered up her spine had Skye gasping in disbelief.

It was Beck.

When she thought she could speak without giving anything away, she said, "The universe certainly has an odd sense of humor today. Of all people . . ."

"Out of all the walk-in coolers in all the countries in the world, you had to come walking into mine. And lock us in."

There was something going on with Beck's voice, a certain strain and tightness that was part of why she hadn't immediately identified him as her fellow prisoner. Skye put a tentative hand out in front of her and took one shaky step away from the safety of the door at her back.

"Hey. Are you okay?"

She sensed movement a few paces away, the shift of air against her skin and the whisper of cloth. "Fine" was Beck's terse answer, but Skye wasn't buying what he was selling.

"No, you're not," she said, more certain than ever when he didn't immediately jump to contradict her. "Where are you? M-maybe we should stick together."

There was that huff of breath again, closer this time as she moved deeper into the darkness of the fridge. "Why? Someone will be along any second now, needing cream or eggs or something. Any second, we'll be out of here . . ."

"You sound like you're trying to convince yourself of something you don't really believe," Skye observed quietly. "But it's true. I'm sure we won't be in here for longer than a few minutes. Still, better to keep warm and calm than to freeze our butts off."

"Can't fool me," Beck said, the words sounding bitten off and odd. "You just want to get close to this hot bod."

A wave of amusement briefly overwhelmed the concern rising in her chest. "You caught me," she said, proving he wasn't the only one who could do deadpan. "Let's throw our clothes off and get down, oh baby, oh baby.

Because what could be sexier than pretending we've both been buried alive in a cozy two-person coffin with no view?"

There was a long pause, long enough get her heart pumping faster with a combination of nerves and worry, before Beck choked out, "Okay, nix on the coffin stuff. Shit."

Swiping a careful hand through the darkness, Skye frowned when she still didn't encounter him. Beck was a huge guy, and this wasn't a very big cooler. Where the hell was he?

"You really have a problem with being in here," she said, keeping her left hand on the wire shelving lining the wall of the cooler as she inched her way toward the back. She couldn't move too quickly, because she remembered that the floor of the fridge was crammed with crates of produce, seafood and T-bones and heads of cabbage, sitting there waiting to trip her up.

She couldn't afford a broken ankle right now. Shoot, she couldn't afford to be stuck in this cooler, either—but whatever was eating at Beck seemed more serious than completely understandable frustration at their prep time ticking away.

"It's not a problem," Beck said, but his voice sounded like he'd been gargling gravel. "At least, it won't be once someone fucking notices we're missing and comes to find us."

"Someone will come," Skye said, feeling like she was trying to soothe a savage beast. Should she sing? No, that wouldn't help. "In the meantime, where are you?"

"I'm fine," he said again, proving beyond a shadow of a doubt that he wasn't, and everything inside Skye went on red alert.

"Okay, but maybe I'm not," she said, letting a tremor into her voice. "I'm getting really cold, and a little freaked out, and it would help if I knew where you were so I don't feel like I'm going crazy and talking to myself."

That got another snort out of him, but this time it sounded like simple laughter, and Skye let herself grin. "Come on," she coaxed. "I promise not to bite."

"That's not much of an incentive," he commented, but in the next instant, she felt his large, strong-boned hand slide around her fingers in a solid grip.

Despite herself, a tension she hadn't realized she was carrying melted from her shoulders, as if she'd been holding the sun salutation pose for long, deep-breathing moments and had finally relaxed out of it at his touch.

His palm was sweaty and chilled, which surprised her, even considering how weird he was acting. She'd seen Henry Beck face down a trio of switchblade-happy street kids, their mean, gouging landlord, and her own mother, and he'd never flinched. But somehow, being locked in this freezer with his soon-to-be-ex-wife was really getting to him.

Trying not to take it personally, Skye said, "So. You didn't used to be claustrophobic."

He stiffened and, predictably, tried to pull his hand away. But Skye had, in fact, anticipated that reaction, and she kept her grasp on his fingers snug and secure, and went on talking.

"I know, because if you'd been claustrophobic when we had that apartment on Stockton, you would've had to be on medication just to walk through the front door."

Beck relaxed a little, some of the rigidity going out of his forearm, and Skye risked stepping a little closer to the radiant heat of his big body.

"That place was tiny," he said in a gruff, remembering voice. "And the only window was in the bathroom, way up high over the shower."

"You didn't seem to notice the close quarters back then."

"Maybe I was too busy thinking about other things."

Skye swallowed hard. Now she was remembering, too, and it occurred to her, as Beck's voice slid into that deep, caressing tone, that she hadn't always felt so take-it-or-leave-it and unconcerned when it came to sex.

In fact, in those two years she and Beck were together, she remembered being vitally concerned with sex—at all hours of the day and night, in every position their fevered brains and youthfully flexible bodies could come up with.

Trying to stay on topic, she shot back, "I don't think so. This is new. So what gives?"

"I don't want to talk about that."

Time for a different tactic. "Okay, then. What are you making for your signature dish?"

That got her a frustrated growl, the kind that vibrated through her ribcage as if someone had struck a tuning fork.

"Don't want to talk about that, either, hmm?"

He shifted, his body too big to move without shifting air currents. "I just . . . I don't know what they're looking for. I can cook any kind of fish, any way they want. But I don't have a signature. I'm not some celebrity chef with a catchphrase and a line of condiments for sale. I'm a glorified line cook, and damn proud of it."

Feeling her way, Skye said carefully, "I don't think 'signature dish' has to mean something that people associate with you, like a brand. I think it means . . . a dish that exemplifies what you love about cooking. Your style, your ability to use ingredients and showcase them . . . it's more about what you're trying to say with the dish than the dish itself."

He was quiet for a long moment while Skye felt an embarrassed flush heat the tips of her ears. At least *they* were warm.

"That actually . . . that helps," Beck said, sounding endearingly awkward. Skye fought down the urge to give him a squeeze. "Thanks."

"No problem. Now what else should we discuss? I know . . . how about your sudden claustrophobia?"

Beck jolted, his leather boots squeaking against the floor of the cooler with his sudden movement. "I'm not talking about that."

"Well, I think you should talk about it. How else are you going to get over it?"

She felt a tug on her hand that pulled her off balance, the darkness of the space around them robbing her of her center of gravity and tilting the world into instantaneous vertigo.

But only for a second, because Beck was there to catch her against his chest, her clumsy feet tangling with his as her long skirt wound itself around his legs like an affectionate cat.

"You know what works better than talking?" Beck purred, the rumble of his voice vibrating against her breasts and all through her body. "A distraction."

And before she could gather her scattered wits to protest, to argue, he'd brought his mouth down across hers and the urge to argue was swept away in the onslaught of pure, raw sensation.

So hot, so hungry, his tongue stroked between her teeth and ignited a fire that had been banked down deep inside her for years. In a flash of wet friction, clutching fingers, and a breathless moan from deep in someone's chest, Skye remembered the one place she and Beck had always been able to communicate . . . in bed.

Or, in this case, in a walk-in freezer.

Right here and now, it didn't matter that Beck had been out of her life for years. It didn't matter that every moment they were together was shadowed with uncertainty and insecurity about where she stood with him.

Right here and now, she knew how he felt without being told in words, because as his iron grip curled around her waist and jerked her closer, their bodies spoke a language older than time.

He wanted her.

And goddess above, but she wanted him right back, with a soaring, surging passion that gripped her like a riptide and spun her dizzily into the dark.

She wrapped her arms around the solid thickness of his muscular shoulders and opened herself to him.

Beck was on fire.

Heat throbbed through him, where only moments before he'd been chilled to the bone, fighting the shakes with every ounce of his strength.

The desire for her burned through him, scorching away every thought and fear and feeling that wasn't connected to the silkiness of her hair gripped in his fists or the satiny glide of her tongue as she welcomed him in.

Skye Gladwell's kiss. There was nothing like it, anywhere in the world.

Without even meaning to, Beck had used the memory of this kiss—the sweet strawberry taste of her, that bitten-off moan in the back of her throat, the eager press of her lips—as the baseline against which all other kisses were measured. Every kiss he'd had in the years since he left Skye had been too wet, too dry, too reserved, too sloppy—just . . . not this.

And as her body molded against his as if they were two measuring spoons nestled in a drawer, Beck felt something deep inside himself slot into place.

Unwilling to examine just what that meant, he burrowed

his hands deeper into the curly mass of her hair, fingers searching until he cupped her delicate skull in his big, rough hands, and deepened the kiss until they were both gasping for breath.

Beck was the one who broke away, sucking at air so cold it felt like a knife in his lungs after the heated passion of the past few minutes. A surge of fierce joy went through him when he felt her go up on tiptoe, swollen mouth puffing hot breaths against the sensitive side of his neck.

With everything he had, Beck wished he could see her face clearly, but even his killer night vision couldn't pierce the complete darkness of a commercial-grade refrigerator.

But he could imagine how she looked. Hell, he'd imagined it so often over the years, he could probably sketch her expression from memory—the wide daze of her summer-blue eyes, the hectic flush of pink on her milky cheeks, the slick, plump softness of her ripe, just-kissed mouth.

Oh yeah, he knew exactly what Skye looked like after being kissed to within an inch of her life. And in that moment, he swore to himself that he'd see it again with his own eyes.

Because no one who kissed him like that was completely over what they'd had.

"Henry," she breathed, a fine tremor shivering through her body, and Beck had to fight down a shiver of his own, because damn. That name he'd hated hearing for a decade suddenly didn't sound half bad, when Skye moaned it in that soft, yearning way.

But the sound of her own voice seemed to snap Skye out of whatever haze their kiss had put her in, and she struggled a bit in his arms.

"Oh goddess," she groaned, reason returning with a

sharp edge to her voice, and Beck regretted it. Especially when she tried to jerk away from him.

"Stop that," he ordered, pulling her closer and tucking her more firmly against him, because her shivers were getting worse. "We need to conserve body heat."

It was cold in here, he knew, but it was a clinical sort of knowledge experienced at a distance, the way Beck had learned to process pain from a wound and keep going, keep moving, keep working.

The cold kept him alert, and as she subsided, dropping her arms to wrap around his waist and tucking her cold nose against his chest, Beck's head finally cleared completely.

Priority one was to get them both out of here.

Priority two? Get his team into position to win this damn competition, because he had to have her one last time.

Chapter 11

Over her years in the male-dominated world of magazine publishing, Claire had learned to read a room.

It was a useful skill, one that had served her well in front of editorial boards, irate advertisers, and banquet halls full of chefs whose restaurants she'd reviewed—not always favorably. It had helped ensure that as her workplace dynamic gradually shifted to accommodate the influx of highly educated, determined, career-minded women, Claire remained at the head of the pack.

Glancing around the frenetic San Francisco kitchen as the challenge clock wound down to zero, Claire saw a number of interesting things.

Devon Sparks had arrived on an early flight that morning, and Eva had been touring him around the kitchen, getting him up to speed on where things stood in the competition.

Now they were standing by the back wall, having what looked like a very serious conversation; it was the first time Claire had seen her young friend without a smile on her face since they'd left Chicago.

Claire frowned; either Devon was sharing upsetting

details of his pregnant wife's recent illness, or Eva was in a funk for some other reason.

Tilting her gaze to the right, she checked out Danny Lunden to see if he looked similarly frustrated—that would mean there was trouble in paradise, and Claire could expect to spend a good portion of her evening dispensing chocolate, martinis, and "poor baby"s.

However, although Danny cast the occasional concerned look in his true love's direction, he didn't appear to be suffering from anything worse than a pan of sadly flat-looking ladyfingers. Making a disgusted noise, he scraped the sponge cake cylinders into the garbage and started fresh while Claire turned back to her perusal of the room.

All the teams were rushing around, spilling sauces and cursing sticky pressure cooker lids and praying that the blast chiller could firm up their from-scratch, oddly flavored ice creams. The Midwest chefs, in particular, appeared to be floundering—there was quite a bit of red-faced shouting coming from their team leader, Ryan Larousse.

Danny's teammates from the East Coast team appeared to be doing well, although one of them seemed a bit behind after having gotten caught in exactly the situation Claire had warned them about.

One of the most interesting things she'd observed all morning had been the state of Beck and Skye Gladwell when they'd tumbled out of the walk-in, clothing askew and hair mussed, after that chef with the dreadlocks had tried to get into the cooler for a carton of buttermilk and found the door jammed.

Dreadlock Boy had pried it open with the help of his West Coast teammates, and there they were, the intimidatingly large, dark-haired chef wrapped around the petite, zaftig hippie with the messy red curls like something off the covers of the romance novels Claire kept as her secret indulgence.

They'd broken apart instantly, claiming the embrace had been all about conserving body heat, but Claire was no fool. She knew how it could be when circumstances threw one into contact with an old flame.

So really, she had nothing to feel guilty about in regards to Beck and Skye, just because two chefs had found themselves trapped in the large commercial refrigerator during the challenge even after she'd warned them! They'd surely enjoyed themselves.

So what if she might have had a chance to get the door latch fixed, had she not been so busy having a moment with Kane Slater?

Guilt was an entirely unproductive emotion. As was regret.

Fear, however . . .

Claire's gaze fell on Kane where he stood watching the chefs, bouncing on the balls of his feet like a child too excited to stand still. Claire felt a visceral tug toward him, as if he'd hooked her behind the belly button and was now reeling her in.

Claire dug in her heels and resisted the pull, feeling a need to maintain some distance—both professional and physical.

When she was with Kane . . . it was all too much. She felt too much, hoped too much, cared too much, and she was smart enough to know that an ounce of fear for the future would save her an infinity of regret when this affair inevitably ended.

So she turned resolutely away from her young ex-lover, and most certainly did not notice the flex and play of muscles in his tanned arms, bared to the elbow by the rolled sleeves of his hipster-plaid button-down.

A loud buzz jerked Claire's attention back to the wall clock, which now read 00:00 in flashing red digits.

"Time's up," Eva called, moving front and center.

"Step away from your stations." She glanced at Claire, who gave her an infinitesimal nod.

Taking a fortifying breath, Claire assumed her best blank expression and stepped forward, heels clicking loudly against the tiled kitchen floor.

Showtime.

There were times when Skye thought if she could choose to have inherited anything from her parents, it wouldn't be her mother's artistic brilliance or her father's genius for political satire.

It would be the single quality they both shared: complete and utter confidence that everything they did was right and good.

Even after tasting her parmesan-chive meringue—even after forcing every person on her team to taste it—Skye's belly was still clenched tight in terror of the judges' reactions.

Fiona, who knew her too well, leaned over close enough to hiss, "It's going to be fine. Stop looking so nervous! They're going to think you sneezed on their plates or something."

Skye laughed because she knew she was meant to, and the bands of tension around her midsection eased a little.

She stared down the long stainless steel table where each team was presenting their finished dishes to the judges. Why did the West Coast team always have to go last?

"I can't help being nervous," she whispered to Fiona, who shot her a sympathetic look that somehow also conveyed a very strong "buck up" vibe. "Everything is riding on this!"

"Not everything! Just your entire life." Fiona smirked and faced forward again, nudging her shallow square plate of jiggling Jell-O shots in line with the rest of her team's dishes while Skye went back to fretting.

If they finished last, the way they had in the practice challenge, they were through. Out of the competition and heading back to the Queenie Pie Café in disgrace.

At her parents' next salon, she'd have to tell them she'd lost. She could already hear her mother's sympathetic but exasperated voice saying, "Well, what did you expect? You're wasting your talents, puttering around a kitchen like some fifties housefrau." And her father would raise his sleek dark brows and take a languid puff of his joint before adding, "Maybe now you'll let go of this ridiculous retro fantasy and do something meaningful with your life." She could picture it all so clearly.

Probably because she'd lived through it a time or two already.

The judges were moving down the line, dragging Skye closer and closer to the moment of truth, and she resolutely blocked out everything they were saying to the other teams.

She didn't want to know. It wasn't about doing better or worse than anyone else, she told herself. All she could do was her best, and hope it was good enough.

And besides . . . if she noticed the other teams and how they were faring with the judges, she'd have to be reminded that not only did she need to win this challenge to avoid dealing with her parents' perennial disappointment—she needed to stay in the competition because Jeremiah was coming home, all the way from Burkina Faso, just to see her cook.

Skye swallowed around a sudden lump in her throat. There was no way she could face her heroic, save-the-world-one-village-at-a-time boyfriend if she failed at a stupid cooking contest.

The deep rumble of a masculine voice roughed over Skye's skin, catching at her and reminding her that she had enough to be ashamed of as it was.

Stop it, she lectured herself. *Don't think about how you're going to tell Jeremiah about Beck. Don't think about—oh God—kissing Beck, or the way your whole body came alive the minute he touched you. Don't think about anything other than getting through the next five minutes.*

It was good advice, but when Beck threw his head back and laughed—actually laughed!—at something Kane Slater said about his dish, Skye knew she wouldn't be able to follow it.

As much as her whole life and a ridiculous amount of her self-worth were tied up in winning this challenge . . . there was no distraction big enough to keep her mind from wandering to Henry Beck.

Especially when he turned his head suddenly and caught her staring.

Heat seared up the back of Skye's neck, flooding her cheeks with warmth, and she immediately dropped her gaze to the table in front of her. But there was no way to block her ears, and she listened to every word as Beck explained how he'd come up with his dish.

"Actually, I'd planned to do salmon," he told the judges. "But you've seen that from me before. And then I had the chance to take a few minutes alone with one of the chefs from another team . . ."

Skye kept her eyes stubbornly trained on her own plate, ignoring the inferno in her blood.

"And she talked some sense into me about what a signature dish really is. So I decided to do this take on linguini with clam sauce. Because for me, cooking is all about taking what you've got, and turning it into something better."

"Flour, egg, clams, white wine, lemon juice," Devon Sparks counted out as he twirled another bite of pasta around his fork. "Very basic ingredients, but you made them sing. Well done, Chef Beck."

That wasn't a glow of pride she felt, and it definitely wasn't satisfaction that she'd helped Beck crystallize his dish, Skye told herself. Nope.

No way.

Finally, it was the West Coast team's turn to be judged. Skye stood up straighter, pulling her shoulders back, but not so far back that she was in danger of poking anyone's eye out with her overlarge chest.

It was a fine line to walk, but she managed it.

The judges strolled down the table, looking cool and fresh and relaxed, and just generally giving off the air of people who hadn't been brawling their way through a crowded competition kitchen for the past five hours. Skye blew an errant curl off her sticky, sweaty forehead and tried not to miss the chill, dark confines of the walk-in cooler.

"Chef Gladwell," Claire Durand said in her cool, precise voice. "What do you have for us today? Your team sourced all the ingredients for these signature dishes from . . ."

"Chinatown," Skye confirmed. "Which, honestly, if I'd chosen first? I still would have picked Chinatown. It's my favorite neighborhood in the city."

"Oh?" Claire wasn't really looking at her. All her attention was focused on the plates in front of her, but Skye nodded anyway.

"I used to live there," she babbled nervously. "Above a Chinese grocer, actually, so I'm super familiar with the local shops and what they offer."

"So even though you drew the short straw, you kind of lucked out," Kane Slater observed, giving her a friendly smile that somehow didn't relax a bit of the tension holding Skye's shoulders in a rigid line.

"Yes. And I hope you enjoy what we've prepared for you." With a practiced flick of her wrist, Skye turned her plate and presented it to the judges. "I know you said 'signature dish,' which could mean something we're known for. But I wanted to stretch a little, and honestly, to me, I think my signature as a chef is the willingness to treat simple, perfect ingredients with love and respect. This dish definitely works for that. It's a savory meringue, with chives and parmagiano reggiano to give it some bite, with a topping of sweet onion confit and whole basil leaves."

Each judge had a spoon, and they took turns digging in.

Skye studied their reactions anxiously, holding her breath. Was this too out there? Not out there enough? Would they think she'd tortured the concept of a meringue, pulling it too far off course and taking too many liberties, or would they be impressed that she'd managed to solve the sugar problem?

But when "Intriguing . . ." was the first thing out of Claire's mouth, Skye knew she had them. Her shoulders dropped at least two inches, sending relief all down her spine and through her lower back.

Claire Durand looked her in the eye and said simply, "I'm impressed. You've achieved something I didn't think was possible."

Relief flooded Skye's system. They were so in!

The judges had more comments, but Skye barely processed them, her whole body alight with hope and joy. She definitely wasn't still tingling with the aftereffects of Beck's kiss. No way.

The rest of her team did well, as she'd known they would; Fiona's playful take on Jell-O shooters was an especially big hit.

Devon Sparks couldn't stop admiring the brilliant little squares of jewel-bright gelatin flavored like Fiona's favorite cocktail, the French 75. Fi spent a bunch of time explaining how the French 75 got its name when it was invented during the First World War—for having a kick like a

75mm artillery cannon—-but Skye had a feeling that Devon wasn't listening to her.

The calculating look on his movie-star-handsome face made Skye think grown-up Jell-O shots might be making an appearance at his New York restaurant in the near future.

Nathan's summer vegetable tart was always a favorite on the Queenie Pie menu, and the judges appeared to agree that it was awesome. Oscar had quietly, stubbornly, made carnitas, the way he did every single Sunday at the café, over Nathan's strenuous vegetarian objections, and the judges were impressed with the perfectly caramelized crust on the tiny chunks of juicy pork.

They even liked Rex's unapologetic fish and chips, especially the way he battered the potatoes before frying them, making them extra crispy.

All things considered, Skye thought they had a good shot. But then, she'd thought that before and wound up extremely disappointed. So when the judges headed back to the front of the room to make their announcement about who would stay in the competition and who would be going home, Skye couldn't help but hold her breath.

Chapter 12

Tension filled the kitchen like smoke from the grill, so thick Beck wondered why it didn't set off the fire alarms.

On one level, he could see why everyone was jacked up. Shit was about to go down. It was tempting to let his heart rate increase, get his adrenaline pumping in case action was called for—but it wasn't.

They all just had to stand there and take it, whatever the judges said.

Beck crossed his arms over his chest and set his jaw. There was nothing he could do about it now. Whatever was going to happen would happen, regardless of what he wanted.

It reminded him a lot of being in the Navy, actually. Decisions were made. Orders were handed down. And it was up to grunts like Beck to execute.

Wanting didn't enter into it.

But if he could want something . . .

The tiny rebellious voice in the back of his brain, the one that had gotten him into so much trouble when he was a stupid kid—the one that had nearly gotten him tossed out of recruit training—piped up with one single wish.

Like it was Beck's inner eight-year-old blowing out the candles on the last birthday cake anyone had ever made for him.

If we make it through to the finals . . . I wish I could be the one to take us all the way.

Stupid, he told himself. It was so freaking stupid to want what he couldn't have. It didn't even make sense. If they made it as far as the final head-to-head culinary battle, it would be Jules up there going at it, not Beck. Or maybe Max, if Jules had to step aside for some reason.

Although, the way those two fought when Max first showed up to advise the team, Beck was pretty sure it would take something on the level of a severed hand to make Jules step aside.

All of which made it that much more unlikely that Beck would get his stupid, stupid wish.

So he ignored it, the way he'd learned to ignore the bone-deep need for sleep, the ache of overtaxed muscles, the hollow scrape of hunger. And he focused on what the judges were saying.

"It's been a long road to get here." Claire Durand surveyed them gravely, her shoulders so straight and still she almost looked like she should be in uniform. "And you've all done remarkably well. We, the judges, would like to thank each of you for the wonderful flavors and techniques to which we've been treated in the last few weeks."

She looked at her co-judges, who both nodded.

"It's good to be back," Devon Sparks said. "I look forward to a lot of delicious food and some impressive cooking, now that we're getting close to the finals."

Beck noticed new lines carved by worry and sleeplessness on Devon's face, but there was a bright sheen to his electric blue eyes as he looked at the group of assembled chefs. "I want to thank you all for the concern and the well wishes about my wife, and I'm very happy to be able to inform you that as of this morning when I talked to Lilah, she was doing great, feeling better, getting plenty of rest . . ."

He paused, his whole body strung so tight with emotion, he appeared poised for flight. Beck tensed instinctively, bracing for impact, even as his gaze sought out Skye's pale face.

"And actually, we just found out . . ." Devon's throat worked for a heartbeat before he managed to keep going. "We're having a baby girl!"

Everyone clapped; a couple of people even cheered. Devon was a celebrity chef with a reputation for throwing his weight around, but over the weeks of the RSC he'd proven himself to be tough but fair as a judge—and totally, completely, irrevocably in love with his wife. The combo made him pretty well liked by the chef contestants, and there'd been a lot of worry when he'd had to leave. Beck understood that everyone was glad to have him back, and glad to hear that his wife was okay.

Beck was glad, too, of course he was. But as he stared at the look of tremulous, complicated relief on Skye's heart-shaped face, what Beck didn't understand was why the sight of it, and the sound of the Sparks's happy news, made him want to smash the entire kitchen to smithereens.

Get a grip, Beck.

"Right on," Kane Slater added, slapping his palms against his thighs with a big, blinding grin. "Way to go, Devon. And yeah, what Claire said. You're all rock stars!"

That got more cheers. Beside Beck, Winslow was bouncing like he'd jumped onto a trampoline.

Claire held up a hand for silence. "All true. Which only makes this more difficult, to say goodbye to one of the last three teams. But it is now that time."

Beck had to give it to her. Now that the moment had arrived, she didn't drag it out. No glancing at her co-judges for last-minute validation, no waffling around. All she did was take a deep breath in and let it out slowly before turning her gaze to the right of Beck.

Where the West Coast team stood.

Mouth suddenly dry, Beck experienced a moment of panic that felt like free fall. Shit, was she about to cut Skye out of the competition?

No. I'm not ready.

"Chef Gladwell, in answering the challenge today, you and your team exemplified everything the Rising Star Chef contest stands for. You presented your signature dishes with authority, never backing down from the bold, idiosyncratic flavors you showcased, and you told us exactly who you are. Very, very well done."

Beck's head floated down out of the ether and back onto his shoulders. That sounded pretty good. After all that about showing who they were as chefs, and with the way Claire was nodding at them in obvious approval, there was no way she was sending Skye packing.

But it wasn't until Claire said definitively, "West Coast team, you will be competing in the final round of the Rising Star Chef competition. Please choose your lead competitor and one sous-chef," that Beck finally managed to draw in a shaky breath.

Of course, that was the instant he realized that the fact that the West Coast team was in meant that he and his own team now stood a fifty-fifty chance of being cut.

Well, fuck.

Claire left the West Coasties to their exuberant celebrations and cast a sympathetic look over the two remaining teams, standing there quaking in their leather cooking clogs, waiting to hear their fate.

"East Coast team and Midwest team." She spread her

arms, looking back and forth between them. "You both did well today. The Midwest team has shown us some of the most consistently avant-garde, innovative plates throughout this competition, and today was no exception. Chef Larousse, although we loved your crab consomme and the delicacy of the avocado foam, some of the judges felt that you relied too heavily on showy techniques and not enough on the food itself.

"And East Coast team . . . your ability to bring classical preparations into the new millennium has been exciting to watch—and even more exciting to taste. Chef Lunden—" she nodded at Max, who straightened up like a kid who hadn't expected the teacher to call on him.

"Your barbecued pork belly ramen was a triumph, as was Chef Beck's clam linguini."

Holy shit. Beck blinked. She'd called him out specifically. Well, that was just . . . cool.

Holding his head up, he told himself to enjoy this moment, to let it make the outcome of the next few minutes unimportant . . . but he still tensed all over when she drew in another deep breath.

Accent heavier than usual, Claire lifted her chin and announced, "East Coast team . . . you will be competing in the final round of the Rising Star Chef competition . . ."

The rest of her instructions about choosing a lead competitor and a sous were lost in the ear-splitting whoop Win gave, pumping his fist in the air and throwing his arms around the chef nearest him. Who happened to be Beck.

Beck barely noticed. It felt like fireworks were detonating in his chest, sparking in his belly and knocking him around from the inside as his team fell spontaneously into a group huddle and howled with glee.

"We're in," Max crowed, while Jules cackled joyfully into his shoulder.

"If I could have everyone's attention for just one moment." Claire's round, elegant tones cut through the ringing in Beck's ears and the chatter of his teammates.

He got himself upright again, hauling Winslow to his feet as he went, and cast a quick glance at the Midwest team.

They were already filing out of the kitchen, looking pissed and exhausted and beaten down. Their team leader, Ryan Larousse, cast one final glance over his shoulder and snagged on Beck's stare.

A man wasn't defined only by how well he bore up under a loss. He was also defined by how he behaved in victory—and Beck hated a bad winner. Gloating wasn't just pointless and petty. In some parts of the world, in certain situations, it could be deadly.

So Beck nodded at Larousse, man to man, and waited to see what the little shit would do.

After all, this was the piece of crap who'd actively tried to hurt Skye; this was the guy Beck had completely lost his cool and snapped on, taking him down to the kitchen mats with his fists in a display of raw temper and uncontrolled anger that had scared everyone present—Beck, most of all.

Some intense emotion spasmed across Ryan Larousse's face, and Beck could see the muscle in his jaw ticking as the guy ground his back teeth together.

But in the end, all he did was nod back and follow his team out of the kitchen.

Beck wished he didn't respect the guy for that, but he sort of did. After all, he knew exactly how badly Larousse had wanted to win. And instead, he was on his way back to Chicago with his tail tucked firmly between his legs.

That had to suck.

Meanwhile, Claire seemed to have asked the two finalist teams to state their choices for lead chef and sous-chef, because Skye was stepping forward, determination firming her soft little chin.

"I'll be competing for the West Coast team," she said, voice completely unwavering. But Beck could read the nerves in the quiet jingle of the bangle bracelets around her wrists, before she clasped her hands in front of her to still the sound.

"And your sous?" Claire asked.

Glancing back at the pixie-ish platinum-blonde woman behind her, Skye said, "I'm bringing Fiona Whealey to the finals with me."

"Ah," Claire said, interest sparking in her voice. "An all-female chef team in the finals? Theo, correct me if I'm mistaken, but I believe this may be a first for the RSC."

"No, you're right." Theo Jansen who'd sauntered into the kitchen after the tasting, looked as proud and smug as if he'd personally trained Skye and Fiona. "Best of luck, ladies."

"Who needs luck when you've got this much skill?" Fiona flexed her wiry arms with a wink, making the intricate spoon tattooed on her bicep bend like something out of that *Matrix* movie.

Beck's desire to clap Skye on the back was rivaled only by his urge to slap the look of fatherly approval off Theo Jansen's smug face. Beck had seen assholes like that in the service—guys who said the right things about wanting women to succeed, get promoted, whatever, but all with this air of "Aren't they cute for wanting to strap on a gun and defend their country?"

Which was hilarious, considering that the toughest submariner Beck ever met was a five-foot-three petty officer, third class, named Marianne Wells.

Beck took a moment to be glad Theo was no longer a judge.

Claire Durand looked as if she was suppressing the

urge to laugh at Fiona Whealey's posturing as she turned back to the East Coast team.

"And you? Who will be going head to head with Chef Gladwell?"

Their team leader, Jules, arched a brow in Theo's direction. "If you think one all-female team was exciting, you'll love this. I'll be competing for the East Coast team, with Winslow Jones as my sous."

Beck didn't acknowledge the slight sinking in his gut. The sharp disappointment was fleeting and meaningless.

"Well, isn't this something!" Theo clapped his hands together, pleased as punch. "This is the year of the woman!"

"Um, hello?" Win raised his hand and pointed at himself. "I like women fine, as friends and stuff, but . . . not actually a woman, over here. All man, with man parts. I just want to be clear on that."

"Oh!" Theo looked surprised, then embarrassed. "No, of course not, Chef Jones. I didn't mean to imply . . . anything."

Sometimes it was hard not to believe in karma. Act like a fool? Look foolish. The end.

"All right." Eva Jansen swooped in to take control of the conversation and rescue her floundering father. "Congratulations to both the final teams—hundreds of chefs would kill to be in your clogs right now. And now that you've chosen your competitors, we're going to let you go so we can start setting things up for the final challenge, which will be announced here in the competition kitchen tomorrow morning. Everyone, take the night off. You've earned it."

That got maybe the biggest cheer of the entire day as ten chefs who'd spent hours on their feet, rushing around, stirring, chopping, folding, and whipping realized that they didn't have to set foot in a kitchen until the next day.

"Don't party too hard tonight!" Kane Slater called

over the din. "You're all on deck to help your competitors plan and get started once we reveal the final challenge."

"Yeah, fuck that," Max whispered out of the side of his mouth as the crowd of celebrating contestants stumbled en masse toward the kitchen doors. "We are going *out* tonight, my friends. Where's the closest chef-friendly bar?"

This was one of Beck's favorite things about cooking on the line in a restaurant kitchen instead of in the galley of a submarine. When the shift was over, instead of racking out and catching a few hours of sleep in a space no bigger than the average bathtub, restaurant chefs tended to take all the built-up adrenaline of battling through a dinner rush and head into the night for a second shift of drinking, carousing, and general bad behavior.

A sharp elbow in his side had Beck oofing out a breath. "Watch it," he said, peering down at Winslow.

Win stared up at him unrepentantly. "You're a big boy, you can take it." His light green eyes went wide and expectant as he tilted his shaved head at an exaggerated angle.

He was obviously trying to communicate something, but Beck had no idea what. His hesitance only seemed to spur Winslow on to bigger head gestures and wider eyes, until Beck finally said, "Dude, I've got nothing. Seriously, what?"

Making a sucking noise with his front teeth, Winslow gave Beck a disgusted look. "Man, you've got no grasp of innuendo. Let me ask you this. Who, here—" Win spread his arms wide to encompass the larger group of chefs, "might know where the good late-night hangout is in this 'hood? Hmm."

As if Winslow had put a hand on Beck's chin and pushed, Beck turned to glance at Skye talking to the big Latino guy from her team on the outer fringe of the crowd.

Setting his jaw, Beck gave Winslow the most impassive look he could come up with.

"Aw, come on, homes. Go talk to your girl. One itty question isn't going to kill either of you."

In other words, nut up.

He cuffed the side of Winslow's head on general principles before dropping out of the herd to hang back and wait for Skye.

Chapter 13

"Come on, Oscar, you know Fi is the right choice. She works fast and clean—"

"And she's the best at keeping you from spinning out and overthinking shit. I know."

The big guy still didn't look all that happy. Skye bit her lip. She abhorred this kind of drama. The back-and-forthing and he-said-she-said and one-upmanship of jockeying for kitchen positions was her A-number-one least favorite part of running her own small business.

Because every dispute, every argument, every ridiculous bet had to be settled by just one person: the boss.

In this case, Skye. Who hadn't understood when she opened Queenie Pie that she was letting herself in for a long, distinguished career as a mediator/therapist.

Except right now, Oscar didn't seem to actually be arguing with her decision to make Fiona the sous-chef for the finals.

"So you agree she should compete with me?"

Oscar shrugged, his barrel chest barely flexing with the movement. "I guess. Just . . . I don't know."

Skye resisted the urge to scream. "You *do* know."

"It feels like a stunt," he blurted, black brows beetling over his unhappy brown eyes. "What that Jansen guy said . . ."

Oh, Skye remembered. Pushing aside the irritation she always felt, every single time some reporter singled her out as one of the best *female* chefs in the city, or part of the new crop of talented *female* chefs opening their own eateries, Skye said, "Ignore him. We're going to win this thing because we're solid, we rock the kitchen, and we cook great food. Not because we've got ovaries and breasts."

The dark, velvety voice from behind her sent chills to tighten the sweaty hair at the nape of Skye's neck.

"There are so many places I could go with that."

She told herself it was ludicrous to blush at the fact that her soon-to-be-ex-husband had heard her say the word *breasts* when he'd not only seen but touched hers. Multiple times. Not that remembering those occasions helped her cool down at all.

"This guy gonna be a problem, boss?"

Nobody, Skye reflected, loomed like Oscar. He even managed it when the man he was looming over was his equal in size and strength.

Beck didn't exactly look intimidated, however. His calm, questioning gaze turned to Skye. "Am I a problem for you, Skye?"

"Of course not," she snapped, which played right into his hands, but what else could she say? Other than "We're fine, Oscar, go catch up with everyone else. I'll find you later."

Casting a deeply suspicious glare in Beck's direction, Oscar did as she asked. As the kitchen door closed behind him, Skye arched a brow at Beck, determined to be as aloof and uncaring about all this as he was.

"You got what you wanted. We're alone. So what happens next?"

Silent laughter glittered in the depths of Beck's dark eyes, although his mouth never even twitched. God, how she used to live for those brief moments of secret amusement.

"I was hoping for a quick word, just to ask a question. But if you've got something else in mind, I'm all ears."

Skye's pulse raced uncomfortably, but she managed a credible yawn. "You know what? I'm too hot and sweaty to play word games with you all night. Just tell me what you want."

Beck shook his head as if he couldn't believe the way she kept setting him up, but instead of going the obvious route and teasing her about how hot and sweaty he'd like to get with her, all he said was "My team's looking to blow off some steam. You got a recommendation for a good after-hours spot, chill enough to not care if things get rowdy?"

Somehow, that wasn't at all the question she'd anticipated. Blinking swiftly, she said, "Yeah, sure. In fact, if they just follow Fiona and the rest of my crew, they'll be headed in the right direction. I'm pretty sure they were on their way to the Grape Ape."

His expression didn't change, but somehow he conveyed the sense that he was rolling his eyes on the inside. "Yes, the Grape Ape," she confirmed testily. "It's a jazz club with a hookah bar on the side, and a list of small-batch indie liquors a mile long."

Actually, now that she thought about it . . . she grinned maliciously. "You're going to hate it."

Beck had never liked her taste in music; he used to complain that jazz sax sounded like someone blowing into the wrong end of a cat.

And the whole hookah scene? She almost wanted to go along with everyone to the bar, just to see the look on his face.

Although, knowing Beck—who'd somehow become even more stone-faced in the ten years they'd been apart—there wouldn't be much to see.

"Sounds awesome," he said, dry as cornmeal flour. "Can't wait."

There was a short pause while Skye tried not to think about the fact that her clothes were stuck to her in some unfortunate places, stained with who-knew-what.

Finally, Beck said, "So. Will I see you at this Grape Ape place?"

"Later, probably," she said vaguely, plucking at the green tank top she'd worn under her chef's jacket. "I've got some things to take care of first."

Maybe she was turning into an old fuddy-duddy—Fiona certainly thought so, and told Skye so, on a regular basis—but Skye just wasn't as into the late-night, after-service bar scene as she used to be.

Okay, she'd never been *that* into it. But it was what you did when you ran a restaurant, when you were a hard-working, plate-slinging chef who put in the hours and wanted to fit in with the guys on the line, so she'd done her time with the rabble-rousers.

Tonight, though, all she wanted was a little peace and solitude, and the chance to finally cool down.

Being anywhere near Beck? Not conducive to getting what she wanted.

The Grape Ape was exactly as Skye had described it—right down to the fact that Beck hated the place from the minute he first pushed his way through floor-length strands of beaded fringe to get from the entryway into the bar itself.

A miasma of odd-smelling smoke hung in the air, fruitier and sweeter than tobacco but without the herbal grassiness of marijuana. He realized it came from the hookahs, set up on low, round tables throughout the bar.

In addition to cocktails made with artisanal alcohol, the menu featured tobacco flavored with unlikely combinations, such as mint and grape—the Great Grape Ape Special—and tropical fruits like guava and mango.

It smelled like hippies in there.

And the music . . . Beck took another sip of his Balcones True Blue corn whiskey and hoped the satisfying warmth that spread through his belly would offset the discordant screeching in his ears.

He shuddered, noticeably enough that Winslow turned to him with a smirk and a gesture at Beck's nearly full glass of amber liquid. "Rougher stuff than you're used to, tough guy?"

"It's not the drink," Beck told him, wincing as the skinny red-haired saxophone player on the stage in the corner hit a note high enough to shatter diamonds.

"Ah. Not a fan of the most creative, improvisational music ever invented?"

"Not you, too," Beck groaned.

"Me too? Who else—oh, I see." Winslow got that oddly wise look on his boyish face. "It didn't click for me before, but now I get it. Queenie Pie Café, that's cute. I like it."

Beck couldn't help it. He tensed all over, curling his fingers around his glass until the tips of them went numb from cold. "What do you mean?"

"Queenie Pie—that's Duke Ellington's great unfinished musical. Your lady must be a big fan, to name her restaurant after it."

"Ellington. Yeah, that rings a bell. Christ!" He whipped his head around and scowled at the musician onstage. "Why does there always have to be a saxophone player?"

"Duke Ellington was a pianist. God, I love that word. Say it with me three times, fast. Pianist, pianist, pianist!"

It wasn't the kind of place where people turned and glared, which was a good thing, because Winslow nearly toppled off his floor pillow while cackling.

"How old are you?" Beck asked, honestly curious. He couldn't remember ever feeling that young.

"Old enough to know better," Win shot back, "but not so old I've completely lost my sense of humor and fun. God. Anyway, I was saying. What was I saying?"

Nudging Win's third glass of unidentified sugary, vividly green cocktail away from the edge of the table, Beck shrugged.

"Oh! Right. Duke Ellington. One of the greats. Pretty quotable, too. Know what he said about jazz?"

"There always has to be a loud, screechy, annoying sax solo?" Beck guessed.

"No!" Winslow struggled to sit up straight before finally giving in to gravity and collapsing back against the mound of cushions piled at their corner table. "He said jazz was like the kind of guy you didn't want your daughter to associate with."

That caught Beck by surprise, and he snorted before he could stop himself. Winslow, of course, jumped on it. "What?"

"Nothing." Beck swirled the amber liquid in his glass, clinking the dwindling ice cubes together gently. "Just . . . it suddenly makes sense to me why Skye likes it so much."

"Oh, I see." Winslow's Wise, Learned Sage look was back. "Mumsie and Daddums didn't approve of their cherished darling dating a boy from the wrong side of the tracks?"

Beck clenched his jaw, pressing his lips together tightly. Why the hell was he even talking about this? "Christ, it was so long ago," he finally exhaled on an explosive breath.

"Time-wise, maybe, but you can't act like it's not still affecting you, so don't even." Winslow spoke with the slow, deliberate logic of the very drunk—but he was right. Maybe it was time to let some of this garbage go. Or at least figure a way around it so he could move forward.

Besides, Win was wasted. That made it a little easier, somehow.

Surrendering to the inevitable, Beck set his glass down on the table. "You're way off base. I mean, I was from the wrong side of the tracks, I guess. Or the wrong side of the Bay, anyway. But her parents loved me. I was the perfect cause—a troubled youth to cart around to all their intellectual gatherings and show off, to prove how liberal and inclusive they were."

Feeling the corner of his mouth twist up in a humorless smile, Beck regarded Winslow over the edge of his glass. "They would've been all over you."

Win barked a laugh, green eyes sparkling. "Shit, I'll bet. Black *and* gay! I mean, who doesn't love a two-for-one deal?" His smile faded quickly, though, and his gaze went thoughtful. "So when did they stop loving you?"

Beck stared down at his rye, a muscle ticking in his jaw. "About the time I proposed . . . and she accepted."

"Huh. That seems a little bass ackwards, to me."

Shrugging, Beck stared out into the dark, smoky bar. "You have to know Skye's parents, I guess. Arty, hippie types—to the extreme. They weren't married, didn't believe in it. I don't think they meant to have a kid, either—always seemed a lot more wrapped up in their causes and their pretentious art gallery showings and lame-ass pothead friends than in taking care of Skye. But they sure as hell had plenty to say when she wasn't acting the way they thought she should."

Win propped his chin on one unsteady hand and waved

the other in the air. "Keep it coming," he slurred. "This is good stuff."

Of course, that made Beck want to clamp down. "Nah, it's ancient history, man. We got married anyway, they cut her off, whatever."

The wrench of pain in his gut was as familiar as an old friend when he lifted his glass for another sip and said, "It's not like they had it all wrong, anyway. Skye and me, we didn't last. They were right about that."

"What were they wrong about?" Rye burned down Beck's throat as he blinked at Win through the haze.

"What?" Blinking owlishly, Win said, "You said her parents didn't have it *all* wrong. So some of it was wrong. Which part?"

Beck shot a suspicious glance at the neon green cocktail with—what was that? Cucumber slices floating around in it.

"That drink is non-alcoholic. It has to be. No way you're this perceptive after a slew of real cocktails."

Win's eyes shifted guiltily, then he sighed and gave it up. "Okay, yeah. It's just a cucumber water and mint spritzer. But there's a buttload of sugar in it! Enough to make me loopy, I swear. Besides, I knew you'd be more likely to open up if you thought there was a possibility I wouldn't even remember this conversation tomorrow."

"You little shit," Beck said, but he couldn't help the wry smile that tugged at his mouth.

"I was kinda right, though, wasn't I?" Sensing that he was forgiven, Win rolled up to his knees and put his hands up in front of his chest, begging like a puppy. "So come on, finish the story! Skye's parents were right that you crazy kids didn't stay together—sorry about that— but what were they wrong on?"

Okay, that was about enough sharing for one night.

Beck deflected by tossing back the rest of his drink

and slapping Winslow on the back. "They said we'd get divorced, obviously—but we never got around to it."

Although, if Skye had her way . . . Beck's mood darkened.

Visibly, if the way Win's eyes narrowed was any clue. "Yeah. I wonder why. Seems like most people who spend ten years apart do finally manage to break up all the way."

Slamming his empty glass down hard enough to make the remaining slivers of ice jump, Beck growled, "Well, we didn't. But it doesn't matter now. It's over, whether we have the official paper saying so or not."

"Sure it is." The look Beck shot him must have been ferocious, because Winslow started backpedaling fast. "I mean, hey! It's not my fault you and Skye have starcrossed lovers written all over you! And you can glower at me all you want, Mr. Tough Guy, but you know I'm right. There's still something between you."

Beck forced his shoulders to relax, his fingers to uncurl from the fists he didn't remember clenching. "Yeah. Sex."

Star-crossed lovers. Bullshit. Maybe this would shake some of the fairy dust out of Winslow's eyes.

Leaning in, Beck raised a brow as Winslow leaned back, looking nervous. "Want to know a secret? We made a bet, Skye and me. Either way this goes, she gets her divorce. But if our team wins the finals? I get her. For one more night."

See, Beck wanted to insist. *It's over. There's nothing left between us but the way our bodies react to each other.*

But instead of getting a clue, Win got the sappiest smile in the history of the world spreading across his face. "Aw! That's so romantic!"

Stung, Beck sat back. "No, it's not," he said firmly.

"Okay, fine. But it's a start."

Beck crushed down an inarticulate noise of frustration. "It's an ending."

"Oh, Beck." Win shook his head sadly. "God, straight boys are the worst."

"I think we're done here," Beck said, fishing out a ten and throwing it on the low wicker table. "See you back at the hotel."

"Don't be like that!" Win toppled back onto his cushion and lifted imploring hands to Beck. "Come on, sit down. I didn't mean to make you mad."

Beck stood up in a controlled rush, feeling his muscles uncoil gratefully after an hour of being cramped on the floor. "Nah, we're cool. I'm just tired. And I kind of hate it in here."

"Yeah, I know. Thanks for sticking it out so long, and entertaining me with your tale of woe."

"It's not a tale of woe." Beck stuck his hands in his back pockets and looked down at one of the best friends he'd ever had. "It's just my life, man. And that part of my life is finished."

Looking perfectly at home lounging on a tasseled blue velvet pillow like some kind of pasha, Winslow laced his fingers behind his head and regarded Beck seriously. "What part? Love? I hope not, Beckster, for your sake."

"Love." Beck laughed, but the sound tore at his throat with jagged edges. "Jesus Christ. This isn't some romantic comedy, Win."

He expected Winslow to argue with him, extol the virtues of falling in love, take him to task for acting like he didn't know what the word meant.

But Win just blinked slowly and smiled. "You know, we're only going to be here a few more days. Maybe you should take some time to revisit the parts of your life you left behind."

Taking a look around the crowded bar, full of chatter

and laughter and the clink of glasses, sucking in a breath heavy with smoke and the scent of sweaty bodies packed close together, Beck suddenly felt an intense urge for fresh air. And that made him think of . . .

"What are you smiling at?" Win wanted to know.

"Nothing. See you around." Beck hitched up his jeans and headed for the exit, still grinning, an odd lightness filling him at the thought of seeing a particular corner of his past, one last time.

Chapter 14

Beck's worn leather boots skidded on the loose gravel of the faint path, and he shot a hand out just in time to steady himself against the rough trunk of a tall eucalyptus tree.

The whole area around Kirby Cove was covered in eucalyptus, cypress, and pine trees, and the fresh, green smell of them on the cool night air filled Beck's lungs with welcome relief.

Picking his way more carefully, and glad for the hundredth time that he wore his old, comfortable boots in the kitchen rather than the more common leather or rubber clogs, Beck peered up through the enfolding branches and wished for a full moon.

This far off the official trail, he needed all the light he could get.

Finally, he emerged from the woods into the clearing at the top of the bluff overlooking the bay. Beck blinked away the sudden dazzle of the lights of San Francisco in the distance and the glow of the Golden Gate Bridge stretching away from him and out over the black water.

Something in his chest settled as he took in the view.

He might deny it, he might hate it, he might fight against it and vow never to come back here—but no matter what Beck said, this would always be home.

A salt breeze off the bay got him moving again, pulling his T-shirt up and over his head as he clambered down the rocky embankment.

Now that he was here, he found himself in a hurry to get down to the protected inlet, hidden from the campground, where he and Skye used to swim.

Without warning, memories swamped him. Of that first night, the night they'd met, when he'd hiked through the forest after checking his highly illegal crab traps and found a beautiful young girl perched on a rock, like a mermaid or a siren, something out of the illustrated book of myths his parents had given him for his sixth birthday. The one with the cover falling off, and the edges of the pages all worn soft and rounded from constant handling and banging up against the other crap he hauled around in the backpack that carried all his belongings.

Shaking away the vision of Skye as she'd been twelve years ago—pale as the moon shining down on him now, her red hair a waterfall of curls over her shoulders, the soft, smooth curves of her body—Beck ducked a low-hanging cypress branch.

He slung his T-shirt around his neck, his boots finally crunching on the sharp gravel of the beach as he jogged around the last cluster of rocks and got his first real glimpse of the cove.

Their own, private swimming hole, they'd called it, and in all the times they'd gone there, they'd never seen another camper or hiker adventurous enough to bush-whack down to this little inlet and try the water.

Not surprising; it was dangerous to swim in the San Francisco Bay at the best of times—skinny dipping at night was crazy.

Only a lunatic—or a couple of kids convinced they were invincible—would dare.

Beck froze, staring out at the dark water in disbelief. Apparently, he wasn't the only lunatic at Kirby Cove tonight.

A hundred feet away from the rocky shore, a white figure stroked cleanly through the choppy waves.

The compromised visibility made the distance too far for Beck to make out a face, but with a shiver of premonition, Beck knew in his gut who that swimmer was.

A quick recon of the beach proved him right.

Right there, piled at the foot of Skye's favorite sunbathing rock, was a neat stack of folded clothes, topped by a stained white chef's coat.

Whirling to face the water, Beck stared hungrily out into the bay, willing his eyes to sharpen. He had to see her. He had to be sure.

The swimmer paused mid-stroke and hung in place, treading water beneath the surface as she tilted her face up to the night sky. The sound of her panting breaths carried over the open water, as clearly as if Beck were treading water beside her.

Wind kicked up around him, whipping the trees and scudding the clouds that had covered the moon away, shining a brief, milky light over the woman's features.

It was Skye.

Beck flung his shirt to the ground beside her clothes, then went to work on his jeans.

This was dumb. Skye knew it was dumb. If any of her friends went swimming alone at night, even in a nice, safe pool, she'd whack them across the head and warn them about the danger.

Which was exponentially greater when swimming in open water. Notoriously treacherous open water, at that.

But she'd always felt safe at Kirby Cove . . . and besides, she'd needed this like she needed air. And chocolate.

This swim had been essential.

A mere hour of solitude, and she could hear herself think again. Everything seemed clearer out here, away from the noise and bustle and demands of her kitchen and crew. She loved them like crazy, but . . . sometimes *crazy* was the operative word.

Involuntary shudders wracked through her, cues from her body that this water was really too cold, especially when she wasn't doing much more than hanging out and maybe it was time to think about getting out, thank you very much.

A noise, like pebbles shifting and rolling, sent a chill through Skye that had nothing to do with the water temperature.

Right. Because death by drowning wasn't the only thing a solitary swimmer risked.

Heart in her throat, every muscle corded with tension, Skye kicked her legs furiously to turn her in place so she could see the shoreline.

The beach was empty.

Scanning the gravel bank for a hint of what could've made the noise she'd heard, Skye felt her leaping pulse begin to even out.

It was nothing. Probably a rabbit or some other harmless little animal. Still, the peace and serenity of the moment was broken, and she figured it was probably time she got dry and went home, anyway.

Reluctantly pulling toward the shoreline, Skye was just beginning to feel the good, satisfying tremble in her shoulders and arms from the workout she'd given them today when something touched her leg.

Still jumpy, she gave an embarrassing shriek and

thrashed a little, even while her brain tried to convince her it was nothing, some reeds or a harmless fish.

But then the touch came back, and this time it slid from her knee to her thigh, shockingly warm against her water-chilled flesh, and Skye's mind went blank with terror. Throwing all her strength into her stroke, she swam as hard as she could for the beach.

A familiar laugh behind her startled Skye so badly she nearly choked, saltwater burning down her throat and up into her nose.

Coughing and hacking, Skye whipped around to see water pouring in rivulets down Henry Beck's handsome, smiling face and over his broad shoulders.

"You asshole!" Skye could barely see him, shock and adrenaline making her eyes water.

"I'm sorry," he said, slicing through the water toward her. "But it's been way too long since I snuck up on you like that."

"I could kill you right now," she snarled, wiping at her face and kicking her legs to keep out of reach of his long arms, gleaming bare in the moonlight.

"Aw, come on, that's no way for a pacifist to talk."

"You've always been a bad influence," she told him, finally getting her breathing under control. She had to fight the urge to try and smooth her impossible hair down. It wouldn't work, and she'd just make him think she cared what she looked like in front of him.

Which wasn't true. At all.

For instance, she definitely wasn't thinking about the fact that she was swimming in only her currently very translucent pink bra and panties.

Or that she hadn't lost any weight since the last time he'd seen her in her skivvies . . . in fact, she'd done the other thing.

It wasn't easy to keep afloat while crossing her arms

over her chest, and she felt like a tool, so she gave up on that and concentrated on keeping her head above water.

Beck's dark stare dipped to the water line, zeroing in on the plump upper swells of her breasts peeking out over the tops of the bra cups sticking to her skin.

"I thought you were about to get out," he said casually. "How long have you been swimming, anyway?"

Kicking slowly toward the shore, Skye frowned. "About an hour, I guess. I don't know, I came straight here after we left the competition kitchen."

Beck followed her at a slow, deliberate pace. She couldn't seem to stop sneaking glances at the swift, sure stroke of his arms through the water, the bunch and play of muscle in his big shoulders.

Closer to the beach now, Skye felt the mucky ground under her feet and started to stand up.

A sudden gleam in Beck's eyes had Skye sucking in a breath and ducking back down into the water. "You complete shit! You just want me to get out so you can see me in wet underwear!"

"Never said I didn't." Not looking too pissed off at being thwarted, Beck flipped onto his back and floated lazily.

One good thing about being scalded with a furious blush . . . it took some of the chill off the surface of Skye's skin.

"What is *with* you?" she hissed. "You left *me* ten years ago, remember? And after that last phone call . . ." Her voice shook. The memory of that staticky, halting conversation would be with her till she died. Skye firmed her chin and skewered him with a glare.

"After that, not a word. Not a single call, or postcard, or singing freaking telegram, Henry. You could've been dead for all I knew!"

"Sorry to disappoint you."

That was a solid hit, right to the gut. Winded and shocked, a storm of pain rose up and pushed the words out of her clenched throat. "Oh, fuck you, Henry. Seriously, just . . ."

Not caring anymore what he saw or didn't see, Skye stood on wobbly legs and started wading toward the beach.

All she knew was that she had to get away from him, and the memory of those long months alone with her grief.

A soft curse and a splash from behind her was all the warning she got before a hard hand shot out and gripped her wrist.

"Skye, wait . . ."

"No!" Tugging frantically, Skye twisted to get free of his implacable hold.

"I shouldn't have said that. I'm sorry."

His deep, solemn voice drained the fight out of her. Trouble was, it seemed to drain everything else, too, every drop of energy and spirit the peaceful hour of solitude had given her.

Struggling against the urge to wilt completely, Skye swallowed hard. "It's fine. You can let me go now."

Beck made that inarticulate noise she knew so well— the one that meant he was frustrated, hounded by some emotion he couldn't or wouldn't express. "Not yet."

Flexing her wrist against his fingers, Skye played her trump card. "You're hurting me," she said quietly.

He let go as if her skin had burned him, and she began picking her way back up the beach without another word or glance.

This was too hard. Everything with Beck . . . it was too much, and for a brief, horrible moment, Skye saw the dark, gaping mouth of the past surging up to swallow her whole.

"Skye." His voice was raw, ragged around the edges. "Please."

She didn't want to react to that voice, but it called to something deep inside her. Skye stopped walking, ankle deep in cold, brackish water. Chills zipped through her body, raising goose bumps on her arms and legs, but she didn't try to cover herself up when she turned to face him.

He'd seen it all before, anyway. She'd been pudgy back then, she was pudgy now. Five months of pregnancy did that to a person. Maybe nine and a half years should've been long enough to take some of those pounds off, but . . . what difference could it possibly make at this point? She was too tired, exhausted from the emotional roller coaster of the last few days, to care anymore.

"What?" Skye hated the defeat in her tone, but didn't know how to mask it. "I don't understand what you want from me."

His expression tightened, sending his dramatic cheekbones into stark relief. With his chin-length hair swept back off his face, droplets of saltwater tracing rivulets over the smooth, bare musculature of his massive chest, he looked like exactly what he was . . . a warrior.

Battle scarred and battle hardened, changed by what he'd seen and done, he wasn't the same boy who'd signed the marriage license with her in front of the Justice of the Peace.

But when he held out his hand to her, that mute appeal in his fathomless, shadowed eyes, Skye could no more resist the man in front of her than she'd been able to deny the boy anything he asked.

Without conscious thought, without ever making a rational decision one way or the other, Skye lifted her arm and placed her stiff, cold fingers on his waiting palm.

Something bright and fierce flashed across his enigmatic face, too quickly for Skye to read, but she knew exactly what it meant when his hand closed over hers and pulled her in close.

"You're freezing. C'mere," he said, wrapping his free arm around her shivering shoulders and sheltering her from the wind with his big, rangy frame.

And Skye let him, too cold, too tired, too confused to fight anymore. Tucking her nose into his chest, Skye let her eyes drift shut as the deep, steady beat of his heart drummed beneath her ear.

"You left me," she muttered again, but this time it came out sounding less like an accusation and more like a plea. For what, she didn't know—answers, maybe? "Why didn't you come back?"

"After everything that happened, I didn't think you'd want me to" was all Beck said.

How could he think that? Oh, right. Because after she'd sobbed out the ugly, tragic news—that their baby, the baby he'd joined the Navy to provide for, the baby they'd made together, would never be born—she'd paused just long enough to drag air into her tortured lungs and whisper that she never wanted to see him again.

"I was distraught! Eighteen years old, completely alone in the hospital, dealing with a miscarriage."

"I know. But you were right. I should've been there."

Ten years of going over and over and over this in her head, and Skye still didn't get where it had all gone wrong. "No. I was wrong to tell you to stay away. I understood, even then, why you felt you had to join up."

They'd had less than no money, and no support from her parents, who couldn't believe their little love child had run off and taken up the hideous bourgeois state of matrimony. When she'd gotten pregnant, she and Beck hadn't had any insurance, no way to pay for all the prenatal vitamins and ultrasounds and hospital stays . . .

Skye had insisted they'd get by and that they should stick together. But Beck had bigger plans . . . plans that had meant Skye was alone when that nurse came back with their baby's first ultrasound photo and a strained, nervous smile. Skye was alone as she waited for the doctor to come in and explain exactly what was going on, what they'd seen in that blurry black-and-white photo.

She'd been alone when they told her she'd never get to hold her baby.

The memory swamped her, a swell of sadness and longing rushing over her head and dragging her down, catching her in the riptide of familiar grief.

Skye didn't realize she was shaking her head until Beck's fingers caught her chin, stilling the denial and tilting her face up until she had no choice but to meet his stare.

For once, she could read the emotion in his dark eyes, the torment there sharp as glass.

"I hate you," she told him, but her voice broke pathetically as she said it. By the quirk of Beck's hard mouth, she could tell he believed it about as much as she did.

"No, you don't," he said, not unkindly. "You wish you could hate me—it'd be a hell of a lot easier—but you don't, Skye."

God help her. It was nothing but the truth. She didn't hate him at all.

And as she gazed up at him, dazed under the intensity of his expression, the set of his jaw, the rise and fall of his solid chest against hers, she knew the rest of the truth.

In spite of everything, she still loved him.

Chapter 15

Skye stood there, trembling in the moonlight, the creamy paleness of her naked curves glowing like a beacon against the darkness. The sodden scraps of her underwear concealed nothing, clinging to her lovingly. And her expression . . .

She was broken wide open, like an egg dropped on the floor.

But she wasn't denying anything.

Ferocious need swept through him—the need to touch her, to erase the memories from her eyes, the sadness from her trembling mouth, to take her and re-stake his claim on her.

Even if it was for the last time.

Beck didn't want to think about that. He didn't want to think about anything.

Framing Skye's soft cheeks between his palms, Beck brought his mouth down to hers.

It was like taking a deep breath of cool air after hours of working in the galley kitchen of a submarine, with no ventilation and no windows and no way out.

He just inhaled her, taking the freshness and sweetness of her into himself and savoring the sugar-lemon taste of her mouth. Skye opened for him on a gasp, her small hands coming up hesitantly to clutch at his waist, and Beck immediately seized the tactical advantage by thrusting his tongue between her pink lips.

She molded her body to his, the soft ripeness of her flesh a perfect contrast to his hard, tensed muscles. Beck swept his hands down the sides of her neck and over her shoulders, curling around to her back to press her even closer.

The chill of her skin was replaced by a warm flush. He thought he could actually feel the hot blood pumping through her veins, pushed through her by the rapid beating of her heart.

He ate at her mouth hungrily, and she met his attack with a ferocious need of her own. Her hands, no longer hesitant, gripped and pressed firmly. She seemed to be trying to touch as much of him as possible without breaking the kiss. Beck approved, and twisted his torso like a cat, trying to give her more skin to play with.

Skye made a noise that Beck swallowed instantly, a familiar, kittenish sort of growl that threw him back in time and made his cock throb in his wet, clinging shorts.

He needed to get closer to her.

They were still standing in knee-deep water, their feet sucked into the marshy Bay floor, making it difficult to maneuver.

Not that Beck was about to let that stop him.

Bending down, he got one arm behind Skye's knees and plucked her out of the muck. Primal satisfaction filled him as he pulled her in against his chest.

At some point in the last ten years, though, Skye had forgotten everything he'd taught her about being swept off her feet. She gave a little yelp as the world tilted around her, and flailed hard enough that he almost dropped her before getting a firmer grip on her wet limbs.

"Put me down! You'll throw your back out, Henry, I'm too heavy for this."

"Chill," he told her. "The issue is that you're all slippery at the moment. Other than that?" He hitched her up easily, until her mouth was in kissing distance again.

Stealing a quick one off her parted lips, he grinned down at her. "Other than that, you're perfect."

She melted faster than butter in a hot sauté pan. He could feel the exact moment when she forgot to be afraid of being dropped or worried about her weight as all the tension left her body.

He'd never understood what she was so worried about, anyway. No woman had ever felt better in his arms.

Beck considered his options. The beach was the obvious choice, but they didn't have a blanket, and it's not like it was covered in powdery white sand, which meant they'd run the risk of gravel in uncomfortable places.

Decision made, Beck waded deeper into the water. When he was in up to his waist, he shifted Skye in his arms, letting her legs drop down.

Except she didn't drop them—she kicked up and locked her thighs around his hips, grinding her pelvic bone against the hard ridge of his erection and making Beck want to howl.

Working on instinct and memory, he cupped his hands under her rear to support her new position, his fingers pressing convulsively into the lush, silky flesh of her ass.

The scratch of her fingernails against the back of his neck, the flutter of her pale eyelashes as she tilted her head up for another of those ravenous, sucking kisses . . . Beck had to clamp down hard on his control to keep from shooting off in his boxers.

Being with Skye again, after a decade apart . . . it was as if the years fell away and the rough, scarred outer layer of himself peeled back to leave him new again, discovering the joy of his body and Skye's for the first time.

Not that he'd been exactly innocent or pure—or unscarred—when they'd met.

But she'd always made him feel like that stuff didn't matter. When he was with her, he could be the person he so desperately wanted to be. The person his parents would have been proud of, instead of the kid no one wanted.

And she still had that magic touch, he realized as his heart raced and his blood took up a frantic, pounding rhythm.

No one had the power to make him feel like Skye did. Which made her dangerous, a real threat to the life Beck had built so painstakingly for himself—but it also made her irresistible.

Somehow, the water didn't feel nearly as cold now that Skye was wrapped around Beck's huge, solid form like a honeysuckle vine climbing a fence.

Panting lightly, Skye tilted her head to the side as Beck's mouth went for her neck.

The lights of the Golden Gate Bridge sparkled at the edges of her vision. She knew they were close enough to hear traffic noise, the way sounds carried over water, but all she could hear was the rush of her own blood and the harshness of Beck's breathing.

And when his teeth closed firmly over the sensitive spot where her neck sloped into her shoulder, Skye heard moaning. It took her a second to realize those particular sounds were coming from her.

There was something intensely liberating about being out here, at one with the water and the cool night breeze.

She felt as if she was taking part in some ancient, pagan ritual of sex and fertility, an earth mother goddess being worshipped.

She tingled all over, prickles chasing each other down her arms and legs and up her stomach to tighten her nipples where they nestled against the planes of Beck's broad chest.

She felt alive. Extra alive, as if she'd just woken up from the longest sleep ever, a coma patient suddenly sitting straight up in bed and gasping for that first breath of consciousness.

The whole world was new, charged with sensation and feeling, and Skye surrendered to it completely, let it wrap her up and send her flying.

It was so amazing to be naked and unashamed, to know what she wanted with utter certainty for the first time in . . . way too long.

Although she wasn't totally naked, which she remembered when Beck's fingers shifted on her behind, catching at the lacy edges of her thin panties. The damp material didn't seem to hinder him in any way that Skye could notice—those long, agile fingers had her underwear pushed aside faster than she could blink, giving him complete access to the damp, aching secrets of her body.

"God," he groaned against her neck, the vibrations making her shiver. "You feel amazing."

"I do," she said rapturously. "I really do feel amazing. More of that, please."

But Beck wasn't the type to get carried away—not if it meant dropping Skye on her ass. Instead, he walked a little farther out into the bay, until she floated weightlessly against him, only her locked ankles keeping her close.

Her locked ankles, her hands behind his neck . . . and

the indescribably luscious glide of his fingers under the elastic band of her underwear.

His touch left a trail of fire that seemed as though it ought to be making the water around them steam like a pot over high heat. But above the surface of the water in their protected inlet, nothing stirred.

While below . . .

Skye hung motionless in Beck's embrace, head lolling back and eyes closed, all her senses transfixed by the slow, sure strokes of his strong fingers.

He petted her gently, exploring the hot, wet seam at her core, before spearing first one, then two fingers between her lips.

She shook, nonsense words trapped in her throat, vibrating against the delicate pressure of his teeth where he'd bitten down again and was sucking up a circle of heat that prickled and stung deliciously.

More, more, more was all she could think, and Beck gave it to her, his knife-callused thumb finding the knot of nerves at the top of her slit and flicking it teasingly.

He found a rhythm, a combination of glancing tweaks and deep, smooth invasion, and she followed it blindly, her body parting gladly around the thick intrusion of his long fingers.

When he finally lifted his head, she knew by the possessive glint in his smile that he'd left a livid mark at the base of her neck. She could feel it throbbing, all the blood called to the surface there, an echo of the thob lower down.

Squirming restlessly, Skye whimpered because even this wasn't enough. "More," she demanded, and Beck's eyes flashed.

"Hold on to me," he ordered, and Skye pushed her sore, aching muscles to obey the command.

Without taking his hand from her aching center, Beck let go of her rump and moved his other hand between them.

For a long, liquid moment, Skye was suspended between the water and the sky, held up by nothing more than Beck's maddening touch deep inside her.

Then, without warning, that touch disappeared, leaving her empty and cold.

Mindless with desire, she writhed against him until she realized he'd freed himself from his boxers.

She couldn't see the thick, intimidating stalk of his erection, but she could feel it, blunt and uncompromising, rising high and tight to his flat stomach. The movement of the choppy water pushed her into him, and suddenly her slick, open core was rubbing against the smooth underside of his cock.

As warm as his fingers had been, they hadn't prepared her for the searing heat of his erection.

"Yes," she gasped. "In me, come on."

But Beck's hands slid around her hips, holding her in place, his cock jammed up against her but not doing anything, not going in, just burning into her softness.

She might have whimpered. She couldn't be sure; everything was a little hazy.

"No, like this," he whispered, shifting her weight, and that slight movement, that hint of friction, was enough to send a pulse of sensation straight up her spine.

"Okay," she groaned. "I guess I can be satisfied with—oh!"

Beck's hips were in on the action now, thrusting his hardness up then raking it back down, the ridge of his cock head catching with agonizing regularity on the swollen nub of her clit.

Every thrust drove her higher, towards that shiny, elusive, just out of reach . . . damn it, she needed more!

Skye twisted to drag her taut nipples across his chest. She curled her fingers into the waves of his hair, loving the way she could get a good grip on him, and pulled his head down to attack his mouth with hers.

Her lips parted, inviting him in, and when his tongue rubbed velvety over the ticklish roof of her mouth and began a dance of swift in and out, it was the last bit of sensation she needed.

Skye pushed her hips against Beck's as hard as she could and froze there, quivering as she exploded in his arms. Shivers wracked her frame, aftershocks rocketing through her, and Beck let out a hoarse cry. A moment later, warmth spread between their tight-pressed bellies.

Exhausted and wrung out, Skye tucked her face into Beck's neck, feeling the rapid pounding of his pulse as they began to come back down to earth.

"Skye." His voice was wrecked, guttural and deep. "Christ, I missed you."

She stiffened all over, reality descending with a crash, scattering afterglow like a bowl of fresh peas spilled out onto the ground. Three little words, so close to the words she would've given anything to hear in a voicemail, on a postcard . . . heck, even in a text.

But to hear them now, after all this, reminded her of exactly how long he'd been gone. And what had happened since he left.

Jeremiah Raleigh.

She'd met someone else. A good man, someone she supposedly loved. And yet she'd done this.

Never mind that she and Jeremiah had an "open relationship." Never mind that her parents applauded them for being so sensible and practical, mature and liberal-minded about the outdated sentimentality of fidelity.

Skye had never believed in it. In her heart of hearts, she'd always known that what she wanted was a secure, loving, monogamous relationship, so even though she'd agreed to the open relationship because it was what Jeremiah wanted, she'd never been unfaithful.

Until tonight.

"You can put me down now," she said quietly, shame and self-loathing creeping into her chest and making it hard to breathe.

Beck didn't answer, just waded in a little closer to shore before setting her on her feet.

Shaky, Skye looked up at him and tried to smile.

It wasn't Beck's fault that she'd just betrayed everything she believed in. Tempting as it was to lay the blame at his feet, she couldn't do that.

No, the simple truth was that Skye had been forced to take a look inside herself. And what she'd found was that she wasn't the person she'd thought.

"You okay?"

The words were cautious, quiet. The beautiful openness Beck's face took on during sex was gone. Even as Skye wished it back again, she couldn't blame him. She was acting like a fruitcake.

"Sorry, yeah." She tried that smile on again, and this time it didn't wobble so badly. "Just tired. Been a long day, you know?"

"A long day, full of surprises," Beck agreed as they made their way back up the beach to the clothes piled at the foot of the big, flat rock.

Even the reminder that she and her team had been called first as finalists in the Rising Star Chef competition couldn't lift Skye out of the pit of guilt she'd fallen into. Not all the surprises the day held had been great, after all.

Surprise! You're a faithless tramp!

They got dressed in silence. It wasn't a shocker—Beck had never had a whole lot to say for himself, even when they'd been together. Which had been a big part of the problem.

Silence weighed on Skye. Made her antsy, made her babble just to fill it. Only right now, she couldn't think of a thing to say.

But it turned out Beck had one more surprise for her.

Shaking his head like a wet dog, Beck threw himself upright and slicked the dark waves back with both hands. Turning to watch her roll her crumpled tank top down over her naked breasts—she'd taken off the wet bra and stuffed it in her pocket—Beck went still.

Then he said, "This doesn't change anything."

Skye jerked the shirt on angrily enough to almost rip it. She was terrified that this night had changed everything, her entire future . . . and for Beck, it was, what? A trip down memory lane?

Before she could snarl at him, he narrowed his eyes and pointed at her. "The bet is still on, Skye."

Awareness crashed over her. The bet? He was worried about the damn bet, when her whole life was falling apart?

"You listen to me, Henry Beck—" she started, furious.

He cut her off with, "No. You listen. You want your divorce? Fine. But I'm not through with you yet."

Her mouth dried out as he stalked toward her, prowling like a big, hungry predator. She didn't move, caught like a mouse in a trap, and he leaned in close.

"That was only the appetizer," he murmured, nuzzling her jaw line and starting that sweet thump of desire pulsing through her again. "Next time, I want you naked all the way. I want you under me. And I want more than a taste of you."

Surprise! Skye's brain caroled happily. *You're an* unrepentant *faithless tramp!*

Because as Beck pulled away and grabbed her hand to

lead her up the trail and back toward civilization, all Skye wanted was to tug him down to the forest floor with her and make "next time" happen immediately.

She was such a mess.

Chapter 16

Loud pounding on the hotel room door woke Beck up. Instantly alert, he swung his legs off the bed and padded, naked, to check the peep hole.

It was Winslow, wearing a blue shirt with a simple black line drawing of a bunk bed with the caption *Top or bottom?* and a worried expression.

"Hold on," Beck called. "Gimme a sec to find my pants."

"Okay."

Beck paused. Win didn't say anything else, and Beck realized he'd been waiting for a zippy, vaguely sexual comeback that hadn't come.

Shit, something must be really wrong.

But when he opened the door for Winslow, one hand still zipping up his jeans, the first words out of Win's mouth were "Do you know what's wrong?"

"You're the one who woke me up," Beck reminded him, glancing over to the nightstand for the clock. "At . . . Christ, what is it, oh six hundred?"

Win jittered into the room, nearly sloshing the two white-lidded to-go cups in his hands. "Don't growl. I brought you coffee. And I'm freaked the eff out, man.

Something's up—Jules called a team meeting for an hour from now. I couldn't wait that long, sitting around my room all by my onesie, knowing nothing. Here."

Beck took the caffeinated peace offering and sipped at it appreciatively, letting the dark, smooth roast wake him up the rest of the way. Win had a genius for ferreting out the best coffee shop, no matter where they were.

"You can hang with me," Beck said, crouching to grab a T-shirt from his tightly packed duffel bag. "But I don't know any more than you do. Probably less. What did Jules say when she called the meeting?"

Win threw himself down on the unused bed, rumpling the coverlet. "Just to meet in her and Max's room at seven. But she was definitely wigged, in that tough-as-nails Jules way."

Pulling the navy-blue shirt on, Beck was glad he'd showered the saltwater off the night before. He stood up and went to brush his teeth, grimacing at the crazy mess of his hair in the bathroom mirror.

Gathering the top part of it into a rubber-banded pony-tail, he wandered back into the room just as his cell phone buzzed against the nightstand, where it was plugged in.

His mind leaped instantly to Skye—was she calling him? Did she want to talk about last night? Did she want to plan when they could do it again? Because the trip back up the hill to her car, parked at the Kirby Cove camp-ground, had been mostly silent.

He wasn't used to being unable to tell what she was thinking, and he didn't much care for it.

But Winslow said, "I bet that's Jules calling to clue you in about the meeting, even though I told her I'd tell you. Nobody trusts me to do anything."

Forcing himself to relax, Beck reached for the phone, sure that Win was right. Except the number on the display wasn't Jules's, or even Max's.

"Who is it?" Winslow asked nervously, probably reacting to the frown Beck could feel tightening his brow.

"It's the restaurant," he said slowly, clicking the Talk button and holding the phone up to his ear. "Beck."

"Oh, thank goodness I caught you."

Nina Lunden's warm, motherly voice filtered into Beck's consciousness like a sip of peppermint tea—bracing, comforting, and sweet.

"Nina. What can I do for you?"

"That's what I love about you, sweetie. Always straight to the point!"

She gave a little laugh, and Beck felt his lips twitch in response. Nina was . . . something else.

When she'd hired him to work the hot line at Lunden's Tavern seven months ago, she'd barely glanced at his resume, full of his work history and military service. She'd tossed the papers on the table between them and leaned forward on her elbows, faded blue eyes fixed on his face.

"Well, Henry Beck? Are you ready to be a chef?"

"Just Beck," he'd told her. "And I'm ready. You won't be sorry you hired me; I'll never let you down. I'm a hard worker, Mrs. Lunden."

"Oh, I know you are." She'd cocked her head to one side, those kind eyes of hers going shrewd and sharp. "The question is, are you ready for what it means to be a chef, with the bunch of yahoos we've got working here? And I say that with love, since my husband and son are part of the kitchen crew."

"I'm ready," he'd repeated, as firmly as he could.

Her laugh bubbled up, surprisingly youthful and vibrant. "I wonder. You've got a very stoic look about you, Beck. I'm not sure how long we'll let you keep it, or how you'll like losing it. But there's no way to know unless you give it a try."

She'd led him back into the kitchen and had her husband,

Gus, run him through some hands-on tests of his culinary skills, and that was it. He was hired.

But he'd never forgotten the way Nina Lunden seemed able to peer right inside him, or the way she'd accepted him almost immediately, without hesitation.

That kind of acceptance wasn't something he'd had a lot of in his life, and he treasured it when he came across it. Nina had a special place in Beck's heart from that day on, and even if he didn't show it much, he had a feeling Nina knew.

Remembering all that made Beck gentle his voice now. "Nina, tell me what's going on. If I can help, I will."

Her breath caught audibly, and something in Beck's chest tightened like a fist. "Oh," she choked out. "Well, that's good to hear. Because we're having a bit of a problem here at the restaurant."

Suddenly unable to be sitting, Beck got to his feet and started to pace, the hotel carpet thick and soft under his bare toes. "What kind of problem?"

"It's Gus," she said softly, confirming Beck's fears. "He's been having dizzy spells, a little trouble breathing. And yesterday, he said his chest was feeling tight. Beck, I'm worried about his heart."

Nina had good reason to worry. A mere month ago, Gus had landed in the hospital after collapsing in the restaurant's kitchen with severe angina. It had kept him off the Rising Star Chef team, and he'd stayed home in Manhattan to run Lunden's Tavern with a skeleton crew while the rest of them competed.

"He was supposed to be taking it easy," Beck said. "Let the crew handle the heavy lifting and the worst of the work."

"I know," Nina fretted. "But he's so damned stubborn! And I can't watch him every second—I need to be out front, managing the servers and the bar, and the reserva-

tion line's been ringing off the hook. You wouldn't believe how much business is booming, just from our team
having made it so far in the RSC! We're packed every
night. Which is what we wanted. But it's taking its toll on
Gus, and I'm just worried . . ."

"That's all you have to say." Beck stopped her before
the tremor in her voice could get any worse. "I'll catch the
first flight to New York and get back in the kitchen to help
out with the rush and keep an eye on Gus."

And if Beck was surprised at the need to muscle
through a painful stabbing in his gut at the thought of
running out on Skye after last night, well, fuck it. The
Lundens were the closest thing to a family that Beck had
found in years, and Skye had made it pretty clear that she
wanted him out of her life for good.

Ignoring the voice in his head that whispered how
Skye hadn't seemed all that through with him out in the
water last night, Beck tucked the phone against his ear
and started packing the few things he'd removed from his
duffel with swift, economical movements.

Before he could even get his toothbrush off the sink,
though, Nina was saying, "No, no, that's not what I'm saying."

He paused, his attention caught by Winslow, curled over
his own knees on the bed, hunched like he was trying to
disappear.

"What are you saying, Nina?"

Her deep, steadying breath echoed through the cell
network and into Beck's ear. "I don't need you to come
home. I called to ask you for something else, because I
know I can count on you."

Unsure what to say, or how to say it without betraying
the weird lump in his throat, Beck turned away from Win
to stare at the dull painting of the Golden Gate Bridge
that hung on the wall beside the closet. "I promised I'd

never let you down," he managed, ashamed of the rasp in his voice.

"And you haven't," Nina said. "Not once. Which is why I need you to do something for me. It won't be easy, but it's for the best."

Beck braced himself as a familiar calm settled over his mind. He'd felt like this in the Navy, sometimes, waiting for orders.

And just like back then, he knew that no matter what Nina asked of him, he'd do whatever it took to deliver.

"You look like crap on a cracker."

Squeezing her eyes shut, Skye kept her focus on doing up her white chef's jacket. The stupid buttons kept jumping out of her shaking fingers. "Thanks bunches, Fiona. That's exactly what I was hoping to hear the morning I'm officially on the hook for the entire team, carrying all our hopes and dreams for the RSC into the finals."

The morning after I cavorted naked in San Francisco Bay with the husband I'm about to divorce.

"Slap a little makeup on her, she'll be fine," Rex said, running a dismissive hand through his perfectly wavy blonde hair.

"Easy for you to say," Fiona retorted. "You always look like you're just modeling those checked pants and white coat for *Chef's Illustrated*."

Grasping Skye's elbow, Fiona steered her away from the rest of their teammates, tugging her to the back of the competition kitchen, a glint of concern in her pale eyes.

"I'm fine," Skye said, hoping to pre-empt the interrogation she could see hovering on her friend's tongue.

Fiona made a sound that seemed completely incongruous coming from her tiny, pixie mouth. "Right. Tell me another one."

Normally, Skye would have no problem dragging this

out. Normally, she'd make Fiona cross her arms and huff and cajole and do all those things they'd worked out over the course of their friendship to signify that they were about to have a confidential heart-to-heart.

But the urge to confess had been riding Skye's back all morning, and today was not a normal day.

"Okay, look. Last night, after you guys left for the Ape . . ."

As fast as that, she stalled, the confession drying up in her mouth. But Fiona, never one to miss an opportunity, kept it going.

"The Ape, where you didn't join us . . ." Her gaze sharpened on Skye's face as she continued, "Where Beck hung out for an hour or so, and then ditched before the rest of his team had even ordered their third round. Am I getting closer?"

"Yes!" The word exploded out of Skye's chest with a sensation similar to relief, but a lot spinier. "He . . . found me. We talked. And then we . . ."

Fiona waggled her eyebrows delightedly. "Yeah? That's my *girl*! I told you, just needed to get it out of your system."

Skye sagged, trying to get her breath back. "Right. And now that we've . . . done that. Our systems should be clear." She grimaced. "Too bad I can't say the same about my conscience."

"What?" Fiona stared, aghast. "Come on, babe. Is this about Jeremiah?"

"Of course it's about Jeremiah!"

If Fiona rolled her eyes any harder, she was going to be staring at the back of her own skull. "Skye. Sweetie. We have been over this and over this. As good old Jerry would be the first to tell you, it's not cheating when you're in an open relationship. You haven't betrayed him, if that's where your dramatic little brain is going with this."

Skye bit her lip. "I know I haven't betrayed Jeremiah. We have an agreement."

Fiona's exasperated expression softened. "Knowing it and feeling it are two different things though, huh?"

"Maybe I didn't betray Jeremiah, but I betrayed myself."

"Oh babe. It must be pure hell to have a conscience."

That pulled a tired laugh out of Skye. Fiona punched her lightly in the shoulder, clearly feeling that her job there was done.

"Now, come on, boss lady. We've got a final challenge to hear all about."

Tilting her chin from side to side, Skye popped the vertebrae at the base of her neck and rolled her shoulders. "Okay. I'm ready. No more obsessing—it was a one-time thing, and now it's really over."

"Right. So long as you win."

Skye shot her friend a what-are-you-doing-to-me look, and Fiona raised her hands in surrender.

But Fiona was right, Skye mused with a shiver as they rejoined their team and waited for Eva Jansen to swoop down on them with the details of the final challenge.

It was over and done with . . . so long as Skye won the competition. And so long as she ignored last night's most upsetting revelation—that she was still in love with her husband.

Chapter 17

Beck would rather be facing down angry Marines demanding second helpings of rehydrated eggs. He'd rather be cleaning the bilge on the first boat he'd served on, the one with the antiquated waste disposal system. He'd rather . . . well, okay.

What he really wanted to be doing right now involved him, Skye, and miles of naked skin, but that wasn't on the table.

His mission was clear.

Raising his fist, he rapped sharply on the door to Jules and Max's room and stood at parade rest, waiting to be let in. Beside him, Winslow was uncharacteristically still and quiet. He had to know, as well as Beck did, what a giant bomb they were about to drop on the rest of their team.

"Come on in, guys."

Instead of Max or Jules, it was Danny who answered the door, lines of strain bracketing his mouth and muscles pinching at the corners of his eyes.

So they were all here, and everyone was up to speed. Good. That eliminated one step.

Beck strode into the room with a purpose, taking in the scene at a glance. Max and Jules were sitting together at the foot of the king-size bed, while Danny returned to his perch on the edge of the small writing desk in the corner.

"Sit down," Jules said, sighing as she pushed her heavy blonde hair off her face. "We've got some bad news."

But Beck didn't sit. For what he had to do, he preferred to be standing. And it didn't escape his notice that Win stayed where he was, too, standing solid and supportive at Beck's left shoulder, his presence oddly bolstering.

"It's okay," he told her. "We've heard."

Confusion widened her eyes, but from the corner came Danny's exhausted voice. "Of course. Mom called you, didn't she?"

It didn't surprise Beck that Danny was the one who figured it out. Danny was always the one who sat back, observed, and took care of everyone else—which meant he usually had a good handle on the potentially dangerous undercurrents of any given conversation.

Beck gave a short nod. "Nina let me know the situation with Gus."

"Okay, good." Max stood up and started to pace, as much as he could in the confined space of the small hotel room. Which was about three paces in each direction, but it seemed to help him think. "Then you know we've got a problem."

Beck did, indeed. "Someone has to go back to New York ASAP to pick up the slack at the restaurant and take the strain off of Gus."

Which Beck had been fully prepared to do . . . until Nina's quiet, determined plea.

She wanted her sons home. Gus wanted Jules. And they both wanted Beck to be the one to take the team into the finals.

The problem was that Beck was pretty sure no one else here was going to like that solution.

"Right." Jules's eyes were on her boyfriend, worry shadowing her steady gaze as she followed his frustrated pacing. "So we have a few options here."

Beck braced himself. "Actually, we have one option. You're all going. Win and I are staying."

Jules shot off the bed like a torpedo. "What?!"

"It's the only thing that makes sense. Gus and Nina need their family with them now. Win and I are the logical choices to stay behind."

Max stepped over the bed separating them to wrap an arm around Jules's shoulders. "Fuck logic. Jules is our team leader. If anyone competes, it's going to be her." He stared Beck down, anger snapping in his eyes—but underneath the pissed-off vibe, Beck could see the fear and worry.

He didn't allow the sight to gentle his own voice. Beck kept it steady and calm.

"I understand the chain of command, Max, but in this case, we need someone competing who isn't going to be distracted by emotional concerns, half her mind always on something other than the food in front of her."

Jules sucked in a breath, but Beck saw resignation in the way she pressed her lips together.

Danny stood up, propping his hands on his hips. "Beck is right."

"What? Danny, man, come on," Max protested, but his heart wasn't in it.

His brother shook his head, and Beck faded back a bit to let the family hash it out. His part was done.

"You didn't say anything about Nina," Win muttered, cocking his head.

Nina was the one who'd asked Beck to stay and compete. He angled his body to keep their exchange private.

"That would've introduced a whole level of emotion that would've clouded the issue like a squirt of ink from an octopus." Winslow snickered quietly, sobering with a jerk as the rest of their team turned back to them. Max was coiled tighter than a bedspring, but Beck imagined even Max didn't know if it was due to worry for Gus or anger for Jules.

Who didn't look particularly angry, herself, in spite of the fact that Beck knew—they all knew—exactly how much it meant to Jules to be the one to bring home a win for the Lunden's Tavern team.

But it appeared that Danny had done his usual masterful job of making everyone see reason. He was already heading for the phone on the nightstand, probably to check on flights back to NYC . . . but no . . . when the first word he said into the receiver was "Eva?" Beck looked away to give him some privacy as he broke the news of his imminent departure to his girlfriend.

Max and Jules were having one of those silent mind-meld conversations most couples seemed able to have, and when they were done, some of the tension flowed out of Max's stance.

He stuck out his hand and grasped Beck's, shaking it once in a firm grip. "I know none of this is your fault, and you're not trying to supplant Jules or something. Sorry I got a little . . . you know, back there."

"You're concerned about your father," Beck said quietly.

Max shook his head. "That's no excuse to take it out on you. You're right, and I appreciate you stepping up like this, Beck."

Before Beck could brush it off, Jules was right there, her earnest face looking up at him with a complex blend of regret and relief shining in her eyes.

"You've more than proved yourself over the last few

weeks and months, Chef. I know we're leaving the team in good hands."

He'd hoped to eventually make his point and leave things on decent terms with his teammates, but this was a little but more of a love-in than Beck had expected.

Some of the shock must have shown on his face, because Max pulled back with a smirk. "What? You didn't think we'd be mature enough to eventually figure out you're doing us a big favor?"

Time to retake control of this conversation.

"It's not a favor," Beck said decisively. "It's my job."

Jules hunched down to grab their empty suitcase from under the bed and heave it up onto the mattress. "I think carrying the team into the finals of the biggest culinary competition in the nation falls a little outside of the normal sous-chef job description."

Winslow had managed to keep quiet for a long time, but this was apparently too much for him. Bouncing onto the bed beside the suitcase, he beamed around the room at everyone with his brightest, most determined smile. "We're going to rock this! Y'all don't have to worry about a thing. Just head on home, give Gus and Nina big smooches for us, and keep your cell phones handy so we can call and give you updates."

"And get updates on the situation with Gus," Beck said, trying not to make it a command and failing miserably.

Max's shoulders went tight again, but he didn't pause in his manic packing, throwing clothes haphazardly onto the bed where Jules patiently folded them and laid them in the suitcase. She shot him a worried glance, and her eyes were still soft with it when she looked up at Beck.

"I'll keep you informed," she promised quietly.

"Eva's assistant got us on a flight," Danny interrupted, putting down the phone. "But we've got to hustle.

She'll make the announcement to the other team in a few minutes."

Jules squeaked. "Oh my God, look at the time! You've got to get down there." Leaping off the bed, she herded Win and Beck toward the hotel room door with panicky, frantic hand-wringing. "I wish I were going down there with you, I'm dying to know what the challenge is . . ."

Beck didn't doubt that for an instant, but Jules was so much one of the family, her presence was definitely required back home in an emergency. And as scared as she was, Beck saw a steadiness underneath her panicking that he wasn't sure he'd seen in her before—the kind of security that came from finally being sure of her place with the Lundens as more than Danny's friend, Gus and Nina's employee, Max's girlfriend.

She was one of them now, and she knew it.

The knife edge of envy sliced into Beck so cleanly and quickly, he almost didn't notice it until it began to ache when his departing teammates slapped him and Win on the back and sent them down to the hotel kitchen to face the fight of their lives.

It was stupid. Beck would have happily traded this chance to compete for a guarantee that Gus would be okay. Instead he'd be representing the entire East Coast in the final round of the RSC; his hands, his skills, his food would tip the balance and decide whether his team won . . . and whether Beck won his bet with Skye.

When Winslow sighed and gave him a lopsided grin that didn't reach his eyes, Beck figured he knew exactly how the kid was feeling: out of place. Separate. Unwanted.

It was a purely emotional response, nothing rational about it. Rationally, they both knew they weren't related to the Lunden family, by blood or any other bond, but still, it sucked to be the odd men out.

So what? This was hardly the first time he'd been on the outside looking in, and as he knew from experience, life went on. You either went along with it, or you collapsed under the weight of your own self-pity.

Drawing himself up, Beck stood tall.

He clapped a hand on his sous-chef's shoulder and ignored the swoop in his stomach as the elevator carried them toward their destiny. Beside him, Win straightened his spine and tilted his chin, the light of battle brightening his green eyes.

Beck regulated his breathing and his mind, forcing his thoughts away from the Lundens, Gus's heart, the bet with Skye, Skye's skin in the moonlight . . . there was nothing but the contest now. The challenge. The fight.

And they were going to win, or die trying.

Skye was starting to wonder if the East Coast team planned to just concede the fight.

First Eva Jansen had arrived in the competition kitchen, her phone pressed to her ear and a very worried look on her lovely, fine-boned face. Then she'd had that frantic whispered conversation with her assistant, the skinny emo boy with the black-framed hipster glasses and the messy hair, and the assistant had started talking a mile a minute on *his* phone while Eva paced back and forth at the front of the kitchen.

"What do you think is going on?" Skye poked at Fiona, who was busily engaged in yet another bicker-fest with Rex. Honestly, the sexual tension there was so thick, it was starting to clog Skye's pores.

Fiona managed to tear herself away from trying to capture the much-taller Rex in a headlock just long enough to shrug. "Who knows? We were early getting down here, but it must be about time for things to get started."

Skye hated waiting. It made everything worse, and she

was jittery enough already, her stomach roiling with guilt and nerves, and her mind cluttered with images of the night before. And her body . . . she suppressed a shiver. Just thinking about last night sent an unwelcome jolt of sweetness through her veins.

As if her memories had conjured him up, the kitchen doors swung open and Henry Beck stalked into the room, with the East Coast team's sous-chef close on his heels.

The double doors swung on their hinges behind him, closing with a muffled bang.

Where was the rest of his team?

Skye's gaze shot to Eva Jansen, who didn't look surprised or bewildered in the least as she tilted her head to send Beck and Winslow to their places. If Eva looked anything at all, it was sympathetic—and Skye's belly did a sickening flip.

She knew. On some level, somehow, she knew what Eva was going to say before she opened her glossy lips.

"There's been a change to the roster for the final challenge," Eva announced calmly. "Due to a family emergency, Max and Danny Lunden have had to return to New York, and Jules Cavanaugh has gone with them. In their place, Chef Henry Beck will take the lead for the East Coast team. Winslow Jones will assist. Thank you."

And with that, Eva sauntered over to confer with the judges, as calm as if she hadn't just rocked the foundations of Skye's already shaky confidence by pitting her against the one man Skye couldn't resist.

She cut the thought off frantically, closing her eyes and trying her best to call up a vision of Jeremiah Raleigh's rugged good looks, his sun-streaked hair, his tanned, creased face.

The jab of a sharp elbow in her side robbed her of her concentration, and nearly her balance.

Opening her eyes, she snapped, "What?" before she realized Fiona had been trying to warn her.

Beck hadn't gone straight to his station across the kitchen. Instead, he was standing directly in front of her, staring down with a knowing expression in his brown eyes.

He put out his hand. Skye blinked at it for a long moment before clasping it with her own.

Beck's fingers were warm and rough, his hand broad and strong enough to enfold hers with ease. "It will be an honor to compete against you," he said, his gravelly voice rolling through her like thunder.

It took two tries, but she managed to swallow hard enough to say, "You too. I hope everything is okay with your teammates."

His gaze flickered. "They'll be fine."

"I'm sure they will be," Skye said, the urge to comfort prodding her to keep talking. "And I'm sure it helps that they know you're here to carry the team."

Something moved behind his eyes, uncertainty quickly swallowed up by determination. A muscle ticked in his jaw. "Fair warning, Skye. I don't intend to let them down."

The unshakeable vow in his words pierced Skye's heart. Before she could think, her mouth was opening and spitting out, "No, of course not. You'd never let anyone down, would you?"

You told me once that you'd never let me down. Remember?

It hung there between them, her accusation and his silence, chilling the air until she half-expected her next breath to form a visible vapor cloud.

Beck dropped her hand as it were a piece of ice that had numbed him through, and Skye felt the prickle of a flush heating her neck and ears. She'd forgotten they were still holding hands.

She didn't know what she expected him to say. Maybe that he'd try not to let anyone down; maybe an apology; maybe a demand that she let the past go and get over herself already.

Any of those responses would have been better than what he did.

Because after a lengthy, weighted pause filled with the sharp edges of things unsaid, all he did was walk away.

Chapter 18

Beck marched back to the stainless steel table where Win was unpacking their knife rolls. His entire head was filled with Skye's elusive, earthy scent, his pulse throbbing in his ears. His chest pounded with the knowledge that he'd had her last night, and he'd have more of her soon . . . but that none of it made a difference when it came to how she felt.

He'd killed that, and nothing on earth could bring it back.

There was no rhyme or reason to the way that thought scoured his insides out like a sandblaster, and it wasn't going to help him win the RSC to dwell on it.

Thank God for the U.S. Navy, he mused as he took up his place beside Winslow. Without it, he'd never have the training or the discipline to force his mind down a new path, away from the meandering tangle of emotion that was everything to do with Skye.

"You okay?" Win asked out of the side of his mouth.

Beck gave him a short nod and focused all his attention on Eva Jansen, who faced the competitors with excitement flushing her cheeks.

"Good morning, chefs. I know you're as anxious to get started as I am, so let's get right down to it."

Anticipation tightened Beck's sinews, and he consciously slowed his breathing.

This was it.

"We're down to the last two teams, and it's tempting to think about this battle in terms of East versus West. But as epic as the rivalry is between San Francisco's up-and-coming restaurant scene and the more established food culture of New York, I want to go deeper."

Eva clasped her hands in front of her and glanced between Skye and Beck. "The RSC isn't here to decide the debate between San Francisco and New York City. We're here to determine who is the Rising Star Chef of the nation this year. And in order to do that, we need to get to know each of you a little better."

Nervousness skated down Beck's spine and lifted the hairs on the back of his neck.

What the hell does that mean?

For a brief, awful moment Beck pictured a ludicrous version of the Miss America pageant, with himself and Skye tricked out in formal wear and answering questions about their hopes and dreams.

Thank God, Eva's silky voice snapped him out of it. "That's why this year, we did away with the final team battle and turned it into an individual challenge. Two chefs, going head to head, cooking their hearts out . . . and telling us the story of their lives in five courses. Each course will represent a stage in your journey toward becoming the chef you are today."

The words crashed over Beck's head like an incoming wave.

Eva went on to explain in more detail, but Beck could hardly take it in.

The story of my life? Shit. I'd rather strap on a bikini and advocate for world peace.

Beside him, Winslow jittered in place, and Beck shot him a look. Seemed like maybe his sous-chef was as freaked out as Beck was, which should've been bad news. But instead, it gave Beck an outpouring of gratitude that he wasn't alone in being so completely thrown by this.

With a monumental effort, Beck tuned back in to Eva's speech just as she got to the part where she told them they had the rest of that day to plan.

Frowning, she glanced between the two tables set up in the center of the kitchen. Beck and Win stood shoulder to shoulder behind one, while all five of the original West Coast team members were grouped around the second.

"The plan was to allow the full team to consult on the menu," she said slowly, "But that clearly won't be possible for the East Coast team."

Before Beck could open his mouth to tell her it didn't matter, they'd be fine on their own, Skye had one slim hand up in the air and that stubborn, righteous look on her face.

"Ms. Jansen, in order to keep everything completely fair across the board, I'm willing to forego consultation with my team today."

Beck stiffened as Skye's teammates, especially the dreadlocked guy, shot her incredulous glares, but Eva looked relieved.

"Thank you, Chef Gladwell. That's extremely gener- ous of you, and I think it's the right choice. Which brings me to the other choice you need to make."

Beck tensed all over, ready for another twist. Eva didn't disappoint him.

"We've decided that in the spirit of true competition, we want each of you to know exactly what you're up against.

Therefore, you will be cooking and presenting your dishes consecutively—you'll both have the full day tomorrow to prep, then the following day, one of you will cook and present at noon, and the other will go at six. We'd like each of you to join the judges for your opponent's tasting."

Beck allowed himself to relax a bit. That wasn't so bad.

Turning to Skye, Eva said, "Since you won the last challenge, I'll leave it up to you. Would you prefer to present in the morning or the evening?"

Skye licked her lips, an old nervous gesture Beck had always found ridiculously appealing, and said, "I'll go second."

"Which means," Eva cut her eyes to Beck, "You'll be first."

He acknowledged his marching orders with a short nod.

"Okay!" She clapped her hands together, then waved to the judges. "Get planning. The cars will be out front to take you to shop first thing tomorrow morning."

And that was it. She and the judges waved goodbye and trooped out of the kitchen, followed more slowly by Skye's grumbling male teammates. On the way out the door, the dreadlocked guy fixed Skye with a pointed stare and mouthed something at her that looked a lot like "Meat is murder."

She rolled her eyes, then pointedly turned back to her sous-chef, Fiona, when she noticed Beck's attention.

"Well, that was pretty stand up of her," Win commented. "Gotta love a woman who likes an even playing field."

Beck grunted and crouched to retrieve a small, spiral-bound notebook from the outside pocket of his leather knife roll. He carried it everywhere, used it to jot down ideas—maybe the notes in there would spark something.

God knew, he didn't have any other clues about where to start.

"So," Win tried again, nerves pitching his voice higher than usual. "Your life story, huh? That should be fun."

We'll be fine was what Beck meant to say, but somehow, what came out was "Son of a bitch."

"I heard that." Win gave a sage nod and a shrug. "But hey, it could be worse."

It was hard to see how.

Beck flipped through the pages of his notebook, scowling down at his own penciled scratchings. There were lists of ingredients he'd seen at the Ferry Building Farmers' Market, sketches of finished plates he'd dreamed up, one or two new techniques he'd been meaning to try.

All of it was him, Beck the chef, and it should've been a good place to begin. But somehow, it felt like he was failing before they even got going.

"Anything good in there?" Win asked.

Beck shrugged and passed him the notebook. "Maybe a couple of ideas. Shit, I don't know."

Looking up from his perusal of a particularly intricate recipe involving pan-fried skate wings, Winslow cocked his head. "This is really a problem for you, isn't it?"

Beck wondered if it was the tension in his shoulders or the tic in his jaw that had given him away.

"It's going to be fine." There, he managed it that time.

"The life story of the most secretive, mysterious, enigmatic guy I've ever met, in five dishes," Win mused. He looked like he wanted to smile but was holding it back, and Beck felt the roil of emotion that had been percolating since Eva first articulated the challenge threaten to bubble over.

"This is like a dream come true for you," Beck growled, irritation scoring over his skin like fire ants. "The perfect excuse to satisfy your curiosity about whatever mystery you think there is in my past."

He regretted the harsh growl of his tone as soon as the words left his mouth. He knew how intimidating he could sound without even really meaning to, and with all the pressure building in his head, he didn't want to explode all over Winslow. Who might be a busybody but was also a good guy—and, Beck noticed, was not looking the slightest bit intimidated.

"Bitch, please." Win waved a hand. "Get over your bad self. You're not that fascinating."

The twinkle in his green eyes invited Beck into the joke. He chuckled, then laughed out loud when Win's delighted grin spread ear to ear.

And all of a sudden, Beck felt the tension inside him break like the popping of his ears when the boat dove to a new depth. The pressure was still there, but he could handle it.

Holding out his curled fist for a bump, Beck said, "We'll figure it out, man."

"Sure. As soon as you spill your guts."

Beck shifted his weight. "This ain't no therapist's office."

Adopting a ridiculous German accent, Winslow stroked his baby butt–smooth chin and said, "Und how do you veel about zat?"

Snorting, Beck palmed the back of his neck. The muscles under his fingers were corded with tension, and no matter how good Win was at lightening up a crappy situation, Beck still hated the very idea of what they were about to do.

And then an idea occurred to him, like a ray of sunshine striking down through the surface of the ocean, breaking through the waves and lighting up the darkness.

"Listen," he said, lowering his voice. "What if we don't get into the whole feelings and life story bullshit. What if we just come up with the best dishes we possibly can? And once we have a great menu, we'll worry about what story to tell with each dish."

Winslow put his hands on his lean hips, looking doubtful. "That's not exactly what the challenge is about . . ."

But Beck wasn't going to be dissuaded from this course of action. He'd spotted a way through the maze, and he was damn well taking it. "This whole competition is about the food," he said firmly.

Win nodded reluctantly. "Yeah, I guess."

"So that's what we'll be doing." Beck took back his notebook, flipping through the pages of ideas with more purpose. "We're putting the food first."

This was going to work, he was sure of it. And it would be better than if they went through his whole life story, because, shit—how would that menu look? A first course of family tragedy, followed up with a troubled adolescence and a side of utter romantic failure, rounded out by an eye-opening course of military service?

Appetizing.

No, this is the best way, he told himself as he chose a few recipes and concepts to talk over with Winslow.

As they got down to the serious business of planning out the menu, Beck couldn't resist checking in on the other team. Across the kitchen, Skye and her sous-chef were in deep, serious conversation, the kind that made Skye's luminous blue eyes fill with the sparkle of unshed tears.

The sight ripped through his chest, and he ducked his head hurriedly, staring blindly down at the bare, polished metal of the table in front of him.

He knew without asking that Skye wasn't starting with the food—she was starting with her life. She'd draw on her own emotions, fearlessly using them as inspiration for what she created in the kitchen, the same way her bohemian mother painted or sculpted.

Beck wasn't at all sure he could handle hearing the story of Skye's life, her fears and sorrows exposed for the judges. It would be hard to bear, but he'd manage it.

What he couldn't handle at all was the thought of spilling his own past out onto the kitchen floor. Not because of the judges, but because of Skye.

And if that made him a coward, then so be it.

He'd be a coward who kept his secrets.

Chapter 19

From the moment Eva had told the judges what this challenge would be, thoughts of the past had consumed Claire.

The recent past, yes—despite her best efforts, Kane Slater was never far from her thoughts. But the distant past, as well, the events that had formed her into the woman she was today . . . those ugly memories haunted her, too.

So much so that once the contestants were off and running, working on their life story meals, all Claire could contemplate was finding a quiet corner and a cocktail.

Kane had been laughing with Eva about needing a drink just moments ago. And when he slipped out of the kitchen just ahead of Claire, without conscious volition, she found herself following him.

Once out in the hallway, she slowed her steps to avoid overtaking him. She was viscerally aware of how foolish this was, courting an encounter with him after she'd fought so hard for the clean break between them . . . but his last words to her, about being safe, kept swirling through her brain along with the memories that tormented her, until all she could do was hope that Kane was on his way to the lobby bar.

They reached a flight of carpeted steps that led up into a marble-floored atrium filled with potted greenery and architectural flower arrangements on inlaid wood tables. Claire focused on the décor, hoping to distract herself from the delectable sight of Kane taking the stairs two at a time, the wide stretch of his legs drawing his dark blue jeans tight across his muscular derrière.

It didn't work.

Once up the stairs and into the lobby, Claire spied the Boulevard Lounge & Bar sign hanging beside a discreet archway, and quickened her steps. If she hurried, she could be drowning her memories in a digestif within minutes.

Or . . . she could run straight into Kane's back.

"Oof!"

"Whoa, there, are you oka—Claire?"

Kane dropped the hands he'd reflexively wrapped around her upper arms, and Claire missed the warmth of them instantly.

Not that she needed to be any warmer, she realized, as a flush swept up her neck and over her hot cheeks.

"I'm fine, thank you. My apologies, I'm afraid I was a bit too eager to reach the bar."

He huffed out a laugh that didn't sound as vibrant and full of humor as she was used to. "Yeah, I know what you mean."

There was a short, intensely awkward pause while Claire tried to pick her composure up off the floor. Kane broke it by shrugging and saying, "Well, I guess I'll let you get to it, then. Do you think room service will send up a bottle of whiskey, if I ask nicely?"

He gave her a smile that didn't reach his eyes, and all of a sudden, Claire couldn't bear it.

A distance of no more than ten centimeters separated them, but it felt like ten kilometers as she raised one trembling hand to rest just above his elbow.

That simple, glancing touch was enough to stop Kane in the act of turning and walking away. He stood transfixed under her fingertips, the hard muscle of his bicep straining at the soft sleeve of his black-and-white plaid shirt.

It took a ridiculous amount of courage for Claire to say, "At this time of day, the room service staff will think you're an alcoholic. Do you want that story making the rounds of the gossip magazines? I think not. Come with me to the hotel bar instead; there is safety in numbers."

Somewhere along the way, she'd lost the ability to read Kane's expressions. Or maybe it was that he'd lost the beautiful openness that was so much a part of what had attracted her in the first place. The thought that she was to blame for the wary, closed look in his blue eyes tore through her like a lance, even as he nodded and stepped back to allow her to precede him into the bar.

The lounge had only recently opened; the incongruously cheery light cast by the peach silk lampshades fell on clean round tables and unoccupied chaises and upholstered chairs.

The bar, *merci à Dieu*, was not deserted. A lithe young sprite of a bartender gave a mischievous grin as Claire made a beeline for the two empty stools at the end of the polished brass bar railing, as if only the Pegasus hotel chain's impeccable training kept him from winking at them.

Ignoring the leather-bound menus placed in front of them, Kane leaned his elbows on the bar and twisted his head to regard her seriously.

Soft light glinted gold in his hair and shaded his handsome, boyish face in a way that made him look older, jaded, cynical—all the things Claire felt in herself but hadn't ever associated with Kane.

"Now that you've got me here, what are you going to do with me?"

Would this hideous flush never die down? Claire felt as if she'd been walking the beach in Nice for hours with no hat. "I'm going to buy you a drink."

Claire buried her face in the menu, scanning for cocktails before she remembered where they were.

In San Francisco, cocktails weren't king—wine was.

While the flirtatious little bartender would no doubt be able to shake up a fine martini, Claire's years as a food writer had taught her that the best strategy was usually to tailor her order to the specialty of the house. Whatever the establishment was known for was often what they did the best, and would be the most enjoyable to try.

In this case, however, a simple glass of wine wasn't going to be sufficient.

Overcome by a sudden swelling of nostalgia for Paris, Claire said, "I'll have a cognac, please."

There. Cognac was distilled wine. That would have to be close enough.

"The same." Kane shoved the menu back across the bar without taking his eyes off Claire.

Pulling her shoulders back, Claire lifted her chin and focused on the swift, economical movements of the bartender as he unscrewed the top from a squat, round bottle with one hand while stretching up on his toes to snag two short-stemmed snifters with the other.

"I wasn't angling for an invitation before. I told you I was backing off, and I have."

The bitterness in his melodic voice crackled down Claire's spine like lightning, dangerous and shocking and wrong. "Yes, you have," she said quietly. "You did exactly what I asked."

He made a frustrated noise that seemed to come from

deep in his chest. Swiveling on the bar stool, Kane faced her more fully. The twist of his torso tugged at the soft, plaid button-down he wore, outlining his hard chest and gaping open at the collar to reveal that warm, lickable dip where his neck met his shoulder.

"So why do you still look as miserable as I feel?"

For a moment, she struggled to focus on what he was saying—until his words penetrated the dense fog of lust that had briefly overwhelmed her.

Claire was saved from having to respond by the bartender, whose tip was increasing by the moment. He slid two small glasses across the mirror-smooth mahogany of the bar, the gently rounded globes filled with dark amber liquid. Claire's rigorously educated nose detected the faint scent of clove and nutmeg wafting from the spirit.

She lifted the glass to the level of her chin, taking a couple of shallow breaths, and let the caramel notes flow over the back of her tongue. The first sip burned through her mouth, but as the shock of the alcohol tapered off, she tasted the flowery spice she'd smelled before.

It was very good cognac, aged fifteen years or so, and probably from the Borderies. She nodded her approval to the bartender, who did wink, finally, the cheeky thing, before moving discreetly to wipe down the other end of the bar.

Claire turned her attention back to Kane in time to see him tip back his head and down a third of his glass in one swallow.

"God, that's good," he gasped, tongue coming out to catch a drop at the corner of his lips, and everything in Claire's body tightened and heated with arousal.

He was just so alive. So vibrant and voracious, hungry for all the pleasures and excitement the world had to offer.

And that had always been the problem.

Everything with Kane was so *much*. She felt too much, wanted too much, cared too much . . . so she'd pushed him away.

She'd ruined everything they had between them, probably for good. But he deserved to know why she'd done it. She owed him the chance to understand, even if he couldn't forgive.

But before she could gather her courage enough to speak, he'd set his glass back down on the bar. "I know I said I'd back off and let this go, but I can't move on until I say this one last thing to you."

Resisting the impulse to stop him from speaking if it would delay this awful moving-on business, Claire swallowed another sip of cognac and braced herself. "Go ahead."

Kane's face was set in lines of misery. "I hate that I made you think, for even a second, that you—this—was all just a game to me. Because I'd never do that. Even if I weren't in . . ." He paused, his gaze flickering to the side, and Claire sucked in a breath.

"Even with someone I barely knew," he continued, subdued, "I wouldn't treat any woman that way. For one thing, it's rude and disrespectful, and the total opposite of everything I try to be about, with my music and my life."

Guilt that she'd ever doubted him—that she'd made him doubt himself—choked Claire. She put a hand on his forearm and found it rigid, corded with misery. "I know," she said again, feeling helpless and hating it.

"Do you? Because it seems like I've done a shitty-ass job of showing you who I am."

"That's not true," Claire argued. "And as far as your music goes, well . . . As soon as Eva told me you'd be one of the RSC judges . . ." She paused, reluctant to reveal this for some reason.

"What?"

"I may have ordered all three of your albums. As reconnaissance, you understand."

A hint of the usual sparkle lit his blue eyes. "Sure, of course."

Silence stretched between them for the space of several heartbeats before Kane blurted, "So what did you think?"

The moment the question left his lips, he slapped a hand over his reddening face and made a frustrated noise in the back of his throat. "Gah! I'm such a dweeb. I can't believe I asked you that, like some kid auditioning for a part he knows he's not going to get."

Claire laughed, although the reference to himself as a kid clutched at her insides. "Suffice it to say, were it up to me, you'd get the part."

Peering through a crack between his fingers, Kane said, "Really?"

"Yes. I was . . . surprised by what I heard."

A knowing look turned his handsome face sly and mischievous. "Ah, I see. You're one of those who assumed that since the good Lord blessed me with this incredibly gorgeous face and a killer six-pack, that's all I needed to make me rich and famous. I couldn't possibly have or need any musical skill."

"I assure you, when I first purchased your CDs, I had no knowledge of your . . . six-pack. I was more surprised at the broad range of your musical influences . . . a song very lush and lyrical would be followed by something that reminded me of Edith Piaf—soulful and lazy, but with a playful edge."

She shook her head in remembered bemusement, and Kane grinned. "I know which record you're talking about now. Couldn't get much of a handle on me from that one, could you?"

"No." Claire cocked her head, regarding Kane thoughtfully. The familiar teasing glint was back, turning his blue eyes brighter than the summer sky and tugging at the corners of his kissable lips. There was still a certain something hovering over him like a cloud, however, a lingering regret or sadness, and she found she didn't care for it at all. "But since that day, I've learned a great deal about what sort of man you are. And I realized recently that I hadn't given you the same opportunity, when it came to myself."

Claire had never enjoyed opening herself up to others. The very phrase—the graphic imagery calling to mind her vulnerable body slit down the center like an overripe tomato so that all her innards spilled out into the open—set her teeth on edge. But for Kane, she would do it.

Better late than not at all.

Drawing back far enough to be able to look him in the eye was easier than actually making eye contact, but Claire was no weakling. She brought her gaze up and kept her eyes open, allowing Kane unfettered access to whatever his intent scrutiny could discover.

"You asked why I have been making both you and myself miserable—and I don't know if I have a good answer for that. All I have is my past, the history that shaped me. And I offer it to you now in good faith . . . because I trust you with it."

Hunger and interest flared in his gaze, but his voice was gentle as he said, "You don't have to do this."

"Yes, I do." Taking one last sip of her drink, she let the alcohol burn a hole through the knot in her throat, and the words came tumbling out.

"When I was very young, just after I first moved to New York from Paris, I began working as a freelance fact checker at a lifestyle magazine. I would go in, read other people's stories, and then do the work they'd neglected in terms of verifying sources and double-checking information. It was tedious work, but I was ambitious."

"You? I don't believe it." His voice was teasing but his

gaze was keen, and Claire knew he was hanging on every syllable of this unprecedented story from her past.

"*Oui,* very ambitious. And, perhaps, not as subtle as I've learned to be in later years. There was a man at the magazine, an editor. Not my direct superior, but certainly above me in the hierarchy."

Kane bared his teeth in a sudden snarl, the expression cutting off her air for a second before he smoothed it out. "Sorry, sorry. Just . . . I think I know where this is heading."

With a grimace, Claire acknowledged the point. "Yes, mine is not a particularly unique or original story. We became involved, he made and broke promises, both personal and professional, and in the end, I discovered there had been a bet among the editors—all of whom were, at that time, male—to see which of them could get me into bed first."

"Fuck."

The harsh curse in Kane's melodic voice took Claire aback. Her startlement made her realize he hardly ever swore. Recovering, she nodded. "Indeed. I reacted . . . badly, and found myself alone in a strange country, without a job."

"They fired you?" The outrage on Kane's face was a balm to Claire's ruffled soul. She hated remembering that time in her life. Although this part wasn't so bad.

"Well, when I stormed into the editor in chief's office and spilled the entire, sordid story, the editor in chief— also a man—laughed and said something along the lines of 'Boys will be boys.' "

"Gross."

"Agreed."

Curiosity sparking, Kane raised his eyebrows. "What did you do?"

Claire might like to uphold the ethnic stereotype of the

French as coldblooded pragmatists, more practical than passionate, but her behavior that day couldn't be taken as proof of the concept.

Mouth twisted in a rueful smile, she said, "I seized the closest breakable object to hand, a crystal paperweight on the corner of the editor-in-chief's desk, and heaved it at the wall."

Kane blinked, impressed. "Wow."

"One dented plaster wall and a shattered, irreplaceable Award for Excellence later, I was out the door."

"I hate this story," Kane told her.

"Don't worry, it has a happy ending. That magazine folded less than a year after that—I won't say it's because they became involved in several scandals, one right after another, due to shoddy reporting and incorrect facts in their articles, but . . ." She shrugged, kept her voice light. "And then I got a job writing for *Délicieux*, and the rest, as they say, is history."

"Ha," Kane crowed, his delight buoying Claire's spirits in the face of remembered distress. "Suck it, dickweeds."

"My sentiments more or less exactly."

"I changed my mind. I love this story."

A smile twisted the corner of mouth, and she felt her spirits trying to lift. "I thought you deserved to hear it, because I felt it only fair to give you the context for my reaction to what I overheard between you and Theo."

The happiness drained from his face. "Christ. No wonder you freaked."

"I should not have," Claire insisted. "I know that now. You are nothing like those men who made a mockery of my feelings, who used my body as a battleground for their rivalry. Whatever I thought and felt when I heard you talking to Theo, I should not have pushed you away."

Rubbing one finger in a delicate ring around the rim of his glass, Kane slid her a sideways glance. "You've been pushing me away ever since we met. Even when I was inside you—there was still a distance between us."

The truth of it shook her down to her bones.

"I know. And I'm not sure how to stop."

Kane closed his eyes briefly, then suddenly dropped his booted feet to the floor with a bang, pushing his barstool back with a grating sound of wooden chair legs on a marble floor.

"Then I guess you were right all along. We have nothing left to say to each other."

Panic gripped her by the throat, nearly strangling her words as she cried, "Kane, no!"

He paused in the act of tossing a bill down on the bar, his trim, muscular frame rigid with tension.

Claire licked her lips and fought one last battle with herself before saying, "I don't know how to stop pushing away everything that brushes too close to my heart—but I'm willing to learn. I want to try. For you."

Kane's muscles loosened enough to allow him to face her once more, and this time she could see traces of the young, vibrant, happy man she'd met in New York lurking under the hard-jawed stranger before her.

"Well," he said, his low voice resonating through her whole body. "That's a good start."

Chapter 20

Twisting at the hips to realign her spine, Skye pressed both hands to her lower back and breathed in, imagining oxygen flowing into the knotted muscles.

She thought longingly of the Bikram yoga class she'd had to give up when she moved out to Sausalito, and released her breath and the position on a long sigh.

"Tough day at the office?"

She whirled to face Beck and her long skirt flew out around her ankles, whipping at her calves. Off balance, she stumbled against the railing, but Beck caught her before she could do more than stare, shocked, at the churning water of the bay.

His hands were big and solid on her forearms, rough with calluses and unbelievably warm against skin chilled by the breeze whipping off the water.

It was that cold wind making her shiver, Skye told herself, pulling away with a forced smile.

"We made a good start, I think." Finding it stupidly hard to meet his dark, knowing eyes, Skye squinted out over San Francisco Bay, searching the horizon for the fast-moving ferry that would take her back to her parents' house. "What about you? I would've thought you'd be back at the hotel, resting up for tomorrow. It's not like the farmers' market is open this late."

She felt more than saw Beck's shrug. "No, but I'm thinking about using salumi in one of my dishes—thought I'd come check out what Boccalone's got to offer. Somehow I missed it when we shopped here for the last challenge, but Win couldn't stop talking about it."

That surprised her into looking straight at him. They were standing so close together, she had to crane her neck back to catch his gaze.

"Have you forgotten I'm the enemy? I can't believe you'd give me any clues about what you plan to cook."

This time it was Beck who looked away, as if he couldn't quite meet her eyes. "I don't think it matters at this point. Our styles are different enough, we could use all the same ingredients and still come up with entirely distinct dishes. Besides, I know you don't like salumi, and that rasta kid on your team would bust a nut if you put cured meat on your menu."

She laughed, remembering Nathan's grouching about how she'd given up full-team consultation just to avoid hearing him suggest vegan dishes. His parting shot as the team left had been a reminder that animals were her friends, and friends didn't eat friends.

"Yeah, salumi's not really our thing at Queenie Pie," she admitted. "How about you? Already sweating bullets over having to open up about your past?" Not that Skye was looking forward to hearing what Beck came up with to explain his life story, or anything.

He shrugged, massive shoulders jerking up and down in a parody of his usual smooth grace. "Nah, I'm just making the food I want to make. I'll come up with something to say to make it sound good."

Disappointment lanced through her. Skye shook her

head. "Of course you will. God forbid you should actually follow the challenge and tell anyone anything about yourself."

In the distance, a long horn sounded, signaling that the ferry was on its way to the dock.

"Heading home?" Beck's voice was toneless, completely impassive, but Skye still stiffened against the implied criticism.

"It's a temporary situation," she blurted, then snapped her jaws shut on the rest of the explanation. She didn't need to explain anything to him.

Beck appeared to agree, since he didn't ask any more questions. Not for a long moment filled with nothing but the *skreel* of gulls and the wash of choppy water against the side of the ferry dock.

When he finally spoke, his question took her completely by surprise.

"Are you happy, Skye?"

Something about the way he said it, the quiet care she could suddenly hear in his voice, choked her up. Clearing her throat, she tossed her hair out of her face and squinted into the setting sun.

"Sometimes. What about you?"

"When I'm cooking."

The simplicity of his answer gutted her. She kept her face averted, soaking up the dying warmth of the sunset on her skin and trying to breathe around the constriction in her chest.

"Me, too. I miss my restaurant."

"What happened to it?" Beck's frown was as audible as his concern for her, and Skye made herself give him a smile.

"Nothing bad! It's just . . . it's a tiny place, and I don't have a huge crew of reliable cooks. I had to close it down for the month while we compete in the RSC."

"Can you afford that?"

Narrowing her eyes at him, she said, "Normally, here's about where I'd tell you to mind your own damn business. But since part of the start-up money for the café came from what I saved of the money you sent home after you enlisted, I guess it sort of is your business."

He held up a hand. "Hey, no. You don't have to tell—"

"We can afford it," she interrupted. "Barely. But it's a damn good thing we made it this far, and the publicity from getting to the finals should help us make up the lost time."

His fine, chiseled lips were nearly white, they were pressed together so tightly. "Good. I'm glad it's going well for you."

Skye held back a sigh of frustration. She could already feel Beck closing off again, the brief window into his emotions slamming shut. It reminded her of . . . well, pretty much every conversation they'd ever had during their months of living together. And, just like back then, she found herself searching for any possible way to prop that window open for just a little while longer.

"Hey. Would you be interested in seeing Queenie Pie? Considering you're a major investor and all . . ."

That got her a sardonic brow lift. "I thought you had a ferry to catch."

The ferry that would take her out to the quiet, picturesque artists' colony of Sausalito, where her parents would be so busy arguing over politics and bickering over the last joint that they'd barely notice she was there?

"There'll be another one later. Come on, we can catch a cab."

He huffed out a laugh. "Since when?"

The glimmer of humor in his dark eyes called an answering smile from Skye, as instinctive as breathing, and the reflexiveness of the response annoyed her enough to make her voice sharp. "We might not be the Big Apple, but San Francisco has a perfectly adequate fleet of taxis, and great public transportation."

"Right. You always loved those cable cars."

Shooting him a look as they left the Ferry Building, crossing a set of cable car tracks, Skye gestured at the lines running up and down Embarcadero. "Tell me you wouldn't rather climb onto a charming old open-air cable car, zoom around town with the wind in your face, instead of trudging down into the bowels of the earth and packing yourself into a tin can that travels through subterranean tunnels with no fresh air."

Maybe it was her imagination, but she thought he went a little pale under his olive skin. "No arguments here. Subways aren't my thing."

Guilt for playing on his claustrophobia twisted at Skye's stomach. "Well, either way, it's not an issue because we're going to grab a cab. Nothing could be simpler or quicker."

Please, she prayed to whatever god controlled traffic patterns and the sometimes lackadaisical cab drivers of San Francisco. *Please don't make a liar out of me.*

For once, the gods seemed to be listening. Beck and Skye had only been waiting in semi-awkward silence on the corner of Embarcadero and Market for about five minutes when an open cab pulled over.

The awkward silence continued as the taxi carried them over the Bay Bridge and up into the Berkeley hills, and Skye stared out the window wondering what the hell she was doing.

What nutty impulse had prompted her to initiate this little adventure? She was supposed to be avoiding Beck, avoiding the temptation he represented and the catastrophic emotional hurricane he threw her into, not inviting him over for tea.

Exhaustion, stress, worry, and guilt made for quite the mood-killing cocktail, and as the cab sped past the familiar townhouses, bakeries, indie bookstores, and mural-painted walls of downtown Berkeley, Skye felt her mood turning black.

But then the taxi pulled onto the bustling side street that was home to the Queenie Pie Café, and for the first time in what felt like forever, warmth suffused her chest and lifted her heart.

The sight of her restaurant never failed to make Skye happy, and today was no exception. Even seeing it all closed up when it should be bright and busy with happy customers couldn't dim her joy.

"This is it," she told the cabbie, tapping on the thick plastic separating the front seat from the back. "You can drop us anywhere along here."

They paid and got out, Skye nearly tripping over her own feet in her hurry to get inside the café and check on everything. She'd come by when she first got back to San Francisco after the Chicago leg of the competition, but that was nearly a week ago now.

Fumbling for her keys, she dropped the heavy ring once before managing to slot the right key into the lock on the glass door. Pushing the door open with a flourish, Skye turned back to wave Beck inside, vividly aware that her hair was a mess around her flushed, beaming face but unable to care.

"Enter!"

She ducked into the dark restaurant and flipped the wall switch to flood the place with light while Beck hovered, his looming form filling the entire doorway.

He looked more uncertain than she was used to seeing him, and something about the way he held himself reminded her forcibly of the first time she'd taken him to meet her parents. He had that same odd mixture of defiance and supplication, his hands curled loosely at his sides and his stern, strong-boned face set in uncompromising lines.

Skye couldn't help it; her instinct was the same now as it was back then—to treat Beck like a barely tamed wild thing, to be lured and gentled.

"We came all the way out here," she said softly, her heart thudding unevenly in her chest. "Don't you want to see the place you helped me build?"

Something in his closed-off expression opened up as surely as if she'd slipped her key into the right lock.

"This is what you always wanted." His voice was gruff, like sand over glass. "A place to call your own."

She nodded, throwing her arms wide and twirling in a slow circle. "Queenie Pie is mine: every booth, every chair, every cup, every spoon. And I love everything about it, from the broken exhaust fan above the flattop range to the wobbly legs on table thirteen."

Fierce pride lit Beck's eyes to darkly glowing coals. That look, right there—that was why she'd brought him here.

"I gave you this."

He didn't phrase it as a question, but Skye stopped twirling and looked him straight in the face. "The money you sent, and the fact that you were in the Navy, gave me the collateral to get the bank to extend me a loan, yes. A loan I've almost finished paying off."

And wouldn't it be amazing to be free, out from under the burden of that debt? She could hardly wait.

Propping those big hands on his lean, sturdy hips, Beck studied the layout of the space. His laser beam gaze took in everything, from the wood-framed chalkboard mounted on the back wall, still advertising coq au vin blanc and summer vegetable risotto, the night's specials from a month ago, to the mismatched vintage light fixtures she'd found in thrift shops around town.

The soft red of the walls combined with the creamy yellow light to cast a warm glow over his face, his brown hair, tanned skin, and black T-shirt standing out darkly against the cheerful color.

Skye found her own anxious gaze drifting to the tiny imperfections she knew were there: the nick in the countertop running the length of the left wall and serving as a bar, where people could have a cocktail or a glass of wine while they waited to be seated; the one lightbulb that always burned more dimly than the others on the sixties-era Italian brass fixture over the back corner of the café, no matter how many times she replaced it; the scuff marks on the swinging doors that led into the kitchen.

Swallowing down a swarm of butterflies, she made her voice as casual as she could. "So. What do you think? Did you make a good investment?"

He paused long enough that Skye's butterflies threatened to come right back up, but finally he tilted his chin down and met her gaze. "If anything I did helped you achieve this, then I'm proud. And glad. I think my leaving was the right thing to do."

Her instinctive rejection of that last statement nearly strangled her. And as she tried to relearn how to breathe, the truth reached up and smacked Skye in the back of the head.

As much as she loved the café, she would've given it all up if it had meant keeping Henry at her side.

Shaken, Skye dropped her woven hemp satchel on table four and headed for the kitchen, her only thought to grab a few seconds alone to process what she was feeling.

But before she could push open the kitchen door, Beck was there, his long arm propping it open for her. Ignoring the way his bicep stretched the sleeve of his shirt and the corded tension of his lightly furred forearm, Skye reached for the light switch.

In contrast to the mellow softness that lit the front of the house, the kitchen's brilliant overhead lighting buzzed to life in a blinding rush of fluorescence, illuminating every nook and cranny of the small, cramped rabbit warren of cook tops, freestanding tables, and wire shelving.

"Wow," Beck said, his voice rumbling softly above her head, close enough to make her jump as she felt his breath stir the curls at her crown. "Not a lot of room to maneuver back here."

"It's an old building," she choked out, moving away from him as swiftly and smoothly as she could, even though it felt like everything under her skin was jumping.

"I've seen more space in the galley of a submarine."

Her heart skipped a beat, leaving her breathless. He'd never talked about what it was like for him on the boat, not in any of the stilted conversations they'd managed after he left.

Not that there'd been a lot of time—he'd only been gone three months when it happened, and they'd had that final, awful phone call when she'd had to tell him the news. And after that . . . nothing.

Until now.

Her fidgety fingers smoothed over the familiar lines of her workspace, trailing across scarred wooden cutting boards and gleaming-clean stainless steel countertops. The open wire shelves were still stacked with the long-lasting ingredients they used the most often, white plastic tubs of basics like flour, salt, and sugar alongside crates of condiments like Sriracha, Dijon mustard, and jars of Queenie Pie's own canned pickled vegetables.

"So . . . I know why you left me."

He jerked as if she'd shot him, but Skye barreled on, babble filling her mouth like dirt that she had to spit out, or choke on it. "I mean, I know what you said at the time, and I think I even know why you didn't come back—but what

I'm wondering now is why you left the service. Was it because of the . . ."

"What?" he growled, crossing his arms over his massive chest so the muscles bulged.

"You know." Skye waved her hands around helplessly. "The space issue. The claustrophobia."

Surprisingly, he relaxed at that, the tension melting out of his shoulders as he dropped his hands to steady his lean back against the corner workstation Nathan used. "That was part of it. After that last stint on the boat, I never wanted to see another submarine, much less go out in one."

Hungry for any scrap of information, Skye couldn't mask the eagerness in her voice. "Why? What happened?"

She expected Beck to shut down, the way he always used to when she asked questions, tried to get him to talk about anything in his past, but instead he just shrugged, a slight frown touching his mouth.

"Nothing out of the ordinary, except they kept us out there on the ocean for nearly seven months. Which wasn't all that out of the ordinary, come to think of it."

Seven months. She couldn't imagine it. "I thought . . . when you first joined up, they said the submarine operated on a schedule of three months out, three months on land."

He shrugged. "That schedule—it's not set in stone. It can't be. Shit happens, things Command can't foresee. We were used to it." Pausing, Beck shrugged again, more tightly this time. "Doesn't mean we liked it and accepted it with zero bitching, but we got it. We went where we were needed."

When he put it like that, Skye felt like a selfish bitch for the thought that kept running through her head.

But I needed you, too.

Afraid to say anything that might break this confiding

mood Beck seemed to be in, Skye murmured, "That must have been tough."

Somehow, that was exactly the wrong thing to say. Beck pushed away from the counter he'd been leaning against, straightening his spine as his face settled into its usual sculpted stone lines. "It was a job," he muttered. "And it was worth doing."

Stung by the implication, Skye put her hands on her hips. "I never said it wasn't!"

He snorted. "Come on. This is me. I know you, Skye. I know how much you hate war and violence."

"Of course I hate violence! That doesn't mean I hate soldiers, or that I'm not grateful for their sacrifice and protection."

Beck narrowed his eyes as if he didn't believe her. "The way you acted when I told you I'd enlisted, though . . ."

Skye couldn't believe he didn't understand. "I was worried about you," she cried. "I didn't want anything to happen to you."

"No, it was more than that." He had that stubborn, closed look again, and Skye squeezed her eyes shut, tried to control her jumpy stomach and heaving lungs.

"Yes, it was. I didn't want you to go, because I didn't want to be without you."

Chapter 21

Everything inside Beck's head rearranged itself, as if a giant hand had swept through his mind, scattering the building blocks of his memories, all the choices and reactions that made him who he was.

For years, he'd carried the knowledge that Skye hated him for the decision he'd made to go to war. That his sweet, gentle, hippie girl could never forgive him for going against everything she believed in. And now, she was saying . . . what?

"Are you saying you don't care that I joined the Navy?"

She pressed her lips together as if to stop their trembling, but it was no good—she wore her emotions like some women wore makeup.

"No. I care. I wish there was no need in this world for anything like a navy or an army, or for anyone to have to go to war. But that's not the world we live in, and I thank God there are men and women like you who are strong and brave and willing to give up years of their life in service to their country. And I know that makes me a hypocrite for being selfish enough to wish you hadn't gone at all, but I can't help that, because I loved you more than my own life, Henry, and I needed you beside me when I found out about our . . ."

She choked off her word, but it echoed in Beck's brain as if she'd shouted it.

Baby.

Their baby, the baby they'd made together, but never had the chance to hold or touch or see.

The baby Skye had miscarried at five months, three months after she'd begged Beck not to leave her alone— and he'd left anyway.

Their baby, the baby Beck avoided thinking about as much as possible, because part of him was terrified of what would happen if he let himself really feel the loss.

He tried to push the emotion down, box it up and shove it away, but it was too late.

Darkness filled Beck's chest, a crushing weight of grief and guilt that gave him the exact same feeling as being trapped in a submarine, breathing recycled air and longing for sunlight.

"I should've been here," he said, the words torn from him like yanking a knife out of a stab wound. "I should've been with you. If I'd stayed, maybe . . ."

Alarm widened those pretty blue eyes, and the tears that had been threatening spilled unheeded down her soft, round cheeks.

"No! Don't think like that. Henry, oh my God, I thought I explained it on the phone . . . there was nothing anyone could do. It wasn't my fault, it wasn't your fault."

All he could do was shake his head. His memory of that final phone call was vague, blurred by time, distance, and the sound of blood rushing in his ears from the first moment Skye had picked up the phone and sobbed out, "Hello?"

He'd been on liberty, halfway around the world at a port in Italy where the boat had docked to re-provision, and he'd managed to find a phone and snag himself a calling card in the midst of his personal mission to find some fresh herbs and fruit to take back to the galley kitchen for the seven-week journey back to the States.

He tried to call Skye every time he had liberty, but it didn't always work out, and email wasn't reliable, either. Everyone on the boat was only allowed to send out a single two-hundred-word message per week, so he checked in that way as much as he could, but he didn't get her responses immediately. Skye's daily emails to him were held up, read over, and then printed out for him to read, usually once a week.

But for the last month, even that much communication had been suspended, as the boat had dived too deep to transmit anything.

Heart in his mouth, Beck had dialed the complicated series of numbers to make the phone card work internationally, and then waited for Skye to pick up, hoping like hell she was at the apartment and that she'd be happy to hear from him.

Given the way they'd left things, he wasn't always sure if he should even bother calling, knowing how she felt about where he was and what he was doing, but he had to make sure she was okay.

As it turned out, she was at the apartment . . . but she was pretty fucking far from okay.

He knew she'd explained everything that day about what was going on with the pregnancy, and he remembered the words "chromosomal abnormality," but most of it was a fuzzy nightmare of terror and helplessness unlike anything Beck had experienced since he was eight years old.

Passing a hand over his dry mouth, Beck tried to focus on the present. "You said . . . you told me . . ."

Fuck. He couldn't even say it, not out loud. Not to her.

But it didn't matter. Skye's face crumpled anyway, like

a rose clutched in a too-tight fist, and she rushed to him, hands outstretched.

"I told you! It wasn't because I was sad, or stressed, or anything like that. Nothing you could have done would have made a difference if you'd been there. Nothing I could have done would have changed it, either, and trust me, part of me *still* wants to believe that I could have changed what happened if I'd been smarter, healthier, more careful, something. But there was nothing, Henry, nothing. From the moment of conception, our baby had Turner syndrome. The chance that she would survive to be born was minuscule from the very beginning."

Skye had both his hands in hers, the firm grasp of her slim fingers the only anchor in a world that tipped and spun like the boat taking a sudden dive into deep, black waters.

She shook their joined hands, her face fierce and lovely as she stared into his eyes, the grief and determination on her face not letting him look away.

"Do you understand?"

But all Beck truly understood was the one thing he hadn't heard before. "She . . . you said 'she.' Our baby was a girl?"

Skye's lips parted for a long, soundless moment, and fresh tears welled up. Her voice, though, was soft and even. Steady. "Yes. All Turner syndrome babies are girls."

A baby girl.

The knowledge ripped open the box of Beck's suppressed emotions and stole the strength from his bones so that his legs shook. Without the table behind him and Skye hanging onto his hands, he would've crashed to his knees.

Somehow, knowing that made the baby real in a way she never had been before.

At least, not to Beck. Oh, he'd been happy when Skye

found out she was pregnant. Happy, proud, worried out of his mind about how the hell they were going to afford the doctor's bills and diapers and everything else when they could barely make their rent, but the baby had been . . . more of a concept. An idea. A certain loving smile on Skye's face, a new roundness to her hips and sensitivity to her breasts. That was what the pregnancy meant to Beck.

But the baby had been real to Skye from the very beginning, he knew.

Which meant . . . everything he was feeling now, she'd felt nearly ten years ago. And she'd had to go through it alone.

"It would've made a difference." Getting the words out felt like coughing up broken glass, and sounded worse, but he had to say this. "If I'd been home, it would've made a difference."

She shook her head, heaving in a shuddering breath to deny it, but Beck leaned down and pressed his forehead to hers, squeezing his eyes shut.

"Yeah, we still would've lost her . . . but we would've been together. I could've held you."

"Henry," she gasped, clutching at their joined hands and bringing them up to press between their chests. "You could hold me now."

His breath broke in his chest, a mangled, wounded sound grinding out of his aching throat, and he broke her grip on his fingers to wrap his arms around her.

She pressed into his hold, burrowing in until her face was tight against his neck, her hitching breath damp against his collarbone.

She was warm and real and alive. He could feel her heart thudding steadily into his ribcage, as if she were inside of him, and the jagged, broken pieces of Beck started to put themselves back together again.

Skye cried a little more, and he held her through it, his

big frame for once used to shelter and protect, instead of loom and intimidate.

Curved around his crying wife, with the savage burn of tears pricking at his own eyes, Beck had never felt like more of a man.

There were days in the last few years when Skye had been sure she'd cried herself out, that she had no more tears left to shed for the baby girl she'd lost.

The baby *they'd* lost.

And maybe that was it—maybe she wasn't crying now for their little girl, and the life she'd never get to lead, and the hole in her own heart that would never fully close.

Maybe this time the tears were for that little girl's father, and the fact that he'd been tormenting himself, blaming himself, for ten long years.

God. If he believed he was to blame, that his absence had somehow caused Skye's miscarriage, no wonder he'd stayed away.

And it made a vicious sort of sense. After all, she knew Beck—always ready for people to believe the worst of him.

Feeling the need to make sure he understood, once and for all, she tilted her head back until her chin was propped on the smooth, hard plane of his chest. That was as far as she could bear to go.

"I don't blame you," she said, as clearly as she could through the last few tears clogging her head. "I never did."

His arms around her tightened, even though a moment ago she would've sworn he couldn't hold her any closer than he already was, and the look on his face . . . Skye closed her eyes and turned her head down, pressing her mouth to his chest so his expression wouldn't set her off again.

He was so steady, so strong, with a couple more years

and infinitely more life experience—he'd always been a rock for her to lean on.

But with this stuff? Throw anything emotional at him, and Beck was the inexperienced one.

Most of the time, he kept the strength of his reactions buried so deeply, she'd forget how it was for him. She'd start to doubt, to tell herself he was so stoic and impassive all the time because he didn't care.

But when something happened that he couldn't prepare for, couldn't fight down and push away, she glimpsed a side of him that never failed to grab her by the heart.

He kept his emotions locked down so tightly *because* he cared . . . a lot.

And something had taught him early on that showing his feelings was a weakness, a chink in his armor that would instantly let in the sharp point of a knife.

Maybe it was his years shuffling from house to state facility to group home in the foster care system—or whatever had happened when he was eight years old to put him in foster care. She didn't know what had happened to his parents; Beck would never talk about it.

The old hurt tried to surface, an inner voice (one that sounded an awful lot like her mother) whispering that Beck had never shared his past with her because he didn't love her, didn't trust her, didn't want a life together . . . it was a horribly familiar litany that had served as the soundtrack for her entire relationship with Beck, but tonight she managed to squash it.

Tonight wasn't about her hurt feelings. Tonight was about healing, reconnecting, and making damn sure, once and for all, that Beck knew he wasn't to blame.

No matter what else happened between them, she couldn't stand the thought of him walking around with that heavy burden of guilt on his broad shoulders.

At some point during her crying jag, he'd started rocking them, just a gentle sway from side to side, like the chaste, awkward way kids slow-danced at their first boygirl party, and the image made Skye smile into Beck's chest.

No one had asked her to dance, back when she was thirteen and discovering the joys of braces, acne, and hormonal bloating all at the same time. Not to mention the fact that she'd always been That Weird Girl, even in a school full of bohemian artists' kids.

Yeah, Skye hadn't exactly had a lot of interest from boys that year . . . or any of the years that followed.

Until Henry Beck showed up and kissed her under the moonlight on a secluded beach.

He'd been so handsome even then, already radiating the aura of inner strength that had never left him. He'd been more wiry back then, with that lanky, pulled-taffy look some guys had before they grew into their bodies, hands and feet too big for the rest of him, the new width of his shoulders making him carry himself differently.

The body sheltering hers now felt . . . fully formed. The essence of masculinity, all hard, corded muscles layered thickly over his swimmer's frame. Unable to resist, she ran her hands up the sloping plane of his back, feeling the dip of his spine and the smooth tension of his shoulder blades.

The muscles tensed, then relaxed when she touched them, as if her caress over the warm cotton of his shirt gave him chills.

Inhaling deeply, Skye took his scent of sun-warmed sand and salty air into herself, filling her lungs and her head with it until she felt dizzy.

"Skye," he said, his voice rumbling deep in his chest, pushing the vibration into her mouth where she'd pressed it to his collarbone.

There was a plea in that voice, and an ache she knew she could ease—wanted to erase, with every fiber of her being.

She stilled, her fingers mid-knead against the line of his shoulders.

Was she really going to do this? After all her second thoughts and self-shaming this morning, it seemed crazy.

But as Fiona loved to point out, Jeremiah wouldn't care. And Beck would take it for what it was and move on—he'd made his intentions clear on that score.

So who would she be hurting if she gave Beck the comfort of her body tonight? No one but herself.

And as Beck speared one hand into the tumbled mess of her red curls and palmed the shape of her head, she tilted her gaze up to his and knew . . . It would be worth any amount of future heartache to replace the stunned pain in his dark brown eyes with the glow of desire.

Chapter 22

Beck felt . . . hell, he didn't know what he felt. Too many emotions to name tore around inside him in a chaotic mass. Like sharks in a feeding frenzy, all razor teeth and whipping tails and blood in the water.

The warm softness of Skye in his arms was a haven of calm, real and tangible and right there, grounding him in the present. Where she was alive, so was he.

God damn. He'd never felt so alive. Not in combat training, not during the heat of the Rising Star Chef challenges . . . never.

But this moment, right here, where he could feel Skye's living heart throbbing in his own chest and the heat of her seeping into his core, was one he'd remember for the rest of his life.

When her mouth opened against his chest, he felt it like a brand, even through the thin cotton of his T-shirt.

Her name ripped from him in a near-groan, but he didn't know what he meant to ask her . . . all he knew was that he needed her, couldn't let her go, and he wanted her to know.

He cradled her head in his hand and tugged lightly on her hair, suddenly desperate to see her face.

Blinking slowly up at him, Skye had never looked more beautiful. Even with red rimming her eyes, they were bright blue like a rain-washed sky, and the flush of high emotion stained her cheekbones.

Her lush mouth trembled into a smile, lips parted and so, so tempting. He searched her gaze for second thoughts, for denial, but all he saw was acceptance. Recognition.

And a growing flame of desire that ignited an answering fire in him.

As quickly as pouring brandy into a saucepan, his lust shot up in licking spurts of scorching heat, high enough to blacken the kitchen ceiling.

Crap.

They were still in the Queenie Pie kitchen.

Using the last bit of brain function before all the available blood in his body drained south, Beck ground out, "You want to do this here?"

Skye was panting lightly, her fingers clutching hard at his back as her eyes went heavy-lidded and glazed. "What?"

He combed his fingers through her curls, loving the slip and slide of their silkiness over his hands. "Health hazard. Wouldn't want to get you in trouble."

"No. Right." She blinked, shaking her head and nudging it more firmly into his caress as she gestured over her shoulder to a door in the side wall. "Office."

Hell and damn, but he loved reducing her to single-word sentences. Ignoring her shocked squeak of protest, Beck scooped her up in his arms and headed for the door.

Staring down at the frustrating doorknob, Beck fought the urge to draw his leg back and just kick the door in. "Shit, who designed this thing? And why isn't it just a swinging door, like all good doors should be?"

"Sorry." Skye snickered into his shoulder, then twisted her torso to try to reach the handle.

They fumbled together in a quick comedy of errors until Beck finally backed off and let Skye handle it before she laughed herself right out of his grasp.

He got them out of the kitchen and kicked the door shut behind them, juggling Skye around until he could snatch that happy laugh right out of her smiling mouth.

Her giggle died away into a low, breathy moan as he plunged his tongue past her teeth and danced it over the roof of her mouth, licking into her and stealing every bit of her addictive flavor for himself.

For long, frenzied moments, his entire world narrowed down to the woman in his arms, the deliciously squirming weight of her trapped against his chest and the deep, drugging sweetness of her mouth under his.

When the need for air finally forced him to lift his head, he sucked in lungfuls of Skye-scented breaths and buried his face in the red-gold cloud of her hair.

In the darkness of the room, little more than a closet with a couch and a folding-tray table holding a laptop and printer that partly blocked the window on the back wall, Skye's hair looked auburn, the color of aged sherry. Her skin glowed as if lit from within, pale and luminous and spattered with freckles like flecks of cinnamon in a bowl of milk. Her eyes glowed, too, when he pulled back to catch a glimpse of her flushed face.

Licking her kiss-swollen lips, she said, "There's a futon. Want to put me down?"

Beck squinted at the futon, then did a double take. "Is that . . . ?"

"Oh!" She wriggled a little, as if she were embarrassed. "Actually, yeah. I moved it in here when we opened. Couldn't quite stand to get rid of it, for some reason."

It was the futon from their first apartment over the corner grocery in Chinatown. They'd rescued it from the curb and dragged its wooden frame and single, unwieldy cushion eleven blocks uphill to their third-floor walk-up, and for a long time, it was the only piece of furniture they'd owned. They'd slept on it for months before they'd managed to put away enough money for a real bed.

"A lot of memories in that old thing," Beck observed, staring at the futon and remembering how the divot in the center of the mattress had meant they spent every night twined around each other, a tangle of arms and legs and curly red hair.

He wouldn't have been able to throw it out, either.

She raised her pale brows at him. "It's still pretty comfy. Want to take it for a spin?"

They hadn't turned on any lights, and there was something terrifyingly intimate about the moment. Her face was so close to his, the tips of their noses brushed when he breathed. It was exhilarating, as if the two of them were alone in the universe, and the outside world had ceased to exist.

There was nothing but this, nothing but her and the tide of longing swelling inside him.

She licked her lips again, and the wave broke over his head and dragged him down into the undertow.

In two long strides, he was at the edge of the navy blue futon, reluctantly lowering his armful of woman to the mattress. She reclined against the raised back, white arms folding behind her head in an unconsciously sexy pose as she stared up at him with those big blue eyes.

The futon was still in couch-mode, the back propped at an angle instead of lying flat like a bed, but Beck was too impatient to wrestle with the mechanism to unfold it, which he'd bet hadn't gotten any less temperamental and sticky over the years.

All he could focus on right now was Skye, sprawled in front of him, luscious and curvy . . . and wearing far too many clothes.

He wanted to kiss her some more. He wanted to clutch her close, as close as he could get her, and never let her go. He wanted to touch her bare skin, lick every inch of her from head to toe. He wanted to be inside her.

He wanted . . . too much.

Remember your training. Prioritize, he ordered himself, setting one knee on the futon by Skye's hip and leaning over her.

First order of business was obviously dealing with the clothing issue. Once she was naked, everything else would follow.

The problem was how damned distracting Skye was being. The way she arched her back as his hands went to the hem of her clingy tank top; the trembling satin of her belly against the backs of his knuckles as he peeled the stretchy material up and over her head.

The fact that once he'd wrestled the tank top off, she wasn't wearing anything underneath.

He clenched her shirt in his fist and stared down at what he'd revealed, breathing heavily.

Skye's breasts had always been glorious, big and round and silky soft, capped with high, pink nipples that begged for his mouth.

Now, ten years later, the abundant reality of them put his memories to shame.

Red suffused the porcelain skin of her cheeks, flooding down her neck and into her chest. Beck caught the way her hands twitched, as if fighting the impulse to cover herself up, and he couldn't help his instinctive growl.

"You're gorgeous," he told her, hearing the rough husk of his own voice but unable to smooth it out. "Even more than you used to be. I could look at you for hours."

Her breath caught—he could see it in the way her chest stilled, the sudden shift in her breathing doing amazing things to the soft orbs of her breasts.

With the blush still heating her flesh, she lowered her eyes and peeked up at him through her long golden lashes. "Is that all you plan to do? Look at me?"

Beck defied any of the hard-ass, tough-as-nails sailors who'd drilled him at recruit training camp to stick to the mission plan with a distraction like Skye Gladwell staring up at them.

Until Beck had started lifting the hem of her tank top, Skye had completely forgotten that she'd gone for comfort today and worn one of her shirts with the built-in shelf bra instead of a real bra.

So when he got that tank off and she was completely bare underneath, it threw her a little.

After all, her wet pink bra hadn't provided much in the way of coverage in the bay the night before, but it had at least been something.

She could feel herself coloring up, an uncomfortable rush of blood stinging her skin. The urge to hide her breasts like some bashful virgin was immediate and overpowering—and also ridiculous, considering Beck was the guy who'd relieved her of her virginity more than a decade ago.

Besides, Beck obviously didn't want her covering anything up. And when he told her she was gorgeous, all it took was one searing look at the intense heat in his eyes to convince her that he liked what he was seeing.

An unfamiliar but highly welcome surge of confidence flooded her system.

"Is that all you plan to do? Look at me?" The instant leap of flames in his eyes dried her mouth, and she had to lick her lips before she could continue, her voice gone breathy and hoarse. "Because if that's the game we're playing, I think you ought to strip down, too. Just to keep things fair."

That got her a twisted grin, wicked enough to tighten everything low in her body. Skye shifted on the cushion, her thighs rubbing together damply, making her ultra aware of the sensitive, throbbing wetness between her legs.

With a slow, teasing smirk, Beck backed off the futon and stood up, one big hand lifting over his head to grasp the back of the black T-shirt's neck. He pulled the shirt off in one fluid move, shoulders hunching forward and suddenly revealed abs tightening in a swift crunch as the cotton lifted and was tossed away.

Skye stared. At least her mouth wasn't dry anymore, she thought nonsensically, as the sight of the slabs and dips of thick, ridged muscle covering Beck's torso brought on a craving to taste the salty, smoky flavor of his smooth olive skin.

Beck had always been strong, and she knew from the night before that he'd bulked up over the last ten years, that he'd grown into his big, rough frame.

But she hadn't had the chance to really savor the changes in his body. From his powerful shoulders to his hard, defined abs, Beck was all man.

He looked like some ancient warrior king, savage and brutal, the scars she glimpsed telling the story of his conquests. There was a small nick on his left shoulder, she noticed, and what looked like a burn mark slashing over his right bicep, which flexed as his hands came up to unbutton the fly of his jeans.

Skye sucked in air, eyes riveted on the long, blunt fingers toying with those buttons.

But nothing happened.

"Your move, Skye."

Gaze flying up to meet the heat of Beck's expectant stare, Skye reached for that new confidence and hung onto it with all her might.

She hooked her thumbs in the elastic waistband of her

long tiered skirt, snagging her underwear at the same time, because if she was going to go for this, then she was by God going to *go for it*.

For a moment, the awkwardness of lifting her hips off the cushion so she could work the skirt and panties down her legs almost paralyzed her.

But then she saw the way Beck's eyes followed every move she made, like a hawk tracking a rabbit through the underbrush, and she got over it.

With a last tiny jingle from the brass bells on her ankle bracelet, Skye pulled her knees up and kicked her clothes away, and she was naked.

The canvas covering the futon mattress was scratchy and cool against her heated skin, and every shift of her muscles made her shockingly aware of how exposed she was, how much of her body he could see.

To distract herself from worrying about the changes he must see in her, she went back to cataloging the marks life had left on him. She needed to see more; she needed to see everything.

"Now you," she urged, barely recognizing the thready husk of her own voice.

He didn't hesitate, peeling the jeans and boxer briefs down his long, muscular legs, revealing crisp, dark body hair sprinkled over the delicious all-over natural tan she'd envied like crazy back when she was still coming to terms with her own doughy paleness.

Beck looked like he spent an hour a day doing naked push-ups and sit-ups in the full glare of the sun.

And when he twisted at the waist to drop the pants behind him, Skye caught a glimpse of something she'd missed the night before—a tattoo, all black swirls and lines, covered his left shoulder and ran halfway down his back.

It looked like writing, like words, and a bolt of heat shot through her as she considered the possibilities.

Surely not . . . surely there was no way he'd had that particular poem inscribed on his body . . .

She didn't get a chance to see exactly what the design was, because Beck turned back to face her, and the entire question was wiped from her mind. All she could see was miles of smooth, hard flesh, the biteable divots cutting over his hips . . . the heavy, flushed spear of his cock, dark with blood and hard enough that the engorged plum of the head slapped against his ridged stomach when he moved.

Her mouth watered, the memory of his taste stinging the back of her throat. Giving up all pretense of being playful and lighthearted about this, Skye lifted her arms in mute appeal, begging for the hot, crushing weight of his body against hers.

Beck didn't disappoint. With a low sound that seemed to come from deep in his chest, he swooped down on her like that hungry hawk had finally gotten a clear shot at the doomed rabbit.

Skye had never been so happy to be pounced. He felt like heaven, warm and big and there, the reality of him undeniable.

This was no dream, like the thousand other times she'd woken alone in her bed, gasping and sweating and reaching out for something she was sure she'd never feel again.

This was happening. And her body responded to Beck as if it recognized him on a cellular level.

Ten long years were wiped away in the space of one loud, pounding heartbeat.

Her legs fell open naturally, welcoming this man into the cradle of her hips, which pushed up into the delirious pressure of his thick, heavy erection dragging against her slick folds.

Beck's arms went around her, pulling her up and close until there was nothing between them, not even a whisper of air—only the damp, throbbing pulse of passion.

Skye let her head fall back against the futon. It felt too heavy on her neck, outside her control, as all her consciousness shifted to what was happening lower down. Until Beck called her attention back, upward, into her throat as he kissed, licked, and nipped his way across the shivery, delicate skin of her neck.

Someone moaned, a high, reedy sound, and Beck closed his mouth over the thumping pulse in her neck, stilling the vibration before Skye could do more than register that the sound had come from her.

He sucked at her skin, worrying the spot gently, and Skye groaned even louder as she felt blood rushing just under the surface, marking the spot.

Marking her.

The possessiveness of the move should've scared her, or pissed her off—but it didn't. Instead, she was vaguely aware of a tingling rush of heat between her legs that made her want to move, thrust, wriggle her hips until he touched her there.

It was as if Skye's desire, her need, passed directly from her body to Beck's brain. He gave her what she wanted before she could gather the words to beg him for it.

Letting out a deep growl of his own, Beck slid one large palm down her spine and under her hips, lifting her as if she weighed nothing.

One spinny, disorienting moment later, he had his back to the futon and Skye settled atop him, her knees on either side of his lap.

Nice.

Fully enjoying the feeling of being in control, Skye raked her hands down Beck's chest. She tested the thick pads of muscle with her fingertips, taking note of the way Beck narrowed his eyes and clenched his rock-hard jaw when she brushed past a nipple.

The small, brown circle of flesh went taut and needy

under her touch, and Skye couldn't resist the temptation any longer. Bending down, she replaced her fingers with her mouth and the complicated, savory taste of him exploded across her tongue.

His hands wandered up and down her back, sending chills over her whole body as she devoted herself to relearning the texture of Beck's skin. It was all too seductively easy to lose herself in sensation, every one of her senses trained on the man below her.

But Beck didn't seem to be satisfied with a leisurely exploration, and when his fingers brushed down and over the globes of her behind, his fingers curling in to trace where it split like a ripe peach, the hunger for more lashed Skye as if he'd taken a whip to her.

She jumped a little, startled at the liquid response of her body, and Beck gasped out a husky laugh as her sudden movement jolted his fingers further into her cleft.

The naughty, forbidden touch electrified Skye, every hair on her body standing on end, and she sat up so quickly, she overbalanced and nearly crashed to the floor.

"It's okay, I've got you," Beck soothed, his grip on her never wavering, holding her steady.

Which was a good thing, because all the squirming around on his lap and almost-toppling-over business had prompted Skye to grip his hips with her knees like a rider trying to stay on a bucking bronco—and the resulting pressure of the iron length of his cock against her clit made lights flash behind her eyes.

White noise rushed through her ears and when she opened her eyes, she stared down at Beck, panting, open-mouthed, every part of her trembling and yearning for more.

His hands were still cupped around her ass, low down near the tops of her thighs, the tips of his fingers so, so close to where she wanted them.

Maybe the mental telepathy thing would work again.

Giving a tentative thrust of her hips to nudge things along, Skye shuddered anew at the thick wedge of him forcing her folds to part.

The way the silk-skinned penis rubbed at her made her insane with desire, overtaking everything else until all she could hear was her own hoarse voice spilling crazy babble—things like, "Now, please, come on, inside me, Henry, I missed you . . ."

The tightening of his grasp on her ass startled a squeak out of her that thankfully cut off the stream of begging words.

God, his hands were so hot, the palms broad, the fingers long. She wanted them inside her.

She wanted all of him inside her, where she could keep him and never let him leave her again, but that was crazy, of course it was, and she'd settle for his fingers.

Or something even better . . .

Chapter 23

If Beck's mission was to get Skye naked and lick her from head to toe, her mission seemed to be to foil him by being the sexiest thing on the planet.

How had he lived without this for so long?

No woman, anywhere, came close to lighting Beck on fire the way his soon-to-be-ex-wife did.

Even the unwelcome splash of cold water that came with the memory of her demand for a divorce couldn't cool the flames she'd ignited with her responsiveness, her silky body, her generous curves.

In fact, *generous* was the perfect word to describe Skye. A gorgeous, unclothed Lady Bountiful, writhing over his cock like a woman who knew what she wanted from life—and what she wanted was Beck.

After all this time. She still wanted him. And God in heaven, but he wanted her.

He'd thought one last time with Skye would be enough . . . but now he wondered. Would anything be enough?

And if it turned out they wanted more from each other than a goodbye fuck before parting ways forever . . .

How badly did she want that divorce, anyway?

Maybe . . . just maybe he could change her mind.

The notion sent a lighting bolt of energy surging through his veins. He could feel the beat of his heart in the thick heat of his throbbing erection, doubling and redoubling like a train picking up speed until he was hurtling down the track fast enough to break his neck.

Contorting his upper body to reach his pants on the floor was a risky maneuver in light of Skye's balance issues, but the reward would be worth the way she squeaked and immediately tipped sideways if he could just get his fingers on . . . ah.

The foil condom wrapper crinkled satisfyingly as he nipped it out of the pocket of his discarded jeans and held it aloft, triumphant.

Skye was busily trying to right herself, the struggle with gravity and her own center of balance doing amazingly awesome things for her unfettered breasts, and Beck suddenly had to have her.

What was more, he had to be in control.

His mind clicked through the possibilities with tactical precision. He could turn her and lay her lengthwise on the futon, but the angle of the back would mean a lot of bracing and sliding, not the freedom of movement he wanted. He could set her aside and wrestle the futon into its flat, bedlike configuration, but the lever likely hadn't grown *less* temperamental over the years.

That option entailed the unacceptable risk that a long delay might prompt Skye to think better of what she was doing, to remember that she didn't want him anymore, not really. And the longer he sat here, debating and strategizing, the more likely that outcome became.

Making an instantaneous command decision, Beck got a firmer grip on Skye's delectable rear, gathered his balance, and stood up in a controlled rush.

Skye, of course, flailed and clung to him—which was

half the advantage of this particular course of action, as far as Beck was concerned.

The other half came after he'd strode the two steps necessary to place Skye's back against the wall of her office and pin her there like a beautiful, wide-eyed butterfly.

"Oh my God, I can't believe you did that. You're going to give yourself a hernia if you're not careful!"

Burying his face in her shoulder to hide his laugh, Beck shifted her weight to rest on his left forearm—not that hard to do, since she was taking care of a lot of the work of holding herself up by clamping her thighs around his waist and winding her arms around his shoulders.

"I like the way you feel when I pick you up," he told her, meeting her disbelieving eyes. "You're solid. Real."

Red tinged her cheeks, and Beck bit down on a curse. Shit, that didn't sound good. What woman wanted to be solid?

How could he explain what it meant to him to know, in every sinew and with every flex of muscle, that she was there with him? "I like it," he repeated stubbornly. "You feel good in my arms, soft and sexy. Not like some bag of hollow sticks poking at me."

Her cheeks were still red, but now she was giving him a shy smile, and Beck's chest opened up with relief. Giddy with it, he fumbled the condom up to his mouth and ripped the foil wrapper open with his teeth, making her eyes go even bigger.

An instant of one-handed dexterity later, and her eyes went soft and hazy, her pink lips parting on a sigh that Beck felt through his whole body, every bit as intensely as he felt the wet heat of her sex closing around the latex-covered tip of his cock.

He had to concentrate in order to keep his fingers from digging into the taut, quivering mounds of her ass, leaving bruises on her creamy skin.

Instead, with as much delicacy as the throbbing of his erection would allow, Beck relaxed his arms and let gravity slide her down, down, down until every inch of him was sunk into the soft, searing depths of her.

When she came to rest against him, her sex sealed to his pelvis and her thighs trembling with the shock of his penetration, Skye groaned and clutched at his shoulders. Beck devoured her with his eyes, every reaction, every shudder and quake of her responsive body as precious to him as the pleasure overloading his system.

He didn't know how long it had been for her. He reminded himself that he had to go slow. Be gentle. Remember how much bigger he was, how much he could hurt her in his rush to satisfaction, and go easy. Let her set the pace.

But Skye tipped her head back and gasped out, "Move, please . . . oh God," and all of Beck's good intentions went up in flames.

His hips leaped forward, like a racehorse loosed from the starting gate, and jammed his cock harder and deeper into her. He thrust again and again, delirious with the slick, tight clutch of her around him, drunk on the way her internal muscles quivered and pulsed, pulling at him as if trying to milk the orgasm from his body.

Setting his mouth to the spot on her neck that was already becoming livid with the bruise he'd sucked there earlier, Beck licked at the sensitive skin to make her gasp, then set his teeth against the spot and bit down. All he knew was the need to claim her, inside and out.

The drive to make her his, irrevocably and completely, so the whole world would know, pushed him into the last fiery, convulsive thrusts that ground him against her until she tensed and cried out a high, reedy wail of pleasure.

His own climax followed a heartbeat later as lightning shot up his spine and down into his legs where they braced their shared weight against the office floor. He panted through it, openmouthed and silent, with the taste of Skye's skin filling his mouth and the scent of her all around him.

For long moments, they sagged against the wall, spent and overwhelmed. Finally, though, Skye stirred restively, and as she dropped her legs from around his hips, he lowered her to the ground. The movement made his cock slip out of her, which sucked, but he had to deal with the condom anyway.

Making sure Skye was steady enough to lean against the wall on her own, Beck stripped the condom off and tossed it in the garbage can by the desk before turning back to the most gorgeous sight he'd ever seen.

Skye Gladwell, in the glorious, luscious, naked flesh, all languid and leaning and bright-eyed. Her creamy skin still showed the hectic flush of arousal, and there was a soft, satisfied smile curving her pink mouth. Her strawberry-blonde hair tumbled over her shoulders in a silky mass that begged for his hands, the ends curling down almost to the tips of her gorgeous, uptilted breasts.

He stood there, drinking her in, and the moment stretched on until she couldn't help but notice his stare.

For once, though, she didn't make a move to cover herself. She didn't glance away, or blush, or duck her head. Instead, her smile widened and her stance opened, inviting him in.

She lifted her arms from her sides, Beck moved without conscious thought, his feet carrying him into the lush welcome of her embrace.

He was home.

There was a particular ridge in the mattress of the old futon where, over time, the stuffing had gotten pushed and prodded into sticking up.

Before Skye even blinked her eyes open, she felt that diagonal line of hard discomfort pressing into her side.

Not yet fully awake, she grunted in annoyance and wriggled away from it and closer to Beck, who, like always, was taking up about eighty-five percent of the available mattress.

Wait.

Skye's eyes popped open, and she levered herself up on one elbow, trying to figure out where she was and what the hell was going on.

Yep, there was Beck, hogging the mattress, his bare back rising like a mountain from the sparse covering of the ratty cable-knit throw he'd pulled over them last night.

After they had sex.

Amazing, exhilarating, soul-satisfying wall sex.

And then they'd fallen asleep on their dilapidated futon—their marriage bed—just like old times. Skye had even gravitated toward her old side of the bed, uncomfortable ridge and all.

In the moments between sleeping and waking, it had been easy to mistake this morning for any other morning during their brief marriage . . . but those days were over. Or at least, they were supposed to be.

Flopping back down on her back, Skye stared up at the ceiling. There had to be something wrong with her, some terrible moral flaw, because even though she knew she should, she couldn't make herself regret what had happened last night.

Beck had opened up to her, more than he ever had before. She'd gotten a short, searing glimpse into his inner life, the storm that raged behind his dark eyes and stoic facade, and she'd been sucked into it like Dorothy going up in the twister.

She'd wanted to give Beck comfort, to show him with her body, since words hadn't reached him, that she truly forgave him.

But it hadn't been one-sided. Beck had given her something, too. She'd never, in her whole life, felt so desired. So necessary. So beautiful. It was a gift, and Skye hugged it to her chest.

This morning she might have pillow creases in her cheeks and a wild snarl of bedhead turning her hair into a natural disaster area, but last night she'd seen herself through Beck's eyes . . . and she'd been beautiful.

Beside her, Beck stirred and the sheet pulled taut between them, rolling her closer to the decadent, intense heat of his body. Feeling daring, Skye put her hand on the smooth, hard plane of his lower back, just above the sexy dip at the top of his ass. His skin was fine-grained beneath her fingers, like polished wood, but with the living, breathing beat of his heart pounding through it.

In books, people always seemed to look different when asleep—more innocent, or younger. But Beck seemed the same to her: a silent, immovable statue. A mystery.

Even his tattoo . . . squinting in the dim morning light filtering in from the high window above her desk, Skye cocked her head to try to make it out.

It was on the shoulder Beck slept on, and he had his right arm pillowing his head, which twisted the tat and pressed part of it into the mattress. Flicking a glance over Beck's sleeping face, Skye carefully sat up on her knees and put a hand on Beck's top shoulder.

Exerting gentle pressure, she tried to get him to turn over on his stomach so she could get a better look at the swirling pattern of dark blue lines radiating out from his right shoulder blade.

They almost looked like words . . .

Skye *meep*ed as the immovable statue suddenly moved.

Without warning, between blinks, Skye was on her back staring up at Beck's fully awake face, both her wrists imprisoned in his large fists and pressed to the mattress on either side of her head.

For one, terrifying heartbeat, she stared up into black eyes that held no light of recognition.

But then her heart pounded out another beat, kicking painfully at her chest, and Beck blinked. His whole face changed—a slow grin crinkled the skin at the corners of eyes that now sparked with desire, amusement, affection.

"Can I help you with something?"

His morning-rough voice reverberated through her ribcage where they were pressed so tightly together. His weight, which had been crushing in that first instant, was still heavy—but now she felt safe, sheltered, coccooned.

For some reason, the words *I wanted to see your tattoo* wouldn't come out.

Feeling an embarrassed flush spread over her skin, Skye flexed her wrists in his grip and said, "Just wondering if you wanted coffee or something before we have to get back to the competition kitchen." .

The hold on her arms had turned into a caress, more than anything. His thumbs brushed back and forth over her pulse points in a hypnotic rhythm. "I want something before we go . . . but it isn't coffee."

Giddy delight burbled up in Skye's chest. It came out as a breathless laugh, and she squirmed beneath him, loving the rasp of his body hair against her skin, the power of his heavy chest trapping her between the ancient futon and the vivid sensations overtaking her.

Beck's hands trailed down her arms and over her breasts as he moved down the center line of her body, fingers following the shape of her, mouth searching out her sensitive places as if it had been just a day, instead of ten years, since they'd last woken up together.

As he kissed his way over her stomach, Skye fought

the urge to suck in. To distract herself, she concentrated on the sensation, the contrast of his soft lips with the scratchy stubble of beard rasping at her skin.

He kept going down, down, his hands moving to part her thighs as he lay between them, and Skye nearly lost it.

She knew what he was about to do, and she'd never been comfortable with it. Even when they were together before, they'd get to this point and she'd laugh, or pull away and detour him with kisses until he forgot about putting his mouth . . . down there.

There was just something so vulnerable about it. So exposed. But as he pressed a gentle kiss to the crest of pale curls at the top of her mound, he flicked his eyes up to hers as if to say, "Is this okay?"

It wasn't. At least, not yet. But Skye wanted it to be. She didn't want to be the sort of woman who backed away from pleasure, from life anymore. She gave him a short nod.

Then she closed her eyes, because it had to be easier to let go and feel if she wasn't staring at his dark head moving between her thighs. But at the first slow, easy glide of his tongue, Skye's eyes flew open.

Just as she remembered, the sensation was intense, a sharp jangling of nerves that couldn't quite tell pleasure from pain. She tensed, but Beck didn't stop.

He licked her again. Not too fast, not too hard, and her nerves settled down. All it took was one more light swipe against the slickening folds of her sex for her nerves to be entirely sure . . . this was pleasure. Shockwaves of pleasure rolling through her in great bursts, like thunder shaking her mind to pieces until she lost herself, her worries, her fears—everything but this moment and the man cradling her climax between his hands.

She cried out mindlessly, again and again, until the hoarse sound of her own voice was all she could hear.

Time stopped. Her heart stopped. Everything stopped except the relentless coil of feeling at the base of her spine, the knot of sensation between her legs pulling tighter and tighter and tighter until it burst in a shower of sparks.

Breath, sight, pulse . . . everything came back to her slowly while Beck turned his face to the soft skin of her inner thigh and sucked up another red mark to match the one she could still feel throbbing on her throat.

She couldn't speak yet, didn't have the brain power to form words, but as soon as she could lift her arms, she got one hand into Beck's thick, brown hair and tugged lightly, urging him up beside her.

He gave her a smile, like dawn breaking over the bay, and said, "God, I missed the taste of you."

And . . . apparently her ability to feel complex emotions like embarrassment was back online.

Embarrassment mixed with delight, actually, which was beyond complex. It was downright confusing.

"I missed *you*," she said honestly, forcing herself to meet his penetrating gaze.

Something flared in the depths of his eyes, and he licked his lips, almost as if he were nervous.

"Skye." He hesitated, and her heart picked up speed. "Do you think, when the competition is all over, maybe we—"

He broke off abruptly, his entire body going still. Heart in her mouth, Skye poked him in the shoulder.

"What? What about us?"

But instead of finishing his question, Beck shot off the futon and landed on his feet in a single, powerful rush of controlled strength.

Feet braced apart, hands cupped loosely, arms ready— he looked like he expected an army to come marching through her office door any second.

Before she could try to bring his attention back to what

might happen after the RSC, there was a muffled thump from the kitchen.

Clutching the blanket to her breasts, Skye sat up. Another thump, this time closer to the office door, and Skye's blood turned to ice water when the sound was accompanied by a familiar masculine voice.

"Ow! Damn it. Is anyone here?"

It couldn't be, she told herself frantically as she scrambled off the bed and wrapped the blanket around her body like a toga. He was in Africa. Burkina Faso. He couldn't be here, in the Queenie Pie kitchen, on the other side of that door.

He couldn't be. But he was.

The door opened, and Jeremiah Raleigh walked in.

Chapter 24

Beck's mind automatically scanned and catalogued the threat: white male, early thirties, approximately six foot two, a hundred and ninety pounds. In good physical condition, moved like he knew how to handle himself.

When the intruder stopped stock-still just inside the door and blinked in the darkness of the office, Beck noted his darkly tanned skin and shiny hair, light at the tips as if he'd bleached it that way. But judging from his cargo shorts, scuffed brown leather boots, and battered canvas jacket, Beck had a feeling this guy had spent more time under a hot sun than in a stylist's chair.

"Sunshine? You in here?"

Who the hell was this guy? Did he know Skye?

That last question was answered as Skye stepped around Beck, wearing nothing but the blanket from the futon and an expression of dismay. "Jeremiah! What are you doing here?"

"I came to find you," the guy—Jeremiah—answered, glancing back and forth between Skye and Beck.

Who realized abruptly that he was stark naked.

He didn't really want to back down long enough to find

his pants, but when Skye shot him a pleading glance, the embarrassment reddening her cheeks convinced him.

Without taking his gaze off the new guy for longer than a second, Beck crouched down by the futon and felt around for his jeans.

"I went to your parents' house first," Jeremiah went on distractedly, "But they said you never came home last night, so I thought you must have crashed in your office. And I see I was right. Skye, what's going on here?"

Beck snorted as he tugged his jeans up his hips and zipped them up. New Guy must have lost a few brain cells to heat stroke if he couldn't put the pieces of this puzzle together.

"Jeremiah" was all Skye said, sounding helpless. She shook her head as if she'd been dazed by a blow. "I can't believe you're back already."

Beck frowned. She seemed to be really having trouble with this. Was Jeremiah one of her cooks, an employee she'd sent on a *stage* to another chef's kitchen somewhere, and he wasn't supposed to be home yet?

Except he'd gone by her parents' house, so he must be a personal connection rather than professional.

Sticking out his hand, Beck narrowed his gaze on the new guy. "Beck," he said shortly. "And you are?"

"Jeremiah Raleigh," the guy answered, shaking Beck's hand. His grip was dry and easy, firm but not crushing. It was a respectable handshake, likeable, even, but for some reason Beck didn't want to like this guy.

When Jeremiah finished introducing himself, Beck knew why.

"I'm Skye's boyfriend. Nice—and, wow, kind of awkward—to meet you."

"Oh my God," Skye moaned, putting a hand up to her face.

Beck barely heard her; it was all he could do to stay on

his feet. Stumbling back a step, his calves hit the edge of the futon and nearly toppled him.

Everything wanted to topple him—the very air around him felt insubstantial and too thin to breathe, as if he were falling through empty, black space.

"Boyfriend," he repeated. On some level, the gutted rasp of his voice shocked him, but Beck was beyond caring at that point.

"Yeah, but you know," Jeremiah made a waving gesture with one tanned hand. "I'm gone a lot. Peace Corps, you know? We've got an open relationship, don't we, Sunshine? So it's all good. We're cool."

He sounded like he might be trying to convince himself more than anyone else. Personally, Beck was about as far from cool as he'd ever been in his life. Cool didn't begin to describe the chasm that had opened up in his chest—he felt so cold inside, it almost burned.

"Beck, please . . ."

Skye's voice broke into the buzzing in his ears, soft and pleading, with an edge of fear that made Beck realize he was up on the balls of his bare feet. Looking down, he saw his own hands curled into fists, white-knuckled with tension, the corded muscles of his forearms practically vibrating with the need to propel his fists into Jeremiah Raleigh's face.

Then Skye put a hand on Beck's back, soft and almost cold against his overheated skin.

In spite of the rage boiling inside him, her touch had the same effect now that it always did—he felt himself settle, the battle fever cooling to a manageable level that allowed his head to clear.

And all he could think was *Thank God this happened before I made a complete fool of myself, asking Skye to give our marriage another shot.*

* * *

Every nightmare Skye had ever had suddenly paled in comparison to this moment.

Although there were some awful similarities to her standard anxiety dreams—for instance, the inability to find her clothes.

She was a little afraid to stop touching Beck; it felt like her hand on his bare back was the only thing keeping him from lunging at Jeremiah.

Who looked shell-shocked, as if he couldn't believe she'd actually taken him up on the arrangement he'd proposed when they first started dating. Which was understandable, since she never had before in two years of long-distance romance. She'd never even been tempted.

But that was before Beck came home.

He's not home for good, she reminded herself. *You can't count on him to stick around.*

There'd been that moment, though, right before Jeremiah showed up . . . it had seemed like Beck was about to ask her something important.

Silently cursing fate and the gods for stealing that moment before she had a chance to find out what Beck would've said, Skye's mind raced as she tried to figure out what to do.

First things first.

Calling on all her memories of her parents' affairs and their casual attitude the morning after, Skye said, "Jeremiah, can you give us a minute to get dressed?"

He hesitated, his sun-baked face more lined than she remembered it, but in the end, he nodded. "Sure. I'll be right outside."

The sound of the office door closing gently behind Jeremiah echoed like a gunshot through the office.

Skye swallowed and busied herself with tracking down pieces of her outfit from the night before. Tank top over there, underwear . . . there, and, crap, was she using her skirt as a pillow last night?

She unballed the organic cotton and shook it out, lingering over the task to give her hands time to stop trembling.

When Beck spoke, it startled her so badly she nearly dropped the skirt.

"You never mentioned a boyfriend."

She blew out a breath and stepped into the wrinkled fabric, pulling it up her hips. "I know. I'm sorry. It just never seemed like the right time—and, honestly, I assumed you'd be gone long before Jeremiah came home."

Beck stood there, watching her buzz frantically around looking for her bra before she remembered she hadn't worn one. She wished he'd say something, or at least stop staring at her.

"And he really doesn't care that we slept together."

It wasn't a question, the way Beck said it, but Skye was glad the process of working the tight shelf bra of her tank top over her head gave her a second to formulate an answer.

"He shouldn't. The open relationship was his idea."

Of course it had never really come up before, at least not on her end. Part of her wondered if Jeremiah would be quite so liberal-minded now that Skye taking a lover had become a concrete reality rather than an abstract idea.

Very concrete, she thought, stealing a glance at Beck's rough-hewn form while she tried to finger-comb her hair. Beck looked like he'd been encased in cement, rigid and unyielding.

"I would care." His voice was almost subsonic, a growl so low she felt it more than heard it, and the vibration sent a shudder through her system. There was deep contempt in that voice, and a confusion that bordered on anger.

No, Beck wouldn't understand a man like Jeremiah, who cared so deeply about the world at large that he sometimes forgot about the people closest to him. Beck had always been so intent. So focused.

Although Beck had left her to join the Navy, so maybe he had more in common with Jeremiah than she'd thought.

She had to talk to Jeremiah. God, what a mess. She was so humiliated, she could barely look at Beck.

"I would fight for what's mine," he said, moving in a rush almost too fast to see, stepping into her path and blocking the door like a great stone wall.

He didn't want her to leave, she could see that. And it thrilled something inside her—she couldn't hide it from herself. But his words . . .

Shaking her head, Skye said, "I don't want you to fight at all. I never wanted that. What I wanted was for you to talk to me."

Beck jerked his chin in the direction of the kitchen. "That's what you want? That guy out there, who finds you in bed with another man and then leaves you with him to get dressed."

The sneer on his face lit the fuse on Skye's temper. "You think Jeremiah is weak. But I'm telling you now, he didn't walk out of here because he's too weak to fight you, or because he doesn't care enough about me to bother. Jeremiah Raleigh is a hero. He builds houses and schools and clinics in villages that don't have running water. He's the furthest thing from weak there is—and he doesn't have to prove anything to me with fists."

Beck rocked back on his heels as if she'd delivered an uppercut to the chin.

"Is that what you think? That I'm trying to prove something to you?"

Skye breathed in sharply. "You've always had something to prove, ever since I met you. And no matter how many times or how many ways I tried to tell you that you didn't, you never listened."

And he never would, she realized. Beck had been shaped by events in his childhood, a past she knew almost nothing about, long before he ever met her. And no matter what she said or did, it never seemed to be the key to unlocking the cage of his emotions.

The revelation hit her with a vicious slap, nearly knocking the breath from her lungs.

She raised her eyes to meet his fierce, impenetrable glare. "You are who you are, Henry," she choked out. "I get it, and I'm not trying to change you. But I need more than a man who lets his body do all the talking. I need someone who lets me know him, fully and completely . . . someone who wants to know me the same way. And that's not you, is it?"

He clamped his lips shut. Skye knew that look. The conversation was over.

Beck didn't say it in so many words—when did he ever?—but he stood aside, arms crossed over his chest, to let her pass.

She stood motionless for a long moment, letting his familiar silence wash over her while she memorized the sight of him.

Then she walked out, leaving half her heart behind.

Chapter 25

Beck stood in the light, airy flagship Fresh Foods store's produce section, staring blindly at the list in his hand.

The collection of vegetables and fruits and other ingredients he'd listed made sense individually, but when he tried to add them all up into a complete menu, they were nothing but chaos.

Which, come to think of it, made it a pretty good allegory for the story of his life.

Fingers snapping in front of his eyes jerked him out of his head and back into the challenge.

"You awake there, big guy?" Winslow was back, their shopping cart now full of items like chunks of pancetta and bottles of rice vinegar.

Beck stared down into the cart. It didn't look like anything. Usually, at this point in a menu, he'd start to be able to see the individual components as elements of a finished dish. He could visualize what each dish would look like on the plate, how he'd stack the items or what he'd drizzle over top for that last burst of flavor and color, but right now?

It was all cardboard and plastic and paper. Nothing real, nothing substantial.

Nothing of himself.

"Are we doing the right thing here?" he heard himself ask.

Winslow's eyes got big. "Hey. Are you okay?"

Pressing his mouth shut against the words that threatened to tumble out, Beck clenched his fingers on the wire frame of the cart, feeling the metal dig into his palms. The pain grounded him, made it possible for him to mutter "Not really."

Winslow reached out and pried at Beck's hands. "Quit that, you're going to hurt something."

"I already hurt something," Beck said, and shit, now it was all coming out. "Someone," he amended, pulling away from Win and rocking the cart on its wheels with a clang.

And he'd hurt her. He knew he had. The look on Skye's face when she finally got it, finally figured out that she could do so much better than a violent, damaged, mute fucking asshole . . .

"Hey!" The alarm in Win's voice penetrated the black fog hanging over Beck's head. He blinked at his sous-chef and found the kid staring back at him with more than a hint of anger in his expression. "Beck, come on. Do not be doing this to me right now. I need you to get your head out of your ass and focus!"

Beck blinked, his jaw set as if someone had poured cement into the joints. "Sorry," he rasped out. God, would he never be done needing to apologize?

"Don't be sorry, man." Win sighed, his fingers coming back to pluck at Beck's stiff hands curled around the wire cart. "Tell me what's going on. Maybe I can help."

Beck snorted. That was sort of the whole issue in a nutshell, wasn't it? "I never tell anyone what's going on," he said.

Win rolled his eyes. "Well, duh. Kind of noticed that.

And most of the time, who cares, but now is not most times, Beckster. Now is the Big Time, and you need to quit withholding and let me in!"

"Everybody wants in." He laughed, but it scraped his throat on its way out. "Pretty fucking funny, since most of the time I want out. There's nothing to see in here, man."

Beck dropped his head, his hair swinging forward to hide his face. It felt good to hide. Familiar, comforting.

Safe.

He stiffened. Holy Christ, was Skye right? Had he been taking the coward's way out his entire life?

The memory of Skye with Jeremiah Raleigh rose up in his mind, as inescapable as a swarm of hornets. Beck had left Queenie Pie on his own, as soon as he found his boots. The last thing he saw before he pushed through the kitchen and out into the front of the house was Skye wrapped in a warm, loving, tender embrace.

Perfect, good-looking, fucking *heroic* Jeremiah Raleigh.

Jeremiah hadn't yelled or thrown punches or stomped around. He'd opened his arms and invited her in.

And she'd gone.

She'd met his unblinking gaze over Jeremiah's shoulder. Emotions were hard for him to read sometimes, but there'd been something in the deep blue pools of her eyes . . . pain and memories and the release they'd found together in purging some old wounds the night before.

But something else, too. Maybe a plea?

"I never know what people want from me," Beck said.

Win leaned closer, brow furrowed, as if he'd barely caught the words.

Clearing his throat, Beck steeled himself and lifted his head. "No, that's not it. I assume I know what people want, and that I don't want to give it to them."

"Sounds like a pretty unsatisfying arrangement," Win said. "For everyone concerned."

Beck huffed out a breath that could've passed for a laugh. "Yeah. It sure wasn't satisfying for my wife."

Win went on full alert, Beck could tell from the way he straightened as if someone had goosed him. "Something going on with Skye? Other than the whole divorce thing, and the bet about spending one last night together."

Beck was ninety-five percent certain they'd already had their last night together, bet or no bet. "I'm really fucked up," he admitted, the words torn from his chest as desperation got its fist around his heart and squeezed. "I don't know what to do about it. Tell me what to do."

Win sucked in air. "Shit. Are you serious? No one ever asks me what to do!"

That made Beck look his young friend in the eye. "We should," he told him. "You give damn good advice."

"It's true. I am one emotionally healthy motherfucker." Winslow preened for a moment before getting serious again. "Bottom line, man, is you have to decide what you want and what you're willing to do to get it. No one can give you advice about that, and no one can do it for you— you've got to take a real close look at your heart, and then don't puss out about listening to what it tells you."

"Christ," Beck said, feeling short of breath. "You should have your own talk show."

Punching him in the shoulder, Win beamed. "Yeah, maybe on one of those channels where they don't care if you swear a lot. Or Bravo! Bravo loves the gays."

"It has nothing to do with you being gay," Beck said, frowning.

Shit, this was awkward, but it had to be said. *Don't puss out,* he reminded himself, and the surge of amusement gave him the guts to put his hand on Winslow's shoulder.

"It's because you're a good friend, you care about people. And you see things others miss."

This time it was Win who ducked his gleaming shaved head, but only for a second. "Thanks, man. But I just caught sight of my watch, and holy cats, but we need to get moving here. I know I said to have a good long heart-to-heart with yourself, but we don't have time right now."

There was no time; every second ticking down on the clock brought them closer to the moment of truth, when they'd have to check out with whatever product they'd managed to acquire, and that would be what they'd cook.

But as Beck stood there in the produce department between towers of lemons and a bank of greens getting sprayed down with a fine mist of water, he caught sight of his competition racing toward the table full of fresh herbs across the wide aisle.

Skye's chin was firm with determination, her movements swift and purposeful, with an economy of motion that Beck found as beautiful as any dancer. She'd been through so much, been so alone through most of it, but she was still here. Still in it, hoping and taking chances and trying to be happy. She was magnificent.

And he realized he didn't need a lot of time.

His heart had been telling him what it wanted for years; he just hadn't been listening.

And after this morning, he knew he only had one shot at getting it. His mission was clear.

"Dump this stuff, we need a new cart." He fired off the order, feet already in motion.

Win jumped into action with a whoop and a curse, ready to follow his lead, and Beck took the extra five seconds to grab his sous-chef around the shoulders and haul him into a quick, very manly hug.

"What's the plan, boss?" Win said when Beck set him back on his feet.

Beck ripped his prepared list of ingredients straight down the middle and took off at a ground-covering jog for the fish counter.

"We're cooking from the heart."

Skye had never been so distracted in her life. She'd be lucky if she made it through this challenge with all her fingers intact.

Usually cooking was where she lost herself, burying her fears and worries in mounds of juicy diced tomato and drowning them in gallons of homemade chicken stock. But today all she could think about was the look on Jeremiah's face when he pulled back from hugging her and said, "Sunshine, we need to talk."

She blinked, and suddenly the image morphed to Beck walking out of the Queenie Pie kitchen, head down, steps slow but steady, like a wounded lion.

They couldn't leave it like this.

Across the kitchen, Beck and his sous-chef were just finishing stowing their groceries in the walk-in, stacked on a couple of speed racks for quick, easy access once the challenge actually began.

Eva Jansen had arrived a few moments ago with her assistant, Drew, and the two of them were checking through the kitchen, making sure everything was ready to go. If Skye was going to do this, she didn't have much time.

Breathing in a deep breath of serenity and calm, Skye closed her eyes and imagined peace filling her up, like water poured into a cup.

She opened her eyes and saw Beck striding over to his station, his jaw dark with stubble and his eyes fierce, and her cup of serenity shattered.

Crap. That worked a lot better in yoga class.

Now or never, Skye.

Mentally hitching up her skirt, Skye marched over to

Beck's station. His sous, Winslow, saw her coming and got all big-eyed before fading discreetly away to talk to Drew.

Skye was grateful for the gesture toward giving them privacy, but she was very aware that she and Beck weren't alone in this kitchen. Which was why she stopped a few feet away from him.

Distance was crucial to her sanity.

He watched her approach, his dark eyes deep and fathomless, shadowed by the sweep of his hair. It was loose, she noticed, but she knew he'd pull it back and out of his face before the cooking actually started.

She knew little things like that—things like the sound he made when he came, or the fact that he hated scary movies and preferred poetry to fiction. But did she really know him?

"Today we prep," he said quietly, jolting her out of her thoughts. "And tomorrow, we find out who's the next Rising Star Chef."

Fighting down a blush, Skye lifted her chin and stuck out her hand. "Whatever happens, I want you to know . . . I'm proud to compete against you. May the best cook win."

His gaze flared with a bright spark of passion when their fingers met, palms sliding together, but Skye wasn't sure if it was desire for her, or the desire to win. At this point, it hardly mattered.

"I'm ready," he told her. "And I'm looking forward to tasting your dishes. I know they'll be great."

God, so polite and stilted. As if they were strangers. Skye pulled away and tried to find a smile for him. "Okay, well, I'm sure they're going to start the timer soon, so . . ."

"Is Jeremiah coming to the judging?" Beck asked, startling her.

"Oh," she stammered. "I don't know, I didn't think anyone was allowed other than the judges . . ."

"They should make an exception for him," Beck said. "He came all the way from Africa to see you cook."

Sheesh, could this be more uncomfortable? Skye had to swallow three times to get rid of the painful lump in her throat, and before she could manage it, Eva walked up.

"Who came from Africa?" Eva asked, gray eyes bright and avid with curiosity.

"My . . ." Skye broke off. God, what was she supposed to call Jeremiah now, after the conversation they'd had once Beck left this morning? "Friend," she concluded lamely, feeling the flush she'd been suppressing finally erupt like a wildfire and spread up her chest all the way to the tips of her ears.

"He's in the Peace Corps," Beck supplied, his voice unreadable.

"Wow." Eva had a calculating look that made Skye nervous. "Well, I think we should invite him to join us for Skye's tasting tomorrow afternoon. Beck, is there anyone you'd want to invite for your judging in the morning?"

Even in the midst of her dismay over this turn of events, Skye was avid to know the answer to that question. She watched Beck from under her lashes, taking in every shift and nuance of his expression.

Which barely changed at all as he said, "No. There's no one."

Skye's heart, which had already been through the wringer today, shredded a little more.

Clearly taken aback by the uncompromising answer, Eva raised her brows. "Oh! Well, if you're sure . . . then I guess it's time to get this challenge started. I know you have a lot of prep work to do, so please take your positions and I'll start the clock."

Feeling like she'd barely survived an ambush, Skye somehow made it back to her station where Fiona stood sharpening their knives on a honing steel.

"What was that all about?" Fee asked, concern roughening her voice. She'd been worried about Skye since the shopping trip that morning, but there hadn't been a moment to fill her in on the incredible developments of the past twenty-four hours.

Or maybe Skye just hadn't known what to say about it all. Kind of like now.

"Nothing," Skye said, straightening her stance and watching the clock for the moment to start. "Let's just cook."

Everything else would have to wait.

Chapter 26

Beck woke up at oh-dark-hundred, as alert and ready to move as if it were noon. He blinked into the darkness of the hotel room he and Win shared and tried to let himself be soothed by the rhythmic breathing coming from the other double bed.

Knowing what lay in store for him later that day, though . . . it would take more than a little light snoring and snuffling to calm Beck down.

Besides, mental prep was important. At least as important as the cooking they'd done the day before, and the finishing touches they would put on their dishes this morning before serving the judges at eleven thirty.

The judges, and Skye.

Somewhere along the way, this whole competition had boiled down to her. He still wanted to win—of course he did, if for no other reason than to repay the Lundens for everything they'd done for him—but all he could think about as he stared up at the hotel room ceiling was Skye.

His entire menu was a love letter to the one woman in all the world who might be able to read it and know what it meant.

Beck breathed out and marveled at how calm he felt. He would've thought that the knowledge of what he was about to do, how much of himself he'd have to expose, would fill him with the kind of terror and avoidance usually reserved for full-on combat and cleaning out the bilge.

Yeah, his stomach was jumpy with nerves, and his palms felt clammy against the sheet . . . but it was nothing he couldn't push through. Nothing that would stop him from doing what had to be done.

Today was the day he'd make his last stand.

And if he went down, at least he'd go down fighting.

Skye stared at herself in the mirror as she buttoned up her white chef's jacket. Same corkscrew curls, just a shade too light to make her an actual redhead. But she'd gotten the redhead's pasty complexion, which seemed unfair, especially given her tendency to freckle.

Same blue eyes. Same round cheeks and face and, oh hell, everything.

She looked for the woman Beck had seen, that night at Queenie Pie, but she couldn't find her in the pale, tired-looking woman in the mirror.

"Today is going to be a good day," Fiona announced from the door of the bathroom.

Because of this morning's early start, they'd spent the night at the hotel where the competition was being held instead of going home. At least, that was the reason Skye had given her parents when she finally called to check in with them.

That conversation had made it clear they only noticed she was gone when Jeremiah came looking for her at their house, so it was hard to feel too guilty for abandoning them a second time. Although her mother had certainly done her best.

"When is that silly contest over?" Annika's voice was vaguely petulant, and Skye had distinctly heard the snick of a lighter in the background.

"Soon," Skye promised, but her heart wasn't up to the usual round of assurances and scrambling for whatever scraps of caring her mother might toss her way, so all she'd said was "Tell Jeremiah I said good night, okay? You made sure the guest room was made up for him, and that he has towels and stuff. Right?"

"Yes, yes. He's fine. But you should be here with him, not playing around in some kitchen."

Not for the first time, Skye was glad she'd never mentioned the identity of the chef who was her biggest competition in the RSC. She didn't need to deal with her mother's feelings about Henry Beck, as well as her own.

She'd said goodbye and hung up, all the time aware of the fact that recognizing the futility of loving Beck hadn't, in fact, done much to wipe that love out of existence.

It was still there, hours later, throbbing in her chest with every beat of her heart as she prepared to face him for what might well be the last time.

Whichever one of them won, there wouldn't be any reason to see each other again after today.

That knowledge was an endless expanse of open highway spooling out in front of her, a long, lonely road to nowhere.

A slim arm slipped around her shoulders reminded her that she wasn't alone.

Leaning her curly head against Fiona's sleek cap of white-blonde hair, Skye closed her eyes and let herself feel the warmth and acceptance of the embrace.

Her friends, the other Queenie Pie chefs . . . They were her real family. What did it matter if her parents didn't understand why she'd entered the RSC, or even why she'd become a chef in the first place?

She had the family she'd cobbled together from the people she loved and worked with, the people who had her back and kept her sane through the daily frustrations and joys of owning her own small business.

Which she'd still own, even if she lost today. She'd still have Queenie Pie, and her family of misfits and outcasts.

The thought was like opening a valve in her brain. The pressure that had filled her near to bursting gusted out of her on a sigh, and Skye felt lightheaded with relief.

No matter what happened today, she'd still have the life she'd chosen with the people she cared about.

And once she accepted the fact that winning wouldn't make her parents suddenly support her in that life, the serenity and calm she'd been searching for enveloped her in a warm cloud of confidence.

"You're ready," Fiona observed, her pale eyes keen in the mirror.

Skye nodded. "Let's go get 'em."

The competition kitchen felt weirdly empty. No chaos of frantic chefs, no judges . . . just Beck and Winslow, banging through their set list and executing dishes with precise efficiency.

Eva and her assistant were in and out, keeping tabs on the time, watching for rules violations, and just generally being on hand in case anything went down.

But for the most part, Beck barely noticed anything beyond the food in front of him.

He was cooking for his life, for his future, and he knew it.

The clock ticked closer and closer to eleven thirty, when the first course would need to be plated and ready to serve to Eva, Claire, Kane, Devon . . . and Skye.

Stay focused, he told himself, blinking sweat out of his

eyes and rubbing the sleeve of his chef coat over his forehead. *The details matter.*

Everything mattered.

Five seconds before the buzzer went off, he and Win were scrambling to get their first course plated and ready, reaching over each other with spoons full of sauce and sprinkling garnish. But when Eva called time, they stepped back from the table, hands in the air, and looked at each other.

"We made it," Win breathed.

Beck nodded, although for him, the hardest part was yet to come. "One course down. Let's keep up the intensity plating the next."

They each picked up a tray and followed Eva out of the kitchen and across the hall to the judging room.

Beck was watching his step and doing his best to keep his tray level as they entered the room, which was set up with a long, banquet-style table covered in a white tablecloth. The chairs for the judges were arrayed along the back side of the table, all in a row, and Beck closed his eyes for a second to come to grips with exactly how much this was going to be like performing for an audience.

Win started passing out plates as Beck opened his eyes. The first person he saw was Skye, sitting on the end. She gave him a nod, but before he could nod back, or smile, or figure out the right thing to do, Skye tilted her head to indicate the person sitting beside her.

Beck glanced over, then did a ridiculously cartoonish double take, because the person in the chair next to Skye was Nina Lunden.

The woman who'd given him a chance when he had nowhere else to go.

Nina gave him one of her soft smiles, but the look in her eyes was fierce with pride.

"Surprise?" Win's tentative voice at his side nearly startled Beck into bobbling his tray.

"That was you?" Beck asked, handing his tray off to Winslow, who'd already passed out the plates from his own.

Win rolled his eyes, but Beck could tell he was still nervous. "Why do you think I was so gung ho about plating an extra portion?"

Beck, who'd thought Win was exercising a very commendable caution with his contingency plan, clapped him on the back before he could run off to serve the rest of the judges.

"Thanks, man," Beck said, looking right into Win's eyes. He wanted Win to know he meant it, from the bottom of his heart.

Win relaxed enough to send Beck a cocky grin over his shoulder as he walked back to the judges' table. "Come on. Like we'd let you go through all this without any family here."

Beck's breath caught in his throat.

Family.

Nina was still smiling at him when he looked back to her, and she gave him a nod and a discreet thumbs-up just as Eva Jansen cleared her throat.

"Thank you, chefs. And welcome to the final judging of this year's Rising Star Chef competition."

Everyone clapped, which made Beck feel more onstage than he had yet. He quelled the urge to fidget by bracing his legs apart in an at-ease position and clasping his left wrist in his right hand behind his back.

"And a very special welcome," Eva continued with a nervous smile, "to Nina Lunden, part-owner of Lunden's Tavern, who is here to support Chefs Beck and Jones."

"Thank you," Nina said, nodding comfortably at Eva as the younger woman sat back down beside her. "You did that very well, dear. And don't you look pretty! No wonder Danny gets that look on his face whenever he's on the phone with you."

Eva flushed, probably with a combination of delight and embarrassment, and Beck noted Nina's pleased grin as she sat back in her seat.

Nina caught his glance and sent him a slow wink, and that, more than anything else, gave Beck the guts to get on with it.

He cleared his throat and lifted his chin. "Before we begin, I want to thank the RSC for giving me the chance to tell the story of my life through food. Some of the events that shaped me, that made me the chef I am today, are things I haven't talked about much."

He flicked a brief look at Skye, whose eyebrows were somewhere up near her hairline. Beck amended his statement. "Okay, all of them. I don't like to talk about my past. But that's why I wanted to thank you, because I have some things I need to say—and this challenge gave me a way to say them, in a language I know how to speak. The language of food."

A disconcerting hush had descended over the large room, and Beck abruptly wished it wasn't quite so big. He felt like he had to really speak up to push his voice into the corners of the converted conference room.

He cleared his throat again, his vocal cords clamping down tight. But he could do this. He'd survived worse.

All he had to do was keep the objective in mind—to show Skye he could open up. That he wanted her to know him, all of him, including the ugly pieces of his past.

Maybe then she'd understand how much he loved her.

"The first course we have for you today is a play on something my mom used to make me when I was little. Like most kids, I guess, I loved peanut butter and jelly sandwiches—but my mom would do them like grilled cheese, with buttered bread in a skillet. The peanut butter would get all gooey." He swallowed, lost in the memory for a moment. "Anyway, they were great. And this is my take on it—we made everything from scratch, including the peanut butter. The jelly is a raspberry and red wine conserve. Enjoy."

With that, he pivoted on his heel and marched out of the room before anyone could take a bite.

"Time to plate the next course," he muttered to Winslow, but that was only part of the reason.

As he stalked back into the kitchen and put his head down, hands moving swift and sure over the plates already set up on the stainless steel work table, Beck took the opportunity to breathe deeply for the first time in ten minutes. He'd made it through the first bit of his story.

But it was only going to get tougher from here on out.

Chapter 27

At the other end of the banquet table, the judges and Eva busily tasted and commented, making notes and conferring about Beck's classy, adult take on a PB & J.

Skye ran her finger through a streak of red raspberry conserve and wished desperately for a moment alone to process what she'd heard.

Beck had a family. A good family, from what he'd described, which was more than she'd ever known before.

And it certainly didn't seem as if he were making up something to placate the judges, the way he'd planned. She'd never heard anything so intensely personal from Beck, and the way he'd had to brace himself to tell the story, the slow grate of his words as they tore from him . . . no. Beck wasn't faking his way through this challenge.

He was ripping himself open and laying his past out on the table for everyone to see.

But why? What made him change his mind? And what was he going to say next?

Her brain didn't have time to spin out any further because the woman next to her turned and said, "So. You're Skye Gladwell."

Instantly wary, Skye gave Nina Lunden her best smile. "That's me."

Nina nodded, the warm lighting in the judging chamber glinting off the threads of silver in her graying hair.

She had a motherly look about her, Skye thought—well, okay. She didn't look anything like Skye's mother, who was rail-thin and sharply angled, skin leathery and lined from years of sun, smoke, and working with welding tools to make her huge, avant-garde iron sculptures.

Nina Lunden appeared to be built along more classically maternal lines, softer and rounder, with arms that looked ready to hug and a mouth made for smiling. The only lines on her deceptively youthful face were crinkles around her eyes and creases beside her mouth—the lines that came from laughing.

But when Skye met Nina's gaze, all of that sweet motherliness faded away in the piercing sharpness of Nina's stare.

"I'm glad to get the chance to meet you," Nina said, her voice friendly but her eyes studying Skye with that uncomfortably intense edge. "I've heard so much about you from my kids."

Skye swallowed, the saltiness of Beck's roasted peanut butter suddenly sticking in her throat and drying her mouth. She wasn't sure what to say; this was awkward on so many levels.

What had the Lunden men told their mother about her? What did they even know? Beck was so closemouthed, it was possible that all they'd had to share with Nina were their impressions of a fellow competitor, and the fact that she and Beck had a history.

The fact that they were competitors in the finals of the RSC together—that alone was enough to make this a tricky conversation, at best.

"It's nice to meet you, too," Skye hedged, trying not to sound as nervous as she felt.

"When Winslow called me and asked if there was any way I could take a few days and come out here to support Beck, I was so glad to be able to do it. With Jules, Max, and Danny all home and keeping an eye on the restaurant—and on my stubborn husband, who just had heart surgery and really shouldn't overdo—I felt like I should seize the chance. I hardly ever get a vacation. Well, you know what it's like—you own your own place, too, don't you?"

"The Queenie Pie Café," Skye supplied, the familiar surge of pride filling her.

"Then you know all about how it is." Nina sat back in her chair. She had on a pair of black pants and a simple sweater, with a white collared shirt peeking out from the neckline, and it made her look effortlessly chic and very New York.

Skye was suddenly and achingly aware of her own ensemble—a white chef's jacket over a pair of silky, low-slung and wide-legged pants with a purple paisley pattern.

A little wacky, even for her, but she hadn't had her mind on fashion when she'd grabbed them.

"I do," she agreed, beginning to relax a little as the stream of inconsequential small talk carried them along. "Gosh, until the first part of the competition in Chicago, I don't think I'd left San Francisco in five years. Maybe longer."

"It ought to be easier for me." Nina sighed. "Since I've got a partner, in work and in life, to help share the load."

Skye stiffened, feeling the trap spring closed around her. "Well, I'm lucky enough to have great, reliable employees," she said through numb lips. "We help each other out."

"Still," Nina said innocently. "There's nothing quite like running a restaurant with someone who has an equal stake in it."

Skye shrugged and stared down at her plate. What was the woman getting at? Was she just trying to make Skye feel bad, or realize how alone she was? It didn't seem like the kind of mean-spirited thing Nina would do, but then, Skye had just met the woman. There was no reason to feel hurt or attacked.

The door of the judging room opened and Beck appeared, holding another tray. His large, powerful form blocked the doorway, and the overhead lighting cast dramatic shadows on his fierce expression.

He looked like he should be carrying a sword and shield, as if he were riding out to slay a dragon, not walking into a room to serve six people a dish of food.

Beck stepped forward, followed by Winslow, who hurried forward to set plates in front of the judges.

As Win served, giving Nina a secret wink and a grin as he set down her plate, Beck started talking.

"This next dish is a salad of bitter greens with roasted morels and a warm bacon and cider vinaigrette. I wanted to do something a little tough and sharp to symbolize my childhood after the loss of my parents."

He paused and Skye froze with the fork halfway to her open mouth, her eyes riveted on Beck's face.

He stared straight ahead, chin up and shoulders back, as if he were giving a report to his commanding officer. But there were cracks in his impassive mask, she saw, and a sympathetic pain rocked through her even as she hung on his next words.

"My parents were Hal and Lisa Beck. My dad drove a truck for the city; my mom was a nurse. Looking back, I guess we never had much when I was little, but I didn't notice, because we had each other. Everything changed when I was eight."

Beck's gaze found Skye, and a shock went through her as they locked stares. "That was the year the Loma Prieta earthquake hit Oakland. My parents were on the bridge when it collapsed."

A fork clattered loudly against a plate, and someone made a sympathetic noise of shock, but all Skye could see was the image of Beck as a little boy, suddenly alone in the world.

"I didn't have any other family, so I went into foster care. And I don't know if it was the Rule of Six or maybe the fact that I was so pissed off at the entire world, but I got shuffled around a lot until I finally aged out of the system."

He'd been eighteen when Skye met him—newly on his own, and living in a halfway house that he'd never let her see. God, Henry . . .

Clearing his throat, he looked away as if he couldn't bear the sympathy in her eyes—or maybe he was afraid she was about to well up with tears.

Skye swallowed them down. If he could be strong enough to stand up there and tell them the story of his life, she could damn well get through listening to it without blubbering.

"There are wild nettles and dandelion greens in the salad because I got into foraging while I was in foster care. I kept to myself a lot, and sometimes the places where I was staying weren't places where I wanted to spend a lot of time. So I'd go out, take long walks, and when I got hungry, I'd find something to eat. Hope you like it."

And without another glance at Skye, he left, breaking the paralyzing spell his story had woven around her.

Picking up her fork again, Skye speared a bite of greens, now slightly wilted by the warm dressing. She made sure to get a bit of crispy bacon with it, and had to close her eyes to savor the complicated tart-sweet flavor of cider vinegar exploding over her tongue.

The greens were more subtle, an earthy, grassy counterpoint to the acid of the dressing and the smoky-salt meatiness of the bacon.

Skye was at the opposite end of the table from the judges for a reason; she couldn't hear any of their comments, had no idea how they were reacting to this dish. But if they didn't taste and feel the connection between the complicated flavors and Beck's past, she'd lose all respect for them.

She ate every last bite and wished she had some crusty sourdough to mop up the rest of that bacon dressing.

"When Winslow told me over the phone what the challenge was," Nina said quietly, pushing her empty plate away, "I admit, I got a little nervous. But now . . ."

Skye laughed under breath. "Now I'm the one who's nervous! I mean, I knew his food would be wonderful, but part of the challenge is about the story—and I never thought Beck would go this deep."

Nina cocked her head like an inquisitive gull. "Win mentioned that the original plan was very different from what they ended up executing. I wonder what made Beck decide to go this route."

A shiver zipped up Skye's spine. There was only one reason she could think of . . . but no, it couldn't have anything to do with her. Could it?

Beck and Winslow appeared with the next course, saving her from having to respond to Nina's not-so-subtle probing.

This time, though, Skye took one look at the dish Win set in front of her, and knew she was about to lose her battle with the tears that had been threatening since the first course.

Beck couldn't help but watch for Skye's reaction to the third course. He didn't even know if she'd remember . . . but then her eyes went wide as she stared down at the plate of sliced roast duck on a bed of melted scallions, and he saw her grip tighten around her fork until the silver had to be cutting into her palm.

She remembered.

The knowledge made it easier to speak. "This is an updated version of something we used to have all the time when I got my first apartment, a tiny place over a grocery store in Chinatown. Back then, I'd buy the roasted duck from the butcher around the corner, but Winslow and I roasted and hung this one ourselves. We also lacquered it with a ginger hoisin glaze, to give the skin a good, crispy crunch. To me, this dish means home, comfort, warmth—it's from a time in my life when I was happy."

Skye looked up and he got his first good look at her face. Her cheeks were wet, her eyes blue puddles leaking tears, but she was smiling as she took her first bite.

Now for the hard part.

"There's a sweet and sour dipping sauce with red pepper and candied orange peel, and that's meant as a spicy, challenging counterpoint to the simple, homey flavors of the duck. Because not everything in my life was perfect during those years."

Skye stopped eating, and he saw her clutch her napkin as if it were a lifeline, but he had to see this through.

"We married young, and neither of us had much when we started out. And when my wife got pregnant, I knew I had to do something to take care of my family. I had a job as a short-order cook in a twenty-four-hour diner, but the pay was lousy and we needed health insurance. The only way I could think of to help my family involved leaving them, leaving my wife alone, for a long time—and she didn't want me to go. But I went anyway, and it ended us." He paused, forced himself to look Skye in the eye. "At least, it ended that phase of our relationship."

She went still, and he let his gaze slide away from the laser intensity of her stare. Beside her, Nina gave him a slight nod. Her eyes were more than a little damp, too, he noticed.

The judges seemed to be keeping it together better. Devon Sparks had on a very serious, contemplative face as he dunked one of his duck slices in the dipping sauce. Kane and Claire had their heads bent together, murmuring their observations on the flavors, he supposed.

Win nudged him in the side. "I think it's going over. Everyone likes that duck."

"Only two more courses left," Beck said, his eyes drawn back to Skye.

Two more dishes to sum up a lifetime's worth of emotions. He could only hope his message was getting through to Skye.

Chapter 28

The next dish was the main course, a more substantial, complex, structured preparation meant to symbolize Beck's years in the navy.

It took Skye a moment to drag her mind out of the deep pool of memories he'd dropped her into with that last dish, but she didn't want to miss an instant of Beck's revelations.

"During my five years in the service, I saw a lot of amazing places, met some incredibly dedicated men and women, and got used to racking out in a bed half my size. The Navy taught me about discipline, about hard work, and relying on a team. Cooking on a submarine? Taught me I'm not a huge fan of small, enclosed spaces. But, more importantly, it taught me I wanted to be a chef."

Looking down at her plate, Skye realized she'd missed the description of the dish. It was fish, which made sense— a firm white fish that had a subtle, briny sweetness to it when she tasted it.

The fish—maybe sea bass?—had been wrapped in paper-thin slices of potato and pan-fried, giving the potato a gorgeous golden-brown crispness that contrasted beautifully with the succulent fish. It sat on a bed of roasted asparagus spears drizzled with basil-infused olive oil, which gave the whole dish a round, fruity undertone.

The flavors were strong, even masculine, but there was a precision to the execution that impressed the hell out of Skye.

"This is amazing," she couldn't help murmuring as Beck and Win left to plate their next course.

Nina nodded thoughtfully and forked up her last bite, chasing a dribble of basil oil. "Beck is an exceptional chef—but I've never seen him cook like this. He must be feeling very inspired."

What Skye was feeling was overwhelmed. For the first time, she questioned her decision to cook and be judged second. After Beck's next course, she'd have to get up from this table, where she'd learned more in an hour about the man she married than in the two years they'd lived together, and head off to the kitchen for her chance to win the RSC competition. She had to get her head back in the game.

"He wants to win this thing," she said to Nina. She wanted to remind herself, too. "For you, and your family. Beck is very loyal."

"He is," Nina agreed. "But I don't think that's what lit the fire under him today."

Stop it, Skye wanted to yell. *Beck's whole menu isn't for me. It can't be.*

But after the way she'd ended things the other morning, she couldn't help but wonder. And the not knowing, not being sure, wanting to believe but not quite being able to—that was torture.

"Henry Beck is a good boy," Nina said, turning in her seat to pin Skye with a narrow look.

"He's done a lot for my family, and of course we're grateful. But even more than that, he's become one of us.

I love that boy, Skye, as if he were my own—which means that as much as I'd like to keep him around forever, what I want even more is for him to find his place in the world. The place where he can be happy. And after today I think that place might be with you. His wife."

Oh God.

All the emotion Skye had managed to tamp down after the Peking duck dish came rushing back in, making her hands shake and her chest feel too tight to catch a single good breath.

"I haven't been his wife in any way that matters for a long time." Her voice was shattered, raw, and Nina raised a skeptical brow.

"Yes. You seem completely over him."

"That's not what I said," she snapped, then cursed herself as Nina's other brow rocketed up to match the first one.

Dropping her head into her hands, Skye moaned, "God. This is all such a mess."

"You can either see it as a mess, a problem that needs to be solved," Nina pointed out reasonably, "or you can view it as the incredible second chance it is. Up to you, I suppose."

"Nothing is up to me," Skye hissed. "It's not as if Beck has declared himself, or asked me to stay married to him or something."

Hadn't he been about to, though? Skye paused, her breath caught around the memory of Beck's face alight with what looked an awful lot like hope, a question on his lips—in the instant before Jeremiah walked back into her life.

Skye deflated as if someone had punctured her with a fork. "No." She shook her head, shoulders slumping. "He doesn't want me back. I ruined that by not telling him the truth about . . . something," she hedged, not really wanting to spill the whole sordid story of her open relationship woes to the woman Beck saw as a mother figure. "Anyway, I told Beck it's over between us. He has no reason to doubt that."

"No reason to doubt it, maybe." Nina glanced up to the front of the room as the door opened for the last time. "But maybe he's got a reason to try and change your mind."

Skye's heartbeat quickened and she focused all her attention on what Beck would say next, hoping for answers, clues, some idea of what he wanted from her.

And for the first time since she met Henry Beck, he spelled it out, word for word . . . and Skye's entire world turned upside down.

Last dish. Last time he'd have to stand up here and eviscerate himself in front of six people, four of them basically strangers.

Last chance to tell the women who weren't strangers exactly what they meant to him.

Beck swallowed down a surge of eleventh-hour nerves and handed his tray over to Winslow to serve.

"I wanted to give you something to round out the meal, but I'm not a pastry chef. Winslow, here, he's got some game, so he helped me with it. And that's part of what this dish is about—it's a cheese course with one of my favorite French cheeses, Epoisses, and a caramelized fig tart. I definitely needed Win's help to get this one done, and that's a good example of the kind of support I rely on at Lunden's Tavern. The people I work with there . . ."

Beck paused, surprised by the way his throat kept tightening up on him. He frowned and coughed, then pushed on, not quite wanting to make eye contact with Win as he said this part.

"My friends. My family, I guess. That's what I've found at Lunden's, and that's why I want so badly to win this competition. For them. To show them how grateful I am that they took me in and accepted me, and that they can count on me as much as I count on them."

He looked up and caught Nina dabbing her napkin at the corner of her eye and felt like a shit. He didn't mean to make her cry.

But then Win moved back to his side, all five foot five inches of him vibrating with emotion, and Beck got distracted by trying to keep the kid from strangling him with a hug.

The scuffle got the judges to chuckle, so that was okay, Beck guessed, even if it made his cheeks heat with embarrassment.

"I love you, too, man," Win mumbled, pulling back and sniffling. "Now bring this baby home."

Beck nodded, waiting for everyone to take a bite. He knew what they were experiencing—the strong, pungent scent of the melty, almost warm cheese, and the way it went nutty and salty as soon as it hit the tongue along with the fig tart . . .

"This dish is all about opposites attracting," Beck said. "A good pairing, to me, isn't about putting the obvious things together. It's about finding two flavors that bring out the best in each other—maybe bring out elements in each other that don't exist when those flavors are on their own. The buttery, flaky crust and the dark fruit of the filling gets brighter with the cheese—while the cheese, which can be kind of overpowering on its own, mellows right out as soon as you hit it with the fig."

Claire Durand was nodding, Beck saw out of the corner of his eye, which was a relief, but most of his attention was pinned on Skye's reaction.

She gave a full body shiver, visible even from a few feet away, and bowed her head over her plate.

He didn't know what that meant, but he had to finish this. See it through all the way to the end, even if it didn't work.

Voice as rough and raspy as if he'd screamed every word into a void, Beck said doggedly, "They're made for each other. They're only whole and complete when they're together. And that's how I feel about you, Skye. About us."

At the mention of her name, Skye's head shot up, her eyes wide and blue as the ocean. Her face was leeched of all color; even her trembling lips were pale, and Beck had to force himself to go on.

Come on, man. This is the last hour of Battle Stations, you just have to push through the final flood control drill and you're on the other side of it. Push. Push.

Ignoring the way the judges' heads were all swiveling to stare down the table, ignoring the looks of confusion, curiosity, interest, whatever on their faces, Beck narrowed his focus down to just Skye. He stared into her eyes and spoke to her as if they were the only two people in the room.

"I know I'm not what your parents had in mind. And I know I've disappointed you, hurt you, and left you alone to deal with the worst thing that ever happened to either of us. You moved on, after I left, and . . ." he struggled a little, here.

Man up, Beck.

"And I'm okay with that. I mean, I get it. We were over, and I'm glad you found someone that made you happy. He's probably perfect for you in every way—smart, educated, into peace and do-gooding and all that hippie stuff you love—and if you decide to stay with him, I'll understand."

Her lips parted, but nothing came out.

Beck straightened his shoulders, refusing to break down. "But I think you should pick me. Because we're not perfect for each other on paper; I can see that. There's no logical reason why we should work . . . but we do. You know we do. And I'm telling you now, Skye, I love you. And I'm not ready to let you go."

Her eyes squeezed shut and both of her hands came up to clap over her mouth. When her shoulders started to shake, Beck didn't know what to do.

He sent Nina an agonized glance, and she immediately put her arm around Skye's hunched shoulders. Skye turned her face into Nina's neck and clung, the way Beck had wanted to do a couple of times.

The way he kind of wished he could right now, with his whole future in the slim, freckled hands of a woman who appeared to be sobbing her heart out.

He had to get out of here.

Without another word to the judges or a backward glance, Beck walked out.

Winslow caught up with him as he pushed through the kitchen doors. "Well, that went well," Win said brightly.

Beck shot him a look as he moved on autopilot to start packing up his knives.

"No, really." Win hitched his skinny hips up on the counter and swung his legs. "She heard you, man. That's what counts."

Beck leaned over the table, breathing deeply, head down between his shoulders. Win was right. He'd said his piece, and Skye had heard it all. What she decided to do with it now was up to her.

It took both Nina and Eva Jansen's help to get Skye out of the judging room, but she needed a minute to pull herself together, and the judges needed to finish their notes and discussion of Beck's dishes.

So Skye got her breathing under control and tried not to die of shame that she'd just wept openly in front of the people who would be soon be deciding her fate in the competition.

Not that the RSC and who won or lost seemed to matter so terribly much, after everything Beck had said.

"Come on, bring her this way," Eva said, beckoning them down the hall to an empty conference room. Nina, who still had a soft, motherly arm around her, helped Skye into a chair as Eva went off to find her a glass of water.

"I'm sorry to be like this," Skye gasped out, still short of breath and feeling her diaphragm jumping around as if she'd been doing one of those yoga poses where her entire body weight was supported by her abs.

"Like what? Like a human being with emotions? Honey, don't be sorry. You're fine. I'd have been more upset if you didn't cry, after all that. Lord almighty." Nina pulled another chair off the top of a stack leaning against the wall and set it down in front of Skye, close enough to pat her knee.

"Yeah, emotions," Skye hiccuped. "I've got 'em. And this last couple of weeks, they've been all over the place. God."

Eva reappeared in the doorway, followed by Fiona's very welcome, worried face.

Stupidly, Skye felt herself crumble all over again as she held out her arms to her best friend.

"Holy mother of crap, what happened?" Fiona demanded, rushing over to hug Skye.

Skye sank into the familiar peppercorn and lavender oil scent and sniffled pathetically. "Nothing. Except that Henry Beck is the most amazing, wonderful man in the world and he happens to love me. And I'm pretty sure I just gave him the impression that I wasn't happy about that."

Tears threatened again at the thought, but Fiona wasn't quite as maternal as Nina. Fiona gave Skye a firm shake and a narrow look. "Hey, quit that. Breathe. Tell me what's going on, so I can help you fix it."

"What's going on is that Skye has a choice to make," Nina said calmly.

"And, not to be a bitch about it," Eva broke in, sounding apologetic, "but it would be better if you made it quickly. The competition kitchen is ready for you, and I'm going to need to start your timer soon if you want to have the full five hours to cook before the judging at six."

Skye sat up and accepted the tissue Fiona produced from one of the many pockets lining her olive-green cargo pants. "In other words," Skye said, blowing her nose, "I need to get a grip."

"That's my girl," Fiona said, smacking her on the back.

Standing, Skye pulled her wild hair back from her face and secured it in a messy bun. Shudders of fear, love, amazement, and joy still ran through her, but she was learning how to breathe around them.

"Let's go cook." Fiona headed for the door, but Skye took a moment to clasp Nina Lunden to her one last time.

"Thank you," she whispered in the older woman's ear. "I'm so incredibly glad Beck found you and your family."

"So are we," Nina said, pulling back to give Skye a meaningful look. "And we'll always be there for him, the way family should be. But we're not all Beck needs."

Throat closing ominously, Skye compressed her lips and nodded.

The future stretched in front of her, a future she never thought she could have. It was harder than she ever would have imagined, and scarier, to stretch out her hands and take it.

"Come on," Fiona said, impatience making her voice tight. "We've got a competition to finish."

Nina gave Skye an encouraging smile, and Skye nodded again.

Beck had opened up and invited her into the warm,

living heart of him. He'd given her a choice . . . now it was up to Skye to finally fight for what she wanted.

He wouldn't have thought it was possible, considering how wound up—and up in the air—Beck felt after the judging, but as soon as he and Win cleared down the kitchen and went back to their hotel room, Beck passed out.

The restless nights and early mornings finally caught up with him, and he slept the sleep of the emotionally wrung-out for the entire afternoon.

His internal alarm woke him in time to shower and get changed before he had to head back down to the judging chamber for Skye's final challenge.

Already dreading stepping into that room again and coming face to face with the judges, Beck was still in the shower when he heard the hotel room door open.

"Beckster, you almost ready?" Winslow called. "I brought you a coffee from Blue Bottle."

Beck switched off the shower and toweled himself briskly before pulling on a pair of jeans. "Thanks, man," he said, stepping out of the bathroom. "I need this."

"This, too, yeah?" Win tossed the clean black T-shirt that had been lying out on Beck's bed at his head, and Beck caught it one-handed.

He skinned into it, nearly scalding himself with hot coffee in the process, and sat on the end of the bed to put his boots on.

"How you feeling?" Win asked, all casual, as if the answer didn't matter much.

Beck hid a smile. He liked that Win wasn't the most subtle, sneaky guy around. Made him easier to deal with, easier to trust. He bent over his laces and said, "Before the Navy, I used to hate sleeping during the day. I'd always wake up groggy, my body clock all confused. But the Navy taught me to catch sleep whenever and wherever I could."

He glanced over at Win, who blinked. "Wow. When you decide to start sharing, you really go all the way, don't you?"

Beck shrugged. It was sort of like flipping a switch, he figured. Not that he planned to go around spouting off about his innermost whatever twenty-four/seven, but now that he'd broken the seal? It wasn't as hard to open his mouth and let fly with something personal.

"So . . ." Win dug the toe of his white sneaker into the thick pile of the carpet. "I hate to push my luck, but . . ."

"No, you don't." Beck stood up and stamped his feet to get the boots to settle properly. "You live to push your luck."

"Okay, you're right. I do. So since I'm Mr. Pushy, how are you feeling, really? Not about the nap, about going back down there."

Beck grabbed his chef's jacket, not sure if he was supposed to wear it for the judging or not. "Like if we don't head out, we're going to be late."

Win deflated a bit, and Beck rolled his eyes and caved. "And also, a little nervous to come face to face with the judges again."

Perking back up, Win nodded and sipped at his coffee, eyes bright over the rim of the paper cup. "Right, 'cause they've seen your soft, gooey center."

"Okay, *now* you're really pushing it."

Win cackled and ran out of the room before Beck could do more than glare at him. But he was sober again by the time Beck pulled the door closed behind him.

"I wish I could go in there with you. If nothing else, I could keep you from whaling on that guy who's going to be there for Skye. Jeremiah What's-his-face."

Beck came to a complete standstill in the middle of the hall, his mind wiped clean of any thought beyond *oh shit*.

"Christ. I'm going to have to sit through Skye's five-course meal next to Jeremiah Raleigh."

The man Skye was, most likely, going to choose over Beck.

Win made a sympathetic noise. "I know. I saw him a few minutes ago in the lobby, and I hate to say it, but boy is fine."

That got Beck moving again, and Win scurried to catch up with him. "Not as hot as you, though! Obviously. Plus, I'm pretty sure you could kick his ass, if it came down to a fight."

"It won't," Beck swore as he pushed open the door to the stairwell and mentally thanked Eva Jansen yet again for putting him and Win on the lowest possible floor of hotel rooms. The shorter the elevator ride, the better.

He definitely would not throw a punch at Jeremiah Raleigh. Beck was through trying to pummel the world into going the way he wanted it to. Either Skye had heard what Beck told her, and she wanted the same thing he did, or . . . she didn't.

Unwilling to confront the yawning chasm that opened up inside him when he thought about what his life would look like without Skye in it, Beck picked up the pace and got them down to the conference room level of the hotel in near total silence, and with ten minutes to spare before judging was officially supposed to begin.

And there, in the hallway outside the judging chamber, stood Nina Lunden.

Win bounced over to her and threw his arms around her, giving her a smacking kiss on the cheek. Nina hugged him back, but her eyes were all for Beck.

"Hey, I'm going to go get the concierge to call a cab for

you, Nina," Win said, walking backward the way they'd just come. "I know you've got a flight to catch."

And then Win was gone, and it was just Beck, alone in the hall with the woman who'd made him a part of her family.

He felt his throat clamp down on the words that wanted to pour out—gratitude for her flying all this way, just to be there for him, for the way she'd always talked to him and accepted him, for helping Skye earlier when she broke down.

But when Nina came forward and grabbed his hands, all Beck could say was her name. "Nina."

Giving his fingers a squeeze, she said, "I wish I could stay and find out how this all turns out, but I have a feeling I already know. And I've got to get back home—no telling what that stubborn husband of mine has convinced those kids to let him get away with."

Maybe the switch had gotten flipped back, Beck thought, because it was harder than he'd expected to bend down for a hug and say, "It means a lot to me that you came."

He felt her smile against his shoulder. "Well, I had to meet this Skye Gladwell, didn't I? Had to make sure she's good enough for you."

"And?"

Nina stepped back and gave him a watery smile. "She's a sweet girl, Beck. A little confused, and life's given her some good knocks that sent her off course—but if she's as smart as I think she is, she's going to get things back on track real quick."

Suppressing a pang of disappointment that Nina didn't seem to have any information on what Skye had decided, Beck gave Nina's hands one last squeeze and glanced at the closed kitchen door right across the hall from the judging chamber.

Skye was in there, watching the timer tick away the

final few moments of her last challenge in the Rising Star Chef competition, probably hurrying to get her plates clean and pretty and ready to present to the judges.

He could go in right now, ask her to choose, once and for all—but he'd screwed with her enough for one day. For the first time, Beck wondered if it had been massively unfair of him to unload all that stuff on her right in the middle of the final challenge.

Shit. He hoped he hadn't thrown her off too badly. He didn't want to win because he'd undermined his competition with confessions of love and undying devotion.

He wanted to win because he'd finally figured out how to cook from the heart.

But then, that was something Skye had always instinctively known how to do. She'd led with her heart from the moment he met her.

What was her heart telling her now? In just a few minutes, he'd know.

Chapter 29

Of course. Of fucking course, the first person Beck saw when he said goodbye to Nina and let himself into the judging chamber was Jeremiah fucking Raleigh.

The hero.

Already seated in the chair second from the end, where Nina had been, Raleigh had his elbows on the table and his dark-blond head bowed over his hands. Beck watched the guy pick restlessly at the linen tablecloth for a long moment.

He looked uncomfortable. Out of place in his coarse canvas jacket and faded T-shirt, sitting at this beautifully set table, with its crystal stemware and polished silver and fine china.

Beck felt a completely unwelcome stab of empathy.

Delaying the inevitable, he strode over to the judges' end of the table and stuck out his hand.

"However this goes today," he said, shaking Claire Durand's slim hand, "thanks. It's been an honor cooking for you."

"I've enjoyed this year's dishes very much," she said.

"In fact, I'm not sure we've ever had a better pair of finalists. Truly, we should be thanking you."

Beck smiled and shook Devon Sparks's hand, too, but when he got to Kane Slater, the guy looked him right in the eye and said, "Your food was great, but I'll always remember what you said, too . . . about how sometimes things that don't seem perfect for each other go together and make something new and amazing."

Casting a sidelong look at Claire Durand, who appeared slightly pink in the cheeks, Kane finished with, "You inspired me, man. Is it gonna piss you off if I use some of what you said in a song?"

Beck surprised himself by laughing. "No, man. It won't piss me off; I'd be thrilled. I'm a big fan of your stuff."

Shocked delight widened Kane's eyes. "No shit? Well, that is just cool."

"Oh, get a room, you two." Eva Jansen sauntered up to the judges' table. "But not really, because it's time to get started. Chef? If you'd like to take a seat?"

Beck's mouth dried out. He wouldn't like to take a seat, thanks very much, but he didn't see how he had much choice about it.

He sat.

Jeremiah Raleigh gave him a tight smile and shifted in his chair as if he'd been sitting there long enough for his ass to fall asleep.

It was probably petty and immature to be glad about that, Beck decided, but so be it. He'd never claimed to be heroic, unlike some guys he could name.

And then he felt like a dick, so he stuck his hand out one more time and said, "Hey. Glad you could make it."

Which was true; much as Beck might wish the guy out of existence, since he *did* exist and he was obviously important to Skye, Beck was glad Jeremiah was there to support her.

Jeremiah blinked as if he were surprised to be on the receiving end of a handshake instead of a black eye. "Thanks. I wanted to be here for her this time; I guess I missed a lot of other chances to show her I cared."

Again with the reluctant empathy. Beck was abruptly kind of sorry that getting what he wanted meant he'd be taking the most amazing woman in the world away from this sad-looking guy.

Of course, there was no guarantee it would go down that way. And if what Skye decided was that Jeremiah Raleigh would make her happy, then Beck wanted that for her. Even though it would suck out loud for him.

Beck wiped his hand on his jeans and tried to think of something else to say. It was a little like chewing glass, but he managed.

"Look. I'm pretty sure Skye understands why you spend so much time away from her. She called you heroic when she talked about what you do out there with the Peace Corps. It's not like you're off in Vegas playing the ponies or something."

It's not like you left her when she was alone and pregnant to go off and do something she hates, like fighting.

But Jeremiah was giving him a funny look. "Thanks, man." Then he shook his head and made a quiet, laughing, snorting sound. "Now it makes more sense. I didn't get it before."

Before Beck could ask what made sense, the judging chamber door opened and he forgot everything but the fact that he was about to see Skye again for the first time since he blurted out that he loved her, in front of God, the judges, his sort-of-adoptive mom, and everyone.

And there she was in the doorway, holding a tray and looking nervous. He wasn't sure how he could tell she was nervous—her color was better than the last time he saw her, and her eyes were bright blue. She moved into the center of the room with a quick, lively step, no hesitation at all, and she gave the judges a smile.

But still, he could tell she was nervous.

Maybe it was the fact that her gaze darted to the other end of the table, Beck and Jeremiah's end, only once.

After that, she focused exclusively on the judges, speaking clearly and concisely about her dish and what it meant to her.

The white-haired pixie-ish looking woman from Skye's team set a bowl of soup in front of Beck, and he inhaled the steam rising off its pale surface.

"This is an asiago broth with a surprise in the middle— a single butternut squash raviolo with walnuts and brown butter. It's a subtle flavor, and the raviolo is . . . well, I guess that's me, during my childhood and teen years. I felt as if I had to hide who I was, because my parents and their circle of friends had . . . let's just say, very specific ideas about what makes a person worthwhile, and I don't really fit the bill."

She gave a wry, self-deprecating shrug, but Beck still kind of wanted to hit something.

Skye left without looking at Beck's end of the table again, and he tried not to worry about what that meant. Probably it meant she was trying to keep her mind focused on the challenge and not get sucked into personal issues the way Beck had. He couldn't fault her for that.

And once he tasted the broth and the plump, perfectly tender pasta with its burst of autumnal flavors, he couldn't fault her for much at all.

"That's very good," Jeremiah said, staring down at his bowl in what appeared to be real surprise.

"Yeah, she's got something special." Beck savored his last spoonful of salty, cheesy broth. "Hasn't she ever cooked for you before?"

"Not really." Jeremiah shook his head, looking pissed

at himself. "We met at a party at her parents' house, so it seemed like whenever I was in town, we had to spend time with her parents. I don't know, that's just how it developed, and I'm not in country enough to bother keeping a place here, so her parents usually put me up. It's nice of them, but when Skye's with them . . . she's not the woman who could make this dish."

Beck knew what he meant. "Being around her parents always makes Skye dial herself back."

Jeremiah nodded, still staring down at his bowl. "That's part of why I asked her to come back to Africa with me—I wanted to get her out of that house, away from her family."

That went through Beck like a harpoon, hooking his heart. He couldn't even argue with the sentiment; he'd wanted to break the chains that bound Skye to her parents, too. But if she went all the way to Africa with this guy . . . she'd really be lost to Beck.

He shook his head to clear it. Fuck it. Skye didn't need to go to Africa for Beck to lose her.

The door opened, and Skye was back, this time with a small salad of roasted beets, arugula pesto, and bright, jewel-like segments of orange.

"The play of savory and sweet here symbolizes the night I got my first kiss—and all the kisses that followed with the man I married."

Beck stared at her. He knew she could feel it, because her cheeks went almost as red as the beets on his plate, but she still didn't look at him.

"I wanted this dish to be bold, exciting, a wake-up call for the senses, because that's how I felt at that time in my life—as if I was waking up for the first time."

The memory of Skye as she'd been that first night swam before Beck's eyes, and while he was savoring that, the real Skye whisked herself out of the room.

Left with nothing to do but taste her dish, Beck let the

citrus bite of the orange tighten his tastebuds and play with the deep, earthy sweetness of the roasted beets. The pesto dressing had a bite to it, a spiciness from the arugula that Beck loved. She was really bringing it today, cooking with dash and vitality.

He swallowed and allowed himself to realize the truth. There was a very real possibility that he could walk away from this day with nothing at all.

She could very easily win the RSC competition, and then go off to Africa with Jeremiah Raleigh and leave Beck with . . . nothing.

Nothing but the knowledge that he'd stood up and risked it all for the chance to be with the woman he loved.

Spearing up the last segment of orange, Beck knew he'd do it the same way again, if he had the chance.

Skye pushed back into the kitchen and bent over, hands on her paisley-covered knees, for her now-traditional post-serving hyperventilation.

God. She just hadn't counted on how flipping difficult it would be to stand ten feet away from the man she loved and not go vaulting over the table to kiss the life out of him.

"I'm not going to tell you to breathe again," Fiona said, already stacking the next round of plates on the trays. "You never listen anyway. Is there anything I can do that would actually be helpful?"

"You're already doing it," Skye gasped, pushing herself upright and rushing over to check the plates before they went out. The tray held six small, individual cast-iron ramekins, each one filled with a creamy, hot vegetable gratin, the swiss cheese topping golden brown and bubbling. "These look gorgeous, thank you."

"Of course." Fiona studied her for a long moment, and Skye read the worry in her friend's pale blue eyes. "You gonna be okay?"

Skye looked down at the plate, tweaking a fennel frond garnish. "I think so. This next one is the hardest, but it's important."

Unspoken was Skye's conviction that if Henry could break free of a lifetime of tight-lipped, closemouthed silence, she could share a little bit of her grief and loss.

"I'll be right behind you," she told Fiona. "Just give me a second."

Fee nodded and hefted one of the trays, leaving Skye alone in the kitchen. Bowing her head, Skye centered herself and breathed in. She imagined the breath bringing her serenity and calm, filling her up, but all the time, she was aware of that black hole of grief deep inside—the part of her that couldn't be touched or filled or changed.

It would always be there, she knew. Oh, it was smaller than it had been right after she lost the baby. She could go days without thinking about it or noticing it. But it never went away . . . and the truth was, she didn't want it to.

The idea that she might one day forget filled her with horror and a sick sort of fear that made her stand there, breathing deeply and futilely, for another few moments.

There's not enough breathing in the world to make this easier.

"Right," she said aloud, psyching herself up. "You can do this."

Holding her head high, Skye picked up the tray and marched across the hall. Fiona had already laid her plates down on the judging table, and she came forward swiftly to grab Skye's tray.

Immediately missing the weight and purpose of the tray in her hands, Skye found herself twisting the drawstring holding her pants up. She had to force herself to clasp her hands calmly in front of her.

"What we have here is a gratin of roasted fresh fennel, carrots, parsnips, turnips, and fingerling potatoes, with a mornay sauce and Gruyère cheese on top. Please be careful; the ramekins are very hot."

She waited until everyone was looking down at their gratins, blowing on steaming spoonfuls of fork-tender veggies covered in decadent cream sauce, before she spoke.

"This dish represents loss. It's pure comfort food, an upscale version of the casserole you bring to a grieving family—this is the kind of dish I made for myself a lot after . . ." she swallowed, blew out a shaky breath. "After I lost my baby."

Everyone who was eating paused, and she caught an aborted twitch of movement from Devon Sparks. She hated that this story was likely to cause him pain, considering everything he and his wife were going through with her pregnancy, but still, most of her attention was on the other end of the table.

On Jeremiah, who'd never heard about any of this, and on Beck. Most of all, Beck.

She locked eyes with him, and the steady strength of his presence helped her go on. "At my first ultrasound, about five months in, I found out that our baby had Turner syndrome, a chromosomal abnormality that can affect the development of the heart. It's not always lethal—there are Turner syndrome kids who are born healthy and grow up to live happy, normal lives. But in most cases, the condition results in a miscarriage. Our baby wasn't one of the healthy ones."

The silence in the room was so complete, Skye could hear the rush of her own blood and every thud of her fractured heart.

Beck's fierce expression never wavered, but as she lost herself in his eyes, she saw a single tear well up and track down his cheek. He gave her a smile, nothing more than the barest quirk at the corners of his firm lips, but it was enough. Skye lifted her chin and let her gaze take in the rest of the room.

"That was nearly ten years ago now, and I rarely speak of it. Sometimes I feel like society would prefer that I just get over it and move on—as if somehow the loss of a child before it's ever born isn't real. Isn't devastating. But it was. It is, and not just for me—after the miscarriage, any time I opened up about what I'd been through, I'd meet a woman who'd been through something similar. It happens so much more often than you'd think, in this day and age of modern medicine—and far more often than anyone talks about. But I wanted to dedicate a dish in my life-story meal to my daughter, because it happened to me, and my daughter was real. Her loss shaped me as a woman, as a person, and as a cook. And it's time I honored that. Thank you."

She made eye contact with every person behind the judges' table; she saw sympathy and pain on Claire's and Kane's faces, and something like terror in Devon's eyes as his hand fumbled for the cell phone lying beside his plate. Good—she hoped he called his wife. Eva Jansen looked shocked, but not as shocked as Jeremiah, whose brown eyes were wide with surprise and sorrow.

And then there was Beck, who had tears running silently down both cheeks now, but who looked, more than anything . . . proud.

Fiona wrapped an arm around Skye's shoulders and gave her a comforting squeeze, but Skye realized as they turned to leave . . . she was actually okay.

Better than okay. She felt lighter, somehow. Cleaner.

"Come on," she told Fiona. "We're almost done."

Chapter 30

Beck didn't know he was crying until he noticed how cold and wet his face was. But after watching Skye stand up straight and tall under the burden of her grief, he couldn't be ashamed. He just wiped his napkin over his cheeks and took another bite of Skye's version of comfort food.

This was another one of her vegetarian dishes where he didn't even miss the meat. What would diced chicken add to this except bulk? The creamy chunks of potato and starchy parsnip were plenty substantial, while the other vegetables lent a satisfying sweetness to the rich, cheesy dish.

"She's kind of amazing, isn't she?" Jeremiah sounded wistful, almost, as if he'd never truly appreciated Skye before.

"Yes," Beck said shortly. What else was there to say, really?

"I wish . . ." The other guy broke off, shaking his head.

Beck never got to find out what Jeremiah wished, because Skye and her sous-chef returned with their next dish—and instead of six individual plates, this one came out in a single large, round copper pan, mounded with golden rice and studded with black clam shells.

The platinum pixie sous-chef set the steaming pan down in the middle of the table while Skye passed small ceramic bowls to the judges and tasters.

"This is my take on paella, a communal Spanish dish that really embodies the spirit of friendship, togetherness, and many different kinds of people coming together to create a wonderful new whole. In the last few years, my friends have been everything to me—they helped me find myself again, and reach for the new dream of owning and running my own restaurant."

She took a visibly deep breath and sent a tentative smile to their end of the table. Beck watched Jeremiah smile back and felt a chill take hold of his midsection.

"This dish is meant to be shared among friends," Skye continued softly. "It's casual and communal, fun and delicious—not to be taken too seriously, but not to be taken for granted, either. I hope you enjoy it."

Trying his damnedest to let go of the things he couldn't change—and not to push Jeremiah Raleigh out of his chair and stomp on his head—Beck leaned over and scooped a portion of the seasoned rice and shellfish into his bowl. He made sure to dig down to the bottom of the paella pan, looking for the best part: the toasty, crackling crust that formed along the bottom of the pan where it got the hottest.

The paella was as good as any Beck had tasted along the coast of Spain when his boat had docked there. The subtle saffron flavor pervaded the dish, more of an aroma than a taste, and every morsel of shrimp, every fresh, briny clam, was perfectly cooked and juicy.

Skye's soft voice broke into his enjoyment of a particularly tender coil of squid. "This is for Jeremiah—thanks for coming today, and for reminding me that I was alive and I deserved to be happy."

Beck felt his stomach drop into his shoes, and had to swallow hard to keep from throwing up.

That was it, then. Jeremiah was the one.

Beck stared into space in front of him, paella forgotten, and spent long minutes trying to process the disappointment turning his insides to lead. He'd made his play—and he'd lost everything. Including the competition, probably, because so far Skye's meal had been flawless.

But when the door of the judging chamber swung open, Skye came back in alone . . . and empty-handed.

"Is there a problem?" Eva Jansen inquired, perfectly arched brows lifting.

Skye smiled, and in the instant before she spoke, Beck had time to notice that even with her hair flying out of the knot on top of her head and a smear of what looked like tomato paste on her cheekbone, she looked more at ease, more sure of herself, than he'd ever seen her.

"Nope, no problem. But there's no fifth course, either."

A ripple of shock traveled down the table and zinged straight up Beck's spine. Without meaning to, he half-rose out of his seat, but before he could even figure out what he thought he was going to do, Skye pinned him with a look.

"It's okay, Henry. This is my choice. And I choose to present the final course of my life-story meal as an open-ended question. I don't know how things are going to turn out, or what my future holds—so how could I make a dish to illustrate it?"

"My dear girl," Claire Durand murmured, "It's possible you've taken the parameters of this challenge a bit too literally. Are you sure there's nothing you'd like to present?"

Skye swallowed, but held her head high and met the judges' incredulous stares with a calm smile. "I'm sure. And after the stunning honesty and courage displayed by my competitor, Henry Beck, how could I do less than try to match it? My future is a giant question mark—but for the first time, that doesn't scare me."

She looked over at Beck, who hadn't managed to make himself unbend enough to sit down. For the first time since she came into the room, she seemed uncertain. "I'm not scared of my future, because I know who I want at my side."

She held out her hand. Beck could see the fine tremor of her fingers. "Henry?"

He blinked. She couldn't mean . . .

Like a fool, he turned and stared down at Jeremiah Raleigh's blond head. "But what about him?"

Jeremiah tipped his chair back on two legs to stare up at Beck with a quizzical look. "What *about* me? Skye and I are over."

Beck gaped down at the man, reeling, as Eva Jansen stood up and clapped her hands together once.

"Well! This has been a very exciting day for all of us. The judges have some deliberating to do, and it sounds like the three of you have a few things to talk about as well. Why don't you head back to the kitchen, and I'll come get you when the judges have reached a decision?"

Feeling a little dazed, Beck moved on autopilot to follow Skye out of the judging chamber, with Jeremiah on his heels. Once the three of them were back in the relative privacy of the kitchen—give or take a couple of sous-chefs, who jumped apart guiltily when the door opened, clearly in the middle of a gossipfest—Beck rounded on Raleigh. His desperation for answers must have come across as ferocious aggression, because Raleigh took a step back.

"Hey! Ease down. If anyone here deserves to get worked up, I think it might be me. After all, I'm the one that got dumped."

Beck was still trying to process those words, and dial his expression up to something civilized, when Skye smacked her boyfriend—ex-boyfriend—in the arm.

"Oh, come on! Considering you let me stumble all the

way through that break-up speech before telling me you'd met someone else, you get zero sympathy from me, buster."

Jeremiah cocked his head, gazing at Skye fondly. "Well, there is that. Alicia's amazing—maybe not as good a cook as you. Although I'll deny I said that with my dying breath, so don't get any ideas."

Dropping the teasing smirk, Jeremiah grabbed for Skye's hand. "Seriously, though. I see why you didn't want to give all this up to come cook on a camp stove or over an open fire. You fought hard to get where you are—don't let anyone tell you your time would be better spent doing something else."

"Thanks, Jeremiah, that means a lot to me." Skye went in for a hug, and it was all Beck could do not to snarl and push his way between them.

He'd been pulled in too many different directions today, opened too many old wounds and drained their poison out onto the ground. Now here he was. Standing here, fists clenched and chest heaving, watching what ought to be a private moment between two people who obviously cared about each other—even if they weren't together anymore.

Skye and Jeremiah weren't together anymore.

Staggering a little, Beck blinked, and when his eyes opened again, he was sitting on the floor with a very worried-looking Skye kneeling next to him.

And no one else was in the kitchen with them.

"Henry! Are you okay? I think you're dehydrated. When was the last time you had a drink of water? Your sous-chef went to get a bottle from the vending machine down the hall."

Beck stopped the flow of Skye's nervous, worried speech by pulling her into his lap.

"Winslow left to give us a minute," Beck said, lips

pressed to her temple. Skye's spicy-sweet curls tickled his nose and made him smile.

Skye, who'd stiffened when he grabbed her, slowly relaxed against him as her arms stole around his shoulders. "Are you sure you're okay?"

"Are you sure you broke up with that guy?" Beck countered, his fingers automatically shaping themselves to soft curve of her back.

She nodded. Her voice was muffled against his chest, but Beck felt every word. "I told him I couldn't be with him, because I'd realized I was still in love with my husband."

The whole long day of intensity and emotions suddenly crashed to a halt. Cupping one hand around the back of Skye's head, he tilted it until he could look into the gorgeous blue summer of her eyes.

And then he kissed her.

When Henry Beck's mouth covered hers, Skye couldn't stop the inarticulate moan of joy that broke in her throat. When his tongue stroked her, she couldn't stop herself from tightening the grip of her fingers in his hair where it curled against his neck.

And when he shifted both of them so that Skye was on her back on the kitchen floor with Beck covering her like a sexy blanket, she didn't even try to stop herself from arching against him.

Still . . . she tore her mouth away from the kiss long enough to gasp in a breath and said, "Winslow and Fiona . . . they'll be back soon."

"Win's got more game than that," Beck assured her, nuzzling her cheek.

His fingers flexed against her scalp, sending prickles down her arms and legs. Skye had to work hard to keep up any sort of rational thought.

"But the judges . . . I don't think it's going to take them long to decide."

That made Beck pause. Propping himself on his elbows, he stared down at her face from mere inches away.

"Why did you do it?" His rough voice rocked low through his chest where it pressed against her.

Skye didn't pretend not to understand. "I wanted to make a point about where we go from here."

"But." He was clearly struggling with this. "You're going to lose the RSC, and all because you didn't present a fifth dish."

"I know. But I finally realized winning wasn't going to win me my parents' respect—nothing could do that, unless I have a total personality transplant and become someone else. Which I'm not willing to try anymore."

"Is that really why you entered the RSC to begin with?"

"It was a big part of it." Skye breathed in deeply, just to watch his eyes cross when her breasts pushed into his ribcage. She could get used to having lots of long, deep, meaningful discussions with Henry Beck stretched out on top of her. "The rest was about gaining recognition for Queenie Pie, and just making it this far has done that."

Beck narrowed his eyes. "So. No part of you wanted to win, just for the sake of winning?"

Skye felt a tiny pang in her chest, but she shrugged as best she could with her shoulders pinned to the slip-free rubber matting covering the kitchen floor. "I won't lie. It would've been great to win. To be named the next Rising Star Chef . . . but I don't need it." Tugging lightly with her wrists crossed behind his head got Beck's mouth down where she could kiss it. "I got what I really wanted," she whispered into his lips.

"Mmm . . ." he rumbled, nudging his hips deeper into the vee of her parted thighs. "You can get a rise out of this star chef anytime."

"Oh my God, you did not just say that."

"Hey, you're the one who wanted me to talk. Don't blame me if it ain't all poetry."

The words sparked a memory, and in her excitement Skye sat half upright, pushing Beck over onto his side. Her fingers flew to the neckline of his shirt and dragged at it, which made Beck laugh.

"Hey, hold on. Weren't you the one worrying about the judges walking in on us? I'm sure they'd love to see you trying to get me naked."

Skye gave up on the shirt collar and burrowed one hand under the hem of his T-shirt until she could stroke her fingers across the tattoo she'd caught a glimpse of that night at Queenie Pie.

The marked skin over his right shoulder blade felt smooth and warm, no different from the skin stretched taut over the rest of Beck's back. Keeping the tips of her fingers tracing the lines of script she remembered swirling out like a spiraling sunburst, Skye felt a shudder of heat work its way through her.

Not attempting to hide her response to touching him this way, Skye met Beck's hot, intent eyes. "Speaking of poetry. Want to tell me what this says?"

She felt the tense and flex of his muscles against her fingers, but his gaze never wavered.

Skye trembled, but she was almost certain she knew what he was about to say.

"It's not real poetry," he grumbled, and it was as if time turned back and they were cuddled on their futon in the Chinatown studio with Skye trying to get a look at the composition book Henry kept under his side of the mattress.

Instead of arguing with him about it, she tucked her face into the hollow of his neck and snuffled quietly at the warm smell of clean sweat and man. This part always used to be easier for him if she wasn't looking at him. "Tell me."

When he started to speak, she smiled, pleased on a deep, visceral level that she still knew him this well. But when his words registered in her brain, the smile faded from her lips.

What she felt was too huge for a mere smile to contain.

"'But still each morning the girl and the boy belong more fully to each other, until it seems they were born face to face.'"

Her mouth moved, following along silently with the last phrase, her head full of the rest of the poem, line after line of devotion Henry had scribbled down and read to her on their wedding day, in a back office at City Hall.

Those were the words he'd turned into art on his body. That was the life experience he'd wanted to record in flesh and blood, a permanent reminder of Skye and their life together inked into his skin.

The last icy sliver of doubt—the scared whisper in the back of her head telling her she was a fool to think there was any chance of a future with a man who'd changed so much in the last ten years—melted away in the warm rush of love and recognition.

"It's you," she said, the words hitching out of her mouth in breathless gasps. "It's really you. Henry!"

Henry Beck. The boy who'd given Skye her first kiss, who'd woken her body up and made her feel special. Beautiful. No matter how much he might have changed, matured, grown—he was still the same man inside.

And they would have a lifetime together to learn and grow to love those surface differences.

"It's me," he promised, his mouth pressed hot against her temple, his breath stirring her hair. "But this time around, I promise to tell you how I feel. I want you to know. I never want you to think . . ."

His throat clicked as he swallowed, and Skye could feel the jerk of his back under her hand. "I said it in there, in front of the judges and everyone, but I need to make sure you heard me."

Beck pulled back and grasped her shoulders, staring down into Skye's upturned face. Her heart beat at her ribcage like the wings of a trapped bird. She was still straddling his thighs, her knees aching against the rough rubber matting, but all of that disappeared as her vision tunneled down to Henry's deep, velvety brown eyes.

"I know I never said it much before, when we were together. But I felt it every day, and I should've made sure you knew. Skye Gladwell, I love you."

Happiness pushed so hard at her insides, she felt as if she'd swallowed the sun. "I love you, too. Even though I tried, I could never figure out how to stop."

Beck brought his hands up from her shoulders to frame her face. The slow, lazy circles he rubbed against her cheekbones with his thumbs made her shiver. He kissed her again lightly—almost reverently—and it reminded her of the way he'd kissed her that day at City Hall.

She laughed softly against his lips, and he pulled back to raise his brows in a question. "Nothing—I just feel like we're reaffirming our wedding vows, or something."

A thoughtful look swept over his handsome face. "That's not a bad idea. It wouldn't be just the two of us in City Hall anymore—we both have people who'd stand up with us."

Joy fizzed and sparked through her like ice cream dropped into a root beer float, sweet and thick and heady. Grinning her biggest, most unrestrained grin at him, Skye teased, "I don't know, what about our bet?"

"Bet?" His voice was distracted; he seemed more absorbed in the path his fingers were tracing down her neck.

"Those judges are going to come back in here," she

reminded him—reminded both of them—with a shudder of rising arousal. "And tell us that you won. Which entitles me to a quickie divorce, after a night of passion with you."

His gaze snapped back to hers. "Forget the bet," he growled, moving in a controlled rush to roll her beneath him, pinning her once again under the solid, steely weight of his muscular body. "You're not getting rid of me that easily."

"You think this was easy?" Skye laughed, luxuriating in the hot weight of him pressing the breath from her lungs.

"No bet," he told her. "No divorce. We're staying married."

She knew—of course, she knew—that was what he wanted, but to hear him say it out loud, in so many words . . . Skye melted. "The bet's off," she agreed.

Henry Beck stared down at her, and Skye took the moment to memorize every detail of his beloved face. The uncompromising angle of his jaw, the firmness of his mouth, the incongruous sweep of his long, dark lashes. His hair swung forward, coming loose from its band, and Skye reveled in the fact that she could lift her arm and push it back behind his ear.

She could cup that strong, rough-stubbled jaw, and bring those warm, parted lips down to hers.

Beck took her mouth in a heated, wet kiss, devouring her with years of hunger behind every slide of his lips, every thrust of his tongue. Skye gave herself up to it, a matching hunger clawing at her belly and making her arch against him.

They broke apart, panting, and Beck gave her a slow, wolfish grin. Leaning down to nuzzle along the softness of her jawline, he whispered in her ear, "No divorce, but

I'll take the other half of my winnings. You, in my arms, tonight . . . and every night."

And as he tilted his head to claim her mouth again, Skye closed her eyes and threw herself into the storm of passion and love, trust and friendship, and she knew.

She'd never been so happy to lose a bet in her life.

Epilogue

One year later ...

Nina Lunden gazed around the crowd assembled in the waiting room feeling as if she'd taken too big a sip of her husband's famous hot chocolate. Her throat burned a little, but it was good, and the warmth spreading out from her stomach made her sigh contentedly.

Having all her family together in one place—there were no words.

Even if they had to get together in a hospital.

Pushing her worries aside, Nina focused on the positive. Any time spent together was precious, especially now that they were so spread out around the country, with Danny and Eva taking trips all the time, and Beck permanently relocated to San Francisco and working at Queenie Pie Café with his wife.

"Jules and I are heading down to the cafeteria, Mom." Her sweet Max leaned over the plastic arm dividing their chairs and nudged her shoulder. He, at least, was home for good, where she could keep an eye on him—and Nina promised herself she'd never take that for granted.

"Can we bring you back something?" he asked. "Maybe a coffee?"

"Hot chocolate would be nice," Nina said, smiling over at her oldest and his wife. Jules gave her a smile back—she, Gus, and Nina had spent a lot of nights sipping hot chocolate together after a long dinner service at Lunden's Tavern.

"It won't be as good as Gus's," Jules warned. "Anyone else want—" She paused, casting a frowning glance around the bland, sterile little room. "Hey, where's Win?"

"Where do you think?" Danny wandered over after covering his sleeping fiancée with her long fur coat. Faux fur, Eva had assured Nina, who'd had to work to repress a smile.

Eva was a complete darling, once Nina got past worrying that the self-proclaimed party girl was only toying with Danny. But all it took was one dinner at the townhouse she and Danny were renting together for Nina to see exactly how head over heels Eva was, and how desperately the young woman wanted to fit in with Danny's family.

All the young ladies her boys had brought home had that in common, Nina reflected. It was a pretty good gig for a mother-in-law, actually—she'd had zero trouble bonding with Eva, who needed a mother more than anyone Nina had ever met. Jules, of course, was already the daughter Nina and Gus always wanted.

And then there was Skye. Nina would be forever grateful she'd had the chance to sit through Beck's beautiful culinary poem to the woman he loved, right next to Skye herself. That day had formed an instant bond between Nina and Skye, and it was a relationship Nina treasured.

"Ever since Win got that new phone, he's on it all the damn time," Danny complained. "I feel like we need to stage an intervention or something."

"Hey, maybe while we're here we can look into surgical options," Max said, standing up and stretching so hard that Nina heard his spine pop. "There's got to be a doctor somewhere who can separate Win from his phone."

"Leave him alone," Jules ordered. "He probably went outside to call Drew. You know Win gets nervous around hospitals."

"Hey, I can sympathize." Max held up his hands in surrender. "All this waiting is making me antsy, too."

"Come on, itchy feet," Jules said, hooking her arm through her husband's and tugging him toward the door. "A little walk will do you good."

Nina smiled to herself, remembering a time when Jules wouldn't have been secure enough to joke about Max and his tendency to wander. Of course, that was before he figured out that what he'd been searching for all over the world was waiting for him back home. It had been a while since Nina had seen that faraway look in her oldest son's blue eyes. These days, he was more likely to be focused on his work at Lunden's, coming up with new recipes for Jules and Gus to try in the kitchen.

Thinking about her husband had automatic worry tightening her belly, a reflex she hadn't been able to shake since the first time he collapsed in the Lunden's kitchen. Before she could catch her breath, Eva stirred and sat up, rubbing her eyes as Jules and Max hurried back down the hall and into the waiting area.

"You didn't get very far," Nina started to say, but then she saw the doctor approaching behind them, and before she knew it she was on her feet, heart beating an unsteady staccato against her ribcage.

"Any news?" She thought she sounded pretty calm, all things considered, but her two wonderful boys weren't fooled. They moved to flank her, strong arms around her back and across her shoulders, and the weight of their love anchored her to the industrial rubber hospital flooring.

The doctor gave them all a tired grin, and Nina's heart began to throb with joy and relief before the woman even started to speak.

A warm, familiar palm clasped the back of Nina's neck. She'd know those strong, callused hands anywhere.

"Gus, you're just in time!" Jules crowded in closer as Nina leaned back into her husband's broad chest.

"Had to call in to the restaurant. They're slammed but kicking butt. Then I grabbed this kid on my way back in. Couldn't let him miss the big announcement," he rumbled. Gus's steady, strong heartbeat pressed against Nina's back as Winslow Jones bounded over to the group, his nervous energy ratcheted up as high as Nina had ever seen it.

Surrounded by the family she and her husband had made out of the restaurant that was their life's work and their legacy, Nina took a deep breath and faced the doctor once more.

"He's perfect."

Beck stared down at the red, wrinkled face of the tiny baby curled against his wife's softly heaving chest.

Skye hummed in sleepy agreement, her eyelids fluttering as she tried to stay awake.

"Go to sleep," he said. "You earned it, babe. I'll stay right here."

He hadn't moved from her side for the last nine months. He wasn't about to start now.

"I don't want to," she protested, those pretty rosebud lips drawing into a pout that nearly killed him. "I want to remember every second of this."

"We will," Beck told her, resting one palm lightly, protectively on the baby's small, blanket-swaddled back. "I couldn't forget it, even if I tried."

Every instant was emblazoned on Beck's brain, from the first tearful, terrified confirmation that Skye was pregnant to the decision to leave Queenie Pie in her sous-chef's hands so they could come to New York and have Dr. Rosen take care of Skye during her final trimester.

The pregnancy had been textbook from beginning to end, morning sickness to labor pains, but you never would've been able to tell it from how scared he and Skye had been. It was like walking around in a constant state of panic and dread, and it hadn't been good for Skye.

But once Beck came up with the idea of asking Devon and Lilah Sparks for the name of the obstetrician who'd helped them through their difficult pregnancy and safely delivered their healthy baby girl, everything got better.

Yeah, it was stressful to leave the restaurant behind, just as he was starting to find his place there and build a rapport with Fiona, Nathan, and the others . . . but if the tradeoff was Skye being able to sleep through the night without waking up sobbing from nightmares, it was more than worth it.

The fact that in New York they were surrounded by the love and support of the extended Lunden's Tavern clan hadn't hurt, either.

Beck flexed his fingers gingerly, watching the rise and fall of the baby's back. Even through the layers of padding, his son's slumbering form felt impossibly breakable under Beck's big, clumsy hand.

His son. God help him.

As if she could sense him freaking out, Skye's eyes popped open.

"Hey, Daddy. What's cooking?"

Daddy. Oh man.

Beck shook his head and tried to smile around the giant, aching, painful lump of emotion stopping up his throat. "Nothing. Get some rest, I'm not going anywhere."

Uh oh, there went Skye's chin. He'd gotten to where he could translate that determined tilt pretty accurately. "Neither am I. Not until you tell me what's going through that head of yours."

Even after all these months, the long, amazing year of knowing exactly how much Skye loved him and wanted to be with him, it was still hard to just open his damn mouth and say, "I'm a little freaked. But I'm dealing."

Every time, it was a struggle. And when Skye's face softened and he felt the warmth of her loving, concerned gaze, he felt stupid all over again for making such a big deal out of things.

"What are you freaked about?"

She looked so honestly perplexed, he had to laugh. "I love the fact you can lie there after twelve hours of natural childbirth and ask me that with a straight face."

"Yeah." Skye grimaced. "I might have taken the whole organic, natural hippie thing too far with that one. Although next time, I'm thinking it might be easier if we do a water birth at home, maybe have a doula instead of a doctor."

Beck nearly fell off the hospital bed. "Next time?"

"Sure." Her beautiful eyes were shining as she poked one finger into their son's loose fist. "I already know Hank, here, is going to need somebody to play with."

They hadn't wanted to find out the baby's sex ahead of time, so they'd had a hard time deciding on a name. Hearing her say this particular name out loud . . . Beck had to blink a couple of times. Hard.

"Hank, huh?"

Skye met his eyes with a tremulous smile. "I thought . . . he could be a Henry, too. Like you, but also to honor your father. But instead of Hal, we could call him . . ."

"Hank." Every time Beck repeated the name, he felt something settle inside himself. He smiled down at them both. His family, the people he loved most in the world, were right there, close enough to touch, to watch over, to protect and cherish with his life.

Skye nodded, eyes brimming. "I love you."

Bending over them, Beck whispered his response against her lips. "I love you, too."

She grinned into the kiss, which deepened and threatened to turn truly inappropriate until a knock on the door startled them apart.

Nina Lunden's quiet voice had Beck reaching for a pillow to hold over his lap.

"Hello? Everybody decent?"

"We're good. Come on in and meet Hank," Skye called. "While he's all cute and asleep."

"Are you sure?" Nina poked her head around the doorjamb. "There are quite a few people out here who want to say hello to the newest addition to the family."

Winslow piped up from somewhere out in the hall. "Including his godfather!"

"Don't worry," Skye said, settling herself more comfortably against the pillows. "He just had his first-ever bath followed by his first-ever meal. I'm pretty sure a five-alarm fire couldn't wake him up."

That was all it took to have the whole crew piling into the tiny room. Beck could only be grateful that Devon Sparks had used his influence with the hospital and Dr. Rosen to get them into a private room. This crowd would be a bit much to handle for some poor random new mom who had the misfortune of getting stuck as Skye's roommate.

Beck made a tactical retreat to the far side of the bed. Still close enough to keep a watchful eye on the proceedings, but not so close that he risked fatal injury by getting between baby Hank and the descending horde of cooing almost-relatives.

While everyone else was distracted by how unbelievably adorable Hank was in his little blue knit cap with his dark-lashed eyes buttoned up in slumber, Nina Lunden made her way around the bed to stand at Beck's side.

"He's amazing," she said. "I'm really proud of you, honey."

Beck shook his head in instinctive denial. "I didn't do anything."

Nina gave him her patented who-do-you-think-you're-dealing-with look. "Nothing much, except uproot your whole life, face your past, and confront your fears about Skye being pregnant again."

The group clustered around the bed, laughed at something Win said, and the noise roused Hank enough that he stirred fretfully, kicking at the blanket swaddling his legs. As if she'd been practicing for years, Skye shifted him in her arms and cuddled him close, as natural as breathing. Beck's heart skipped a painful beat, then thumped heavily as he said, "Skye's the brave one."

Him? Even though Skye and the baby had come through the pregnancy with flying colors, Beck was *still* terrified. What the hell was up with that?

"Does she know?" Nina's soft question cut through Beck's rising tension.

He didn't bother pretending to misunderstand. "Yeah. I told her."

"Good. You know, lots of men find the whole childbirth thing traumatic—after he fainted when Max was born, I didn't even let Gus in the room with me for Danny's birth. It's normal to find it upsetting to see your wife in pain. And for a man like you, I imagine the inability to do anything to make the pain stop is nearly unbearable. But

I'm sure, Beck, your presence at her side *did* help her through it . . . unless."

Nina's gaze sharpened on his face. Wondering what the hell he'd given away, Beck planted his feet like a statue to avoid shifting his weight uncomfortably.

It didn't work.

"Unless that's not what's bothering you." Nina kept the words low and gentle, but they still sent a spike of panic through Beck's head.

Darting a quick gaze at Skye, he relaxed minutely. Her head was tilted back, springy strawberry-blonde curls cascading over her shoulders as she beamed up at Gus Lunden.

"Don't worry, she didn't hear me." Nina rested a light hand on his back, the touch spreading immediate comfort as if she'd draped a fuzzy blanket over his back. "But she should hear it from you, sweetie."

He shook his head, not wanting to let the garbage inside it ruin this special, amazing miracle of a day for Skye, but Nina stopped him with another look.

This one was kinder, her clear eyes full of sympathy but entirely unyielding. "I mean it, Henry Beck. You've got a brand-new start, here and now. Don't fuck it up by repeating the mistakes of the past." Her voice shook as she finished by saying, "And I know if your mother were here, she'd be giving you the exact same advice."

Jolted by Nina's use of the f-word, Beck was shaken to the core by the truth of her warning and the reference to his mom. All he could do was reach out and wrap an arm around her slim, narrow shoulders to pull Nina in close.

Bending down to touch his forehead to her temple, Beck pushed the words out through his aching throat. "My mom would've liked you a lot."

Then he let her go and pasted on a determined smile so they could rejoin the party.

Thirty minutes later, Hank had been the subject of multiple cellphone camera portraits, the star of a short film (also recorded on a cellphone), and serenaded with "Happy Birthday" by a multiplatinum recording artist—over Eva's cellphone, which she'd used to call Claire Durand, who was in Paris accompanying Kane Slater on the European leg of his new tour.

It was an eventful half-hour. A happy half-hour, full of laughter and the kind of soul-steadying joy that came from sharing such a special time with friends and family—but Beck had to admit that when he closed the door behind Winslow, who was naturally the last to leave, he breathed a sigh of relief.

Hank, who'd woken up in time to turn Kane's birthday song into a duet along the lines of screaming death metal, had been fed and put down in his bassinet where he slept the sleep of an infant who knew that all was right in his little world.

Beck was jealous. He desperately needed sleep himself—even the U.S. Navy hadn't prepared him for the exhaustion of new fatherhood—but with Nina's warning ringing in his ears, he knew he wouldn't be able to close his eyes until he opened his mouth.

Skye turned her head toward him, trying to get comfortable on the flat pillow. Her hair spread out in corkscrews of red and gold against the white cotton. She looked worn out and happy, and so beautiful that Beck's breath snagged in his throat.

"How are you doing?" she asked, and instead of simply nodding and smiling or saying *fine* like he usually did, Beck seized his courage in both hands.

"I'm . . . having an issue. It's lame."

She got that fierce look in her wide blue eyes. "It's not lame! Nothing you think or feel is lame. Come on, tell. I know the pregnancy was rough on you, on both of us, but we made it through! Hank and I are right here, and we're healthy and happy, and with you!"

"I know," Beck said, taking a step closer to the bed. "And that should be enough for anyone. I'm not sure what's wrong with me." His gaze traced the beige chenille of the hospital bed coverlet as Nina's warning echoed over and over in his head. He had to tell Skye the truth and trust that she wouldn't use it against him or turn her back on him . . . and when he thought about it like that, it got easier. Because he knew, with a deep-down, unshakeable faith, that Skye would never do those things.

"I'm pretty sure," he said slowly, forcing himself to meet her clear gaze, "there's something broken inside me."

"Is this about . . ." Skye paused, cleared her throat. "Is this about our daughter? The baby we lost? Because I'm thinking about her today, too, Henry. And I believe wherever she is, she knows we love her and that no matter how many other kids we have, we'll never forget her."

Beck shook his head against the sting behind his eyes. "No, it's not about that—not exactly. But I felt this way when you were pregnant the first time, too. Before we lost her. Before I left, even. I think it has to do with how I grew up."

Skye reached out a hand, and Beck took it gratefully. The warm touch centered him, gave him something to focus on while he tried to figure out how to explain the confusion of losing both his parents at the same time, the gradual horror of realizing they were never coming back, that they'd abandoned him to this new life where no one seemed to want him, where being ignored and forgotten was the best he could hope for.

"I'm afraid I don't remember enough about the good times," he said painfully. "While my parents were still alive. The years that came after that . . . they felt like a life sentence, even though I got out as soon as I could. I just . . . I don't want any part of that to touch you or Hank."

Skye studied him for a silent moment, long enough for Beck to realize that he'd expected her to immediately deny the possibility of the ugliness inside Beck ever touching Hank.

Instead, she withdrew her fingers from his grasp and pointed at the bassinet. "Pick him up, Henry."

He took a step back. "He's sleeping. Shouldn't we let him sleep as long as we can?"

"He's a baby. He'll be doing a lot of sleeping for the next few months. Pick up your son, Henry."

She was implacable. Beck's feet shuffled over to the bassinet. Staring down, he watched Hank breathe.

"Go on. He's less fragile than you think."

Beck didn't see how that was possible. He knew there was that thing about the head being too heavy for the neck and how he had to support it. His palms were damp, clammy with nerves—what if he dropped Hank? He wasn't ready for this. He should've practiced or something. How was there no training course for this? Boot camp for new parents, that's what he needed.

"Henry." Skye's voice was soft, hoarse with emotion. "Hold your son."

Beck could do this. He'd won the entire Rising Star Chef competition, for God's sake. He could pick up one baby.

Holding his breath, he worked his too-big hands underneath that tiny body and lifted as carefully as if Hank were a ticking bomb.

Huh. He wasn't as limp or squirmy as Beck had feared. The blanket swaddled around him so tightly, Hank felt like a pretty secure little package. Heavier than he looked, too.

Beck curled his son high against his chest, cradling the

infant close. Hank's cloudy blue eyes blinked open for an instant, and as Beck stared down into his son's face, he felt all his fears and worries drop off his shoulders.

Why had he ever been afraid of this?

Standing there in that hospital room with his son drooling a wet patch on his T-shirt, Beck knew there would be troubles ahead and plenty of mistakes—but he also knew he had what it took to be a good dad.

"I love you," he whispered to Hank, who'd already slipped back into sleep.

When Beck glanced over at Skye, there were silver tear tracks streaking down her cheeks, but she was beaming the biggest grin he'd ever seen.

"I like holding him," Beck told her.

"See? You're a natural. And he's going to need you. We both are. I'm scared, too, you know. It's not like my parents are the best example of how to raise a happy, secure child."

Beck carried Hank over to the bed and sat down, needing to be within touching distance of his wife. He felt swamped with gratitude—that Skye knew him so well, could read the fear in his eyes and force him to move past it.

"We'll figure it out together. And hey," he said, thinking of their visitors that afternoon. "It's not like we're alone. We've got family to help out."

She blinked. "That's true. It's not just about our parents or our childhoods—we've both managed to put together pretty awesome families that have nothing to do with sharing DNA."

"We're going to be okay. Better than okay. We're going to be amazing."

Skye smiled up at him, at their son, and said, "This. This is the moment I'll remember for the rest of our lives."

Author's Note

I am not a poet. Beck's poem, however, is a real, honest-to-goodness poem written by my dear friend, the talented poet Liz Jones-Dilworth. She wrote it for the wedding between her brother-in-law, a New York City chef, and his fiancée, a former pastry chef! So it's weirdly appropriate for Beck and Skye, and once I heard it, I couldn't get the line about being born face to face out of my head. It just fits them perfectly.

So with thanks to Liz and her in-laws for the use of their poem, I wanted to reproduce the whole thing here, so you can see how completely beautiful and romantic it is.

Falling in love is easy, but no one knows how it's done. The girl and the boy are walking through the market. Calluses touch the spots on a stuffed giraffe, the carved patterns of a spoon, wool spun into yarn. The rubber tire of a stroller, the canvas loop of a leash, honeycomb gleaming in a glass jar.

Love is built one choice at a time. Move the bracket to the left, to the right. To the left. Bolts and washers and the wrong-sized wrench. Splice, twist, cap. Dimmer switch.

Another trip to the store. It's not fun until it is fun, and suddenly no noisy street is better than this noisy street. That's when they decide to get the ice cream. Love is a choice, but who among us can resist it?

Two pairs of aching heels under the same covers, two pairs of eyes blinking at the same screen. Two throats laughing at the same joke, which makes no sense outside this room. That's because what the joke really means is we're together. They might sleep through every alarm, but still each morning the girl and the boy belong more fully to the other, until it seems they were born face to face.

Falling in love is a secret, but we all see it happen. The girl and the boy are down the shore, stirring lemon marmalade and wine-poached figs over a sticky stovetop. They arrive on the bus loaded with brown paper sacks, handles tied with curling ribbon. Inside is the earth and all it offers, their work and their love which has bubbled and boiled until it is on our lips—extravagant unnecessary treats, made of sugars without which we could not survive.

Hot Under Pressure Recipes

MRS. BECK'S GRILLED PB & J

   2 slices of bread
   Softened butter
   Peanut butter (your favorite kind—chunky,
      smooth, whatever)
   Jelly (your favorite kind—raspberry, strawberry,
      grape, whatever)

This sandwich is more delicious than you could imagine
from the simplicity of the ingredients!

Set a sauté pan over medium heat. While the pan is warming, spread a thin layer of softened butter on one side of each
slice of bread. Cover the clean side of one slice with peanut
butter, and cover the clean side of the other with the jelly of
your choice. Press the peanut butter and jelly sides together,
then lay the sandwich, buttered side down, in the hot skillet.

Fry the sandwich for a minute or two, until it reaches the
desired level of toasty golden-brown doneness on one

side, then carefully flip it over. The heat will have melted the filling a bit, so the bread may slide around. Just re-align the bread slices once the sandwich is flipped.

Toast the sandwich on the other side; it will take a little less time on this side, because the pan will be even hotter now. Just keep an eye on it, and remove the sandwich from the pan when it's toasted the way you like it.

Put the sandwich on a plate and slice it in half diagonally. Serve with a tall glass of cold milk for the perfect nostalgic lunch!

SKYE'S ROASTED ROOT VEGETABLE GRATIN

For the filling:

2 medium parsnips, peeled and chopped into
    ½-inch dice
2 medium carrots, peeled and chopped into
    ½-inch dice
1 large bulb fresh fennel, cored and chopped into
    ½-inch dice
1 large Yukon gold potato, peeled and chopped
    into ½-inch dice
1 large sweet potato, peeled and chopped into
    ½-inch dice
¼ cup olive oil
¼ cup water
2 tablespoons butter, plus a little extra
2 tablespoons minced shallots or scallions
1 cup white button mushrooms, thickly sliced
1 tablespoon dry white wine
salt
pepper

You could add and/or substitute peeled, diced turnips, celery root, yams, fingerling potatoes, or any other root vegetable you like. Essentially, you need about eight cups of chopped root vegetables.

Preheat oven to 450 degrees.

In a large bowl, toss the chopped vegetables with the oil and water, and sprinkle generously with salt and pepper.

Spread vegetables in a single layer on a rimmed baking sheet, cover loosely with aluminum foil, and slide into the hot oven. Roast for twenty minutes.

Remove foil and stir the vegetables around on the sheet. Roast, uncovered, for another twenty minutes, stirring occasionally. The vegetables are done when they're tender and their edges are beginning to caramelize.

While the root vegetables are roasting, heat a medium sauté pan over medium-high heat. Melt two tablespoons of butter and add the shallots or scallions. Sauté for a minute or two until softened and translucent, then add the mushrooms. Stir the mushrooms around; they'll absorb all the butter immediately so keep an eye on them and if they start to scorch, turn down the heat. But keep sautéing them until they begin to give back the moisture they absorbed, and grow tender and brown around the edges. Pour the dry white wine into the hot pan and cook it down until it's been absorbed by the mushrooms and shallots, another five to ten minutes. Take the mushrooms off the heat and set them aside until the root vegetables are done roasting.

Grease a gratin dish or a medium-size casserole with a thin film of butter, then spread the roasted vegetables and mushrooms in the dish. Salt and pepper to taste.

Turn oven down to 350 degrees.

For the Mornay Sauce:

> 3 tablespoons butter, plus a little extra
> 3 tablespoons all-purpose flour
> 2 cups whole milk
> 4 ounces swiss cheese, such as Gruyere, grated

In a small saucepan, warm the milk over medium heat until almost boiling, being careful not to scorch it or to let it boil over.

While the milk is heating, melt the butter in a medium saucepan over medium-high heat. When the butter has stopped frothing, add the flour and stir it around with a wooden spoon for at least two minutes. It shouldn't get brown at all, but it should stop smelling like raw flour. This is what's called a white roux.

Pour the hot milk into the roux in a slow, steady stream, whisking like mad the whole time. Keep whisking, scraping any bits of roux off the sides of the pan, until it comes to a boil. Then whisk some more while the sauce boils for a couple of minutes. When it starts to get thick and smooth, take it off the heat and whisk in salt and pepper to taste—at this point, you've got a béchamel sauce. Now add about half a cup of the grated swiss cheese a little bit at a time to help it melt into the sauce evenly, and when it's all mixed in, taste it for seasoning again! Now you've got your Mornay sauce.

Pour the Mornay sauce over the vegetables in the gratin dish, then sprinkle the top of the gratin with the rest of the grated cheese. Dot with the extra butter, just a couple tiny pieces here and there over the top of the gratin.

Bake in the 350 degree oven for about thirty minutes, or until the top of the gratin starts to bubble and brown.

Serves six to eight as a side dish, or four as a main course with a lightly dressed salad.

BECK'S PAELLA (SERVES 6–8)

Paella is a generous, informal dish that is perfect for parties and large family gatherings! It's very forgiving when it comes to proportions and ingredients—basically, it's all about making it the way you like it. There are a few steps to go through, but I promise, it will be worth it when you wow your guests with the finished dish.

Stock Preparation
   ½ cup dry white wine
   1 tablespoon lemon juice
   ½ teaspoon saffron
   5½ cups stock (fish or chicken)
   ¼ teaspoon ground coriander
   1 bay leaf

Mix white wine, lemon juice and crushed saffron in a small bowl and let stand to allow the saffron to bloom.

Bring stock to a simmer in a 3 quart saucepan. Add the saffron mixture, coriander, and the bay leaf to the hot stock. Hold at simmer while preparing vegetables and seafood.

Preheat oven to 400 degrees.

Meat Preparation

- 1 pound spicy sausage, such as linguiça or Spanish chorizo
- ¼ to ½ pound diced ham or bacon
- 2 tablespoons olive oil
- 8 boneless, skinless chicken thighs, cut into chunks

Remove the sausage casing and sauté the sausage in olive oil in a skillet until lightly browned. Break into bite-size pieces while cooking. Remove browned sausage to a platter.

Sauté ham or bacon and remove to platter with the sausage.

Add chicken pieces to the skillet, brown on all sides in the pork fat and remove to platter. Reserve the pork fat.

Seafood Preparation

- 2 to 4 small lobster tails (½ tail per person)
- 1 pound large shrimp
- 2 tablespoons olive oil, divided
- 1 tablespoon lemon juice
- Salt and pepper
- ½ teaspoon dried thyme
- ½ teaspoon dried oregano
- 1 pound squid (tubes)
- ½ pound mussels
- 1 pound clams

Cut lobster tails in half lengthwise; you can use kitchen shears to cut through shell.

Peel and devein shrimp.

Toss shrimp and lobster tails in a bowl with 1 tablespoon of the olive oil, and the lemon juice and seasonings.

Clean and wash squid. Slice squid tubes into ½ inch rings and add to bowl with shrimp and lobster tails.

Place paella pan or large, oven-proof skillet on stovetop over medium-high heat. Add remaining tablespoon of olive oil and 2 tablespoons of reserved pork fat.

Once the oil and fat are hot but not smoking, add lobster tails and sauté for two minutes. Remove to platter.

Add shrimp and squid and sauté for two minutes. Remove to platter, then discard fat from paella pan and wipe with a clean towel.

Clean and wash mussels and clams.

Vegetable and Garnish Preparation
   8 garlic cloves
   1 teaspoon sea salt
   3 medium tomatoes (in season) or one
       (14.5-ounce) can diced tomatoes, drained
   1 teaspoon smoked Spanish paprika, hot or sweet
   2 tablespoons olive oil
   1 onion, sliced into ½-inch strips from pole to pole
   1 red bell pepper, sliced
   3 cups Spanish Arborio rice, or other medium-
       grain rice
   1 cup frozen green peas, thawed
   1 cup Italian flat leaf parsley, chopped
   lemon wedges

Mince garlic and mash to paste with 1 teaspoon sea salt in a small bowl.

Peel tomatoes and remove seeds. Dice and place in a bowl. Stir in smoked paprika.

Heat oil in paella pan over high heat, then add onions and peppers. Stir-fry the vegetables for two minutes, until they begin to soften.

Stir garlic and salt paste into paella pan and stir-fry for one minute, until the mixture becomes fragrant.

Add tomatoes and paprika to paella pan and stir-fry for one minute.

Add uncooked rice to paella pan and stir with tomatoes, onions, and peppers to coat.

Final preparation
Measure hot stock and add stock or water as needed to make 5½ cups. Stir hot stock into rice, tomatoes, onions and pepper mixture and bring to rapid boil on stove. Stir gently and cook about six minutes until liquid thickens and rice appears on surface. You know it's thickening when your spoon starts to make tracks exposing the bottom of the pan.

Turn off heat and add sautéed meats from the platter, then stir in shrimp, squid and peas.

Add lobster tails and push them partly into the rice. Push mussels and clams partway into rice, hinge end down, then drizzle juices accumulated on the platter over the top.

Bake ten to fifteen minutes uncovered on center rack of oven until liquid is absorbed and a crust forms. Rice should be slightly too al dente.

Remove paella pan from oven, cover with aluminum foil or kitchen towel and let stand for ten minutes. Rice will continue cooking and firm up.

Sprinkle paella with parsley and decorate with lemon wedges. Serve with a simple green salad and a nice, crusty bread to soak up the juices!